The Deep Slumber of Dogs

A novel by Doc Krinberg

Honolulu, Hawaii
2016

Published in the USA by Aignos Publishing, Inc.
54-253 Kaipapau Loop
Hauula, HI 96717
www.aignospublishing.com

Printed in the USA

Edited by
Cover art provided by Laura Hatcher (laurahatcherphotography.com)
Art Design by Doc Krinberg, Laura Hatcher, and Liang Han "Kevin" Yu

13-digit ISBN: 978-0-9970020-2-7
10-digit ISBN: 0-9970020-2-6

Aignos Publishing Inc. would like to formally thank and acknowledge Savant Books and Publications for permission to use the haiku, *Deep Slumber of Dogs*, which was first published in the poetry anthology "58 Stones."

Honolulu, Hawaii
2016

Dedication

To Laura and the Tribe of 4

Forward

'There's no point in making a distinction between great trees and unworthy trees'

--- Dr. Yamano

NATSU/AKI

(Summer/Fall)

Doc Krinberg

Chapter 1

Chet Felch adjusted in his seat and belched. He pulled his clip on tie with one hand and settled back into his English language newspaper, *The Japan Times*. There was a stain from something yellow on the top of his stomach that rested in front of him like an opened drawer in a dresser and it drew Warren to look at Felch, even though he despised himself for it. Hypnotized, he would stare many times in a day and this bothered him, feeling as if he knew every oversized pore in the man's hooked, beefy nose and every liver spot he could see through the white crewcutted stubble of hair resembling a fat unshaved chin. Warren would look at the faded baby blue eyes settled back in their sockets like lurking azure crabs over the blood vessel disaster of cheeks and he would agonize when Felch smiled his saurian smile, revealing small unevenly spaced yellow predatory incisors in a molar-less void. The stained, stretched shirt was a sea over the corpulent gut and complimented the gorgle of suet that was his neck; shaking like the flap on a turkey when it ran. Warren cringed when he always noted the small, carnivore's arms that he carried in front of him as if he were a rotund and pink skinned T. Rex. But Felch, like a train wreck, deserved a fair amount of rubbernecking. Warren would just sigh, give in and look again; Felch breathing open-mouthed and unaware of his attraction.

"Transfixed are we like, Warren?" Behind him, Flattery asked, amused in his blarney bullshit brogue. Flattery enjoyed catching Warren in these moments. Warren didn't despise Flattery for catching him more than he despised himself for looking.

Seamus Flattery knew that and it amused him more to expose Warren. He already decided that Yanks believed the Irish were a wistful priest played by Barry Fitzgerald so he affected that self deprecating, sadly amused lilt to his voice when addressing them. He knew Warren believed in no such ideal so employed it even more. The *sadly, amused* came thru loud and clear.

"Why don't you make us a pot o' coffee like, Warren, you wank?" He laughed.

"Why don't you, as we say in the lower 48, take a flying fuck?" Warren smiled. Flattery had been in Japan for ten years and was fluent in the language and mysteries of *kanji* and *katakana* while Warren was still after almost a year and a half practically a newcomer and functionally illiterate in Japanese envying Flattery his language skills and resolve. Warren went back writing his lesson plan for the senior class next bell. Flattery moved to the coffee mess, "Yank shirt lifter," He laughed softly, using his favorite euphemism for homosexual at Warren, who was peering over his *Little, Brown* while peeking at Felch who pulled a hair out of his nose with a root bulb the size of a pearl onion. He cursed himself for looking again and then he just lost the thread of the lesson plan, spiraled and crashed, wiping out in the wave of daydream; the daydream that acted as a salve. California. Hollywood. Lise Dreyfus. The wave he had been riding was high and powerful. He rode this daydream many times, and in each instance fell over the falls; surfer fail.

Chapter 2

Felch burped again and Warren realized he was in the past a little too long. He looked at his wrist and then thought of Lise's; thin and finely tapered and always sporting a huge silver and turquoise bracelet with an intricate Zuni design to hide all the fine white scars like scratches a dog leaves on a glass door to the yard from her attempts as a teenager. Stop it, he thought.

Mr. Riordan and Mrs. Bloom returned to the department of Native Speakers, he was so deep in memory he did not notice the chimes for the end of class. At Kin Tama School there were no bells, only wistful chimes that punctuated the classes. It took Warren a month to get used to it, Pavlovian from his public school bell days. Riordan sighed as he dropped his load of texts.

"Jesus what a class!"

Riordan was new this last year, hired after Warren, and like all student and staff, having trouble getting kick started after the summer break in August. The weather was also brutally humid and since the AC 'shit the bed' as Mr. Marlowe put it everyone felt the soporific effects of the heavy and filthy atmosphere of the Kanto Plain.

"What's wrong, Mr. Riordan, besides being an Irish-*American* wank as opposed to the real thing?" Flattery asked in his best Fitzgerald. He took pleasure in ribbing young Riordan while the latter only desired acceptance as an Irish 'homeboy.' Warren noticed quickly after the younger man's arrival in Japan that while Flattery enjoyed torturing Riordan, he avoided any insults to Marlowe, who was a fish of a totally different stripe.

"Dang kids, I swear if any ever brought their books to class I'd have a heart attack!" Riordan muttered. Everyone within earshot just nodded. The kids were notorious for never being prepared, and apathetic when called out on it. Shaking his head he pulled a wedge of rice, wrapped in seaweed paper with a glob of tuna in the middle and started unraveling the cellophane.

Felch looked up at Riordan as he gathered his roll books for the next class, a minute away, "Hey, Mr. Riordan, do you have a solution to this problem?" He frowned.

"Noooo…" Riordan hated Felch and he knew he was in for some cereal box philosophy as he was chock full of banal homilies and self help answers. Warren suspected Felch as having attended and graduated several 12-step programs.

"Then my friend, you're part of the problem." Felch smiled.

"And what do *you* do, Felch?" He asked.

"Nothing." Warren cut in. "Felch teaches whether they're ready or not, present or not, awake or asleep, or dead for that matter…half the time you need to wake them up in his class anyway. But the show must go on, eh, Felch old pal?"

"Absolutely Mr. Haas. Mr. Haas-been." Felch smiled as he floated out of the department quietly. Flattery followed him smiling, throwing Warren the bird.

"I hate that bastard," Riordan said to Warren, "he's the fucking anti-teacher."

Mrs. Bloom was entering scores in her grade book and as usual was oblivious to the men's' daily dialogue, as if she were the sole woman trapped in a locker room from which she there was no escape or means to communicate. To her it was the same shit, different day. She was the wife of a Sergeant Major in the USAF located at the base in Fussa. She taught part-time and never involved herself in the gossip, intrigue or rumor mongering the men were fanatics about with the exception of Marlowe. She was 39, and very petite; like her Japanese counterparts in the department, almost invisible against the high levels of man-sauce exhibited by the robust posturing the white men took part in. When hired thru the employment service at the base for native speaker jobs, she was surprised that she didn't need any formal educational training and just needed a degree, any degree to teach *eigo*. Warren envied her lack of interest in departmental nonsense and politics, which he let himself get sucked into daily. He studied her when he could and wondered whether she was as detached at home. She came to school, taught, and ate lunch on those days she was there and then left. He vaguely remembered her husband referred to as 'Roy' and then after that, never again. She was always kind, polite and somehow disembodied, as if you were seeing a hologram of the real Mrs. Bloom, changing colors as you saw her from different perspectives. There was something ethereal about Bloom, he thought and it unnerved him. Her smile was aloof, mysterious, a cinematic smile with no true warmth. Warren wanted at times to know more about her, see her inner self, just as he wanted to see his Japanese counterparts' cogs and wheels turning. She displayed no emotions, even in class and when looking at you was friendly yet remote. Another cypher, Warren Haas figured, in a land of cyphers.

Poor Riordan wore his heart on his sleeve, Warren knew, and suffered for it. Flattery and Felch double-teamed him, baiting, cajoling, working him into frenzy over students and classes, politics and women. They would work him into a lather then leave him twitching like a fish on the beach. Mrs. Bloom would smile her non-smile in neither disappointment or approval, and he, Warren, would take Riordan's side, his loathing for Messrs.' Flattery and Felch thinly disguised.

Marlowe was what Warren considered his closest friend in Japan. He had also written a number of short stories with Marlowe as the main character named 'Turner' that gathered dust on his small desk at his flat. With Marlowe he got to golf on the cheap and drink at the officer's club at Yokota, Atsugi or Camp Zama, as Marlowe owned veteran's status and was sponsored by many of the people on base. It was he who helped Warren assimilate and walked him thru many embarrassing social moments. Flattery on the other hand enjoyed seeing him or any Yank commit a social *faux pas* and though well fluent in the language would let you drown at his feet. So, nights with Flattery were replaced early on by cultural sessions at Marlowe's small but smart flat in Ebisu, down in Tokyo, near the Anglo-Japanese bookstore and Garlic Restaurant. Like Flattery he lived in Japan almost a solid decade and when young and a navy brat, living in Yokusaka and Iwakuni when his father, a navy doctor, was stationed at the old dispensaries there. Marlowe explained the subtleties of living in Japan when he could. Where an American would walk around all day with a toothpick dangling from his lips; smoke, drink and talk around it, the Japanese were meticulous in hiding its use behind a hand so as not to offend anyone. On the other hand, the loud slurping and sucking of noodles your mother slapped your hand when you attacked

Campbell's noodle soups were perfectly good manners here. There were so many instances of disjointed culture between the two, and so many different overlaps, when first venturing out Warren felt a constant headache, his hackles up a couple of times being outed for not properly using the hand towel prior to eating. Marlowe tried to smooth it over for him. Once, before they stopped being social, he went out with Flattery to lunch at the Korean style BBQ around the corner from Kin Tama. Warren greeted the giggling hostesses, asked for a table for two and smoothly ordered edamame for an appetizer.

"Well, "Flattery said, sizing him up, " You've certainly become Marlowe's pet Jap." Warren wasn't surprised at the comment at the time because he knew Marlowe and Flattery were tolerant of each other but certainly not holding hands. After that lunch, he never ate or went anywhere with Flattery alone.

Marlowe looked far younger than 48. His eyes seemed to hold light and confidence that made people looking at him feeling as if they were sitting, gazing up at him. Warren felt that way when he was younger, in the days he feared his father, Big Dutch Haas. Warren didn't fear Marlowe but held him in a different place than the other men acquainted with in the native speakers department, or his life for that matter. He was a thoroughbred in a gene pool of donkeys. Big Dutch just always scared the shit out of him and always appeared six times taller than he really was.

Marlowe used to tell him that Felch accumulated so much residual moron time in his body, even when he acted normal it was negated.

"He's a complete ignorant swine." He would pronounce matter-of-factly in the style of a by-product from years of military living. Everybody knew he served but what he actually did was a mystery. Before he worked at Kin Tama, the previous years a subtle inference of having worked at 'language jobs' Presently he occupied a self made cubby in the corner more like a shooter's blind than an accessible space.

Felch was a washed up businessman whose wife directed his flatulent existence as a teacher in the DoD's school system. A teacher for years on the mainland, she decided to try something different as Felch cratered their assets in a succession of poor business ventures, and so they took a chance and after her application was accepted to teach at the middle school at Yokota Air Base and embarked for Japan. They enjoyed the luxury of living on the Base and gained the commissary and P/X privileges as a federal employee. Unlike Marlowe, who took people on base with him to include even the *nihonjin* teachers, Felch took no one nor did he ever invite anyone.

Marlowe also explained Flattery's history. He was a refugee from the JET program and worked at a high school for years before applying at Kin Tama and became a brilliant translator, spoken and written but as a human made Nosferatu have a soul. He stated that Flattery could work well above his present pay grade at the consular level but lacked the ambition, enjoying his niche at Kin Tama.

"I don't know what makes him stay here when he could be making more money and hobnobbing with the attaché/diplomatic crowd, but there's something here he likes." Marlowe shook his head.

Chapter 3

Flattery lived just west of Tachikowa and biking to work along the river, on the raised asphalt embankment. He rode a bike his entire life, never owning a car. Growing up in Dublin he never saw a need to, and in Japan, with its preponderance of riders and easy lock-ups at the *ekis* that suited him just fine.

His flat was a two tatami corner unit in a four-story building that bordered the Ome Line tracks. No one from Kin Tama had ever been in his rooms, and like Felch nor did he invite anyone ever. He also lived that way when attending school in London when he thought he would go into banking or business. He spent time at the pubs and in the dorm rooms of others drinking and studying, but never allowed people to his room. The English students piled on good-naturedly that not only was he Irish, but also a hermit as well. Flattery, while beaming his signature smile and purring his brogue, held them in utter contempt. Even though a Dubliner, his family ties to Ulster and Londonderry were strong. So he perfected his charming act and strived to be the best caricature of an Irishman for the Brits, protected in his stereotyped cocoon. In Japan and exposed to the Yanks, he found them repulsive in their language, their need to be liked and in how they tried to make Japan an extension of California. His personal knowledge from film and literature spoke to his belief that everything the U.S. touched, it tried to remodel or renovate it in American style; cooked in American juices until it ceased to be itself and became what he termed 'hotdog castles.'

He read Warren's novel *True Finery* when younger and actually enjoyed it, but would never admit it to Warren. He still owned a copy of it boxed with his other books from Ireland so many years ago. He could recall certain passages or instances in the book and even an appearance by a much younger Warren on a Sunday morning talk show about books and literature on the BBC when he was riding the success of the book and hadn't as of yet started his descent. Flattery watched the show, smoking a cigarette, drinking coffee with Jameson's in it and wearing the same bathrobe hanging on a hook in Tachikowa. He thought Warren very funny and his self-deprecating humor refreshing for a fucking Yank, and he handled the show's host, an obvious shirt lifter, with class and humor. When he actually met Warren, almost nine years after the fact, and on the verge of Warren turning 40 he was at once in awe and also full of resentment. His awe from meeting a published writer of a book he actually read and resentment that with all that money and hoopla, here he was at what was considered for him the *scrapheap* while Flattery sweated and taken all of his written and verbal exams after almost a decade of immersion in Japan, considered a brilliant linguist and respected at Kin Tama yet he was still in Warren's *scrapheap*. So he took great pride in reminding Warren daily he was in that fucking *scrapheap*.

Chapter 4

The early days of his employment at Kin Tama and his escape from the United States made him reflect on just how bottomed out he was. Initially, the interview went well in Hawaii, when first he met Serazowa, the chief of the Native Speakers Department. He was in charge of the *nihonjin,* the Japanese nationals who taught the English grammar classes and the *gaijin,* non-Japanese who were from native English speaking countries who worked with the students on conversational skills as well as literature/speech and reading comprehension. Warren was at the point of ending back on the sauce full tilt, or worse.

His book royalties all dried up, and before his agent relieved himself of his duties, oversaw several pieces rejected. His immolation in America occurred silently, like the image of a monk burning on a Saigon street in a Bukowski poem. His contract in the English Department at UH wasn't going to be renewed. His status so diminished, his last few classes didn't even know he had been a successful writer. His sophomore book widely panned and ridiculed was out of print in a heartbeat. In the time in between the success of *True Finery* and the failure of *An Unworthy Tree* he'd been vilified on a television station that blew the story to a national level, and having several run ins with the authorities and a DUI while speeding did not help matters. A wrongful death law suit lawsuit filed against him by Loren Oppenheimer, Lise's loyal husband that bled him before its dismissal accompanied a drop by a few lucrative sponsors and no more invitations to *Vanity Fair* parties.

Before his interview with Serazowa he looked around his 400 sq. ft flat in Waikiki, on the *wrong* side of Kuhio Street, and needed to talk himself off the ledge of having one drink to get some nerve. He took out the last unwrinkled tailored suit he owned, after showering and shaving, and went to meet his new maybe future employer in the visitors' conference room at the Sheraton on Kalakau where the interviews were being held. It mattered not to Serazowa that Warren, in the estimate of America, had crashed and burned. There was a dog-eared copy of *True Finery* on the table and he asked Warren to write a small dedication in it, to the headmaster of Kin Tama. That he was an author was a selling point. That he was a degreed teacher of English Lit before and after his writing career was a solid foundation for the students. His notoriety was welcome, regardless of his past problems. For Kin Tama, all was in the past. Serazowa, addressing that issue in his odd preternatural way over his shoulder after the interview spoke to Warren without turning to face him, his voice a philosophical afterthought.

"Haas-san…we live many lives, and in your cycle, you have started anew."

Since that day, Warren came to realize his future belonged more to Serazowa than himself.

Serazowa…the biggest cypher he encountered; quiet, seeming almost asleep yet aware of everything, and everyone. His mere presence in the department rearranged the atmospheric pressure in any and all discussions or arguments. It was as if he surrounded himself with eggshells when at his desk. No one dared approach him. All correspondence was either put into a memo or initiated verbally only by him. Warren watched when Flattery cursed in English. That turned Serazowa's head; he addressed Flattery in rapid Japanese. Flattery, realizing a serious breech of etiquette in Serazowa's presence, took what all believed to be a tongue lashing, answering only in submissive *hai's* after each burst of speech from the department head.

Serazowa, earlier in his career, taught abroad in the west and also in Saudi Arabia, which, Warren discovered, he preferred. One day, while listening to a debate in geography and whether teaching parts of TE Lawrence's *Seven Pillars of Wisdom* was essential to young Japanese students, Serazowa cut in and started waxing about his time in the Middle East.

"I was teaching at a men's university in Riyadh, and I must agree with them in how they treated their women, and how they based their society. In the West, all this *equality* of the sexes is a confusing and distracting issue. Each day, I catch girls who insist on rolling their skirts at the waist to make them shorter. I question why they are here in the first place." Mrs. Bloom kept to writing her lesson plan when this small speech occurred, showing no emotion whatsoever. The two Japanese women who were present, not having grammar classes that bell period, modeled Mrs. Bloom's stoicism. He continued:

"I also witnessed the refusal to allow women to drive, or be seen in public, and after spending a day in the city, visiting Meiji Shrine and taking in a sumo event, I can agree with them there as well. Some of the modes of dress were quite scandalous. We seem to be reliving America's 1960's here in this free spirit silliness." He rose up then, with some papers in hand, and exited the department.

"Welcome to Kin Tama, Warren." Marlowe smiled.

Chapter 5

After *his* wave rolled back Warren repeatedly sought to locate a high-water mark and found nothing save the self-inflicted ligature marks on his neck of a blown up career. Sitting in his flat at the El Norte on North St. Andrews in nothing but board shorts he barely heard the guy in the Stetson on TV speaking about *hanging* but this subtle and whispered advice had prompted Warren to try and exit his 7th floor window. Sadly he thought he had pretty much been hanging for quite some time and though ripe and rotted, no one apparently displayed the good manners to cut him down. And he couldn't open the window, so he sat there and poured another drink and wondered what he would get if he couldn't open the window and hurl himself out.

"Hung out to dry!" he laughed, drinking. Out of money, so out of Johnny Black and sailing on Cutty Sark...*not* the high water mark of scotch either. Unlike Lise, he could stare back over it now at the age of 36 and see just how many incarnations he had used up to finally get to Japan, by way of failure in Hawaii. Mr. Johnson had said the last refuge of a scoundrel was patriotism and Warren had paraphrased that to read that the last refuge of a writer was to teach. Then get fired.

His mind daily sought the solace of the past and wandered back to the El Norte in Hollywood. Warren liked the 1920's apartment building because it was old Los Angeles, somewhat stylish and at times creepy, half expecting Rondo Hatton or a dapper George Raft to emerge quietly from the shadows. A good place to croak one's self as there was privacy and almost total solitude since he had fallen from grace and his standard old black rotary phone silent, his answering service long since departed. But the windows sometimes stuck from age and a zillion coats of paint and leaping was out of the question. Leaping days were over, chum; bed-to-bed, city-to-city, all gone. Just a reflection of his peccadillos and a Dale Robertson western behind him ready to hang some poor bastard…low budget all the way. The heavy oak chair worked out better, the glass exploding down on the gardeners below, the chair barely crushing a scampering man.

The crest of the wave had been the publishing of *True Finery* on his 31st birthday that Lise Dreyfus had edited for him when she was still alive and worked that craft and magic. He had wooed them and had entered his 15 minutes without style and had managed in the end to lose a minute or two here and there. And probably much more in the company of Lise who made time shaving an art having had her body shaved in half in an early October evening out with Warren, stopping her clock without a whimper.

Before that day, they had mastered time and the use of each other in any way possible to stay ahead of the clock. Her husband, Loren, was accommodating to a point but Lise's merciless reminders of his lack of potency kept him off balance and bottled. Loren had at times been deployed as a 'den mother' to care for the two of them in times of poor judgment and folly. Saint Loren, or Rabbi Oppenheimer, what Lise called him when in that special *state*.

What happened? Riding high in April shot down in May as Frank sang it. That was Lise's theme song (after *Sister Morphine*). And Warren was a jellyfish trapped in the swells and riptides of her strength, her realm, much the same as Loren. But while Loren sat home 'knitting' as she cattily described his home functions, Warren played. He was walking the walk, and paying for every step. He knew Loren had to be walking cautiously at times too. She could be painful as unseen shards on the floor after a miscue with stemware.

"Can you believe Loren never lets me see him naked…as if he were my *dad*. He actually looks good for a guy his age." She told him one night they were in bed at the Sunset Towers on the Strip.

"You treat him like shit. My dad listens to his radio show all the time, especially after his trip to the Netherlands." He stubbed out his Lucky Strike.

"He's Jewish---he's used to women treating him like shit. My father is used to it. I treat him like a prince compared to that ancient fucking mommy of his back in Shaker Heights." She had curled her foot around his leg, " I like you Warren because you're a heartless goy who while Dutch, to my family that's synonymous to being a Nazi! You're strange fruit, and with an uncircumcised dick, you're pretty far from Jewish." He remembered she laughed as she took out her little brass mini-coffin that held her works. He could never watch her fix so he would stare at the ceiling or go sit by the window, watching the city below stretch out and twinkle like phosphorous waves on a dark breakwater if the moon was just right. He never lectured her or questioned her. Her habit was just so much a part of her fabric, as infidelity and alcohol and a gift for editing the written word also were. So he accepted it. It seemed in those days he had accepted quite a bit, never rocking the boat they precariously clung to. Even the phone calls from Lise in the middle of the night while Loren slept. She was a gravedigger. A dead of night worker who chain smoked Luckies and hammered her word processor relentlessly. She was sought after by many writers and quite a few of the new West Coast wave that made their bones on her sharp directions, senses and focus. Her Dr. Jekyll reigned supreme in literary circles while her Ms. Hyde kept a tight whip hand on Loren and Warren, who paid the toll to the troll in diverse yet similar ways.

Loren Oppenheimer was a radio personality for travel and touring as well as teaching a history of Modern Europe class nights at UCLA. He was 30 years older than his one and only wife and was very established, very rich and very enamored of the young nuclear device he had wed. They had met at a book signing for Loren's work at the time on his latest Euro travels, she at the time a young hustling go-fer with one foot in the editor's door and the other doing PR slave work. She had a disarming way she went about things. Her voice, soothing and encouraging wrapped up Loren like a baby in a swaddle; the plate men eat from. And while she talked and looked into your eyes she could empty your pockets, use your credit cards, extract gold teeth, and after shaking hands goodbye excise your watch from your wrist without a feeling. Loren knowingly overlooked these lethal qualities and fell into the abyss immediately. Lise wore her blue-black hair cut *kokechi* doll style and affected silk Chinese style blouses and dresses that accentuated her gymnast physique. At first glance people mistook her for Asian with her almond shaped eyes and style of dress until they saw the opaque grey iris in which they felt as if free falling thru clouds and any second the ground would rush up to meet them. Lise enjoyed the power of those almost invisible eyes and used them as a whip. 'Beat em like a red-haired stepchild' she would laugh around her Lucky Strike to Warren. He sometimes experienced that vertigo that Loren and all the other fools had felt at one time or another when gazing into them. In semi-darkness she looked eyeless, and he avoided them as sure as a vampire overlooking a cross; frightened of the outcome. He at times had wondered if Loren's impotence was caused by them…his prick turning to mush in their cold translucency.

Another reason to jump out that window, and he had come pretty close to jumping that evening. He had envisioned himself as a dangling corpse on the end of a tether. Lise had been dead six months due to what she would probably amusingly refer to as 'excesses and an all around disregard for safety.' All her Harold Lloyd style of predicaments, her Perils of Pauline moments well documented and Loren on the sidelines with a towel, her cheerleader and janitor.

Warren stood at the precipice of what he saw as a blurred and untidy life. He had ushered in this mess and tried to find an end game to fix it, but was at a loss. His first instinct was to find blame like the child who gets caught and hastily looks around for an accomplice to cast shade on and at a loss to frame anyone for it had only to look in the mirror; and loathing that he couldn't stand the sight of himself anymore. When he lost himself gazing at Felch, whom he loathed, he knew he was looking back into that mirror. Like Kurtz, all he could mutter was 'the horror.'

Loren had the patience of paint. He would sit and watch Lise play as if she were a child at a picnic running in the distance wildly with other kids; to jump in only if she got too far away, too close to danger. But he was sometimes too slow to react and Lise would spin out of orbit, a runaway train. On occasion Warren thought he detected a bemused anticipatory look in Loren's eyes as if he were hoping for a train wreck he couldn't fix. Something to alleviate the situation…divest him of the dreadful job of watching her self destruct, but Lise was a yoyo that seemed to spring back up to his index finger each time she dangerously brushed the ground; her daily or weekly bungee jump from the marital bridge that he was a spectator from. Warren would study him when the three played their ersatz *Jules et Jim* psycho-drama night and day. He tried to pierce Loren's serenity; his glacial crust. He seemed unplugged, unfettered, and peaceful. When Warren had first laid eyes on the Daibutsu, the great sitting Buddha at Kamakura his immediate thought was of Loren. It had the same effect on him as when he would encounter those moments of retreat on Loren's face. As if he knew true peace, contentment and strength yet had no power to deter Lise from her nonsense. In the presence of the Daibutsu one could simply end it all without a problem, the beautifully peaceful Buddha in all its omniscient aura of silent witness...perhaps this is how Lise felt and Loren's acquiescence of her nature, and her comfort in his knowing that.

Like all intelligent people run amok, it was a waste of time to mention it or lecture her. She would just look to Loren from that edge she ran on and wistfully smile as if he were some doting, over indulgent father she knew she could manipulate easily. And she did. Warren also knew that Loren studied him back, wanted to understand and see his side of the attraction; knew there were moments when Warren just wanted to blurt out a 'what the fuck?' and find some rationalization for his own behavior, and not Loren's. He understood Warren wanted off the hook for his behavior, his guilt from his crimes associated with all things Lise to include the sex and heroin use. Loren referred to him as The Flying Dutchman to Lise's Pandora, swept away by their own fates; Warren tied to the wheel of his ambitious ship and Lise the storm tossed sea he was attempting to navigate upon but had to sail regardless of risk. But Loren knew he was romanticizing the whole set up that way and deep down he never really understood Lise's sprint to her end, and Warren also had less sway than he realized or concluded over her and both men knew they were over their heads.

What Warren thought was the serenity of the Buddha on Loren's face was a ruse; he knew all along he was being observed and so affected that look. He would become what he considered a sphinx that Warren couldn't discern or penetrate. And Warren would indeed wonder. He would write, in his own mind, various descriptions of Loren, and always swaying between them, around them was Lise in her death dance. Warren sometimes paid more attention to Loren then he did Lise when they were all three together. This was when Warren was in the chips, making the rounds, and didn't need references for his narcotics purchases, first cabin and cash. He also bought the small powerful machine that ultimately would be the last Lise rode in.

"What are you thinking Warren?" Loren broke his silence.

Warren just stared over the other man's shoulder, not making eye contact, "You, Loren."

Loren smiled, amused, "You always do."

Warren had shivered hearing that declaration, "You're right."

"Yes, but why am I so wrong about her?"

"None of us----and I hate to tell you cuz there's more of her minions than just you and I----understand her." Warren was feeling the effects of Lise's distance from him as she had started another editing job.

Loren laughed weakly, " She's a cult. Do we need to be de-programmed?"

"Jesus, dude…if you only knew Loren. If you were a fly on the wall you'd want to have your wings pulled off, let alone de-programmed!" Warren said as he ran his hand thru his hair with agitation.

Loren gave him the sphinx.

Chapter 6

"Hey, Haas-san." Felch barked at him as he caught Warren poring over some detail from *Gatsby* he wished to go over with his lit course kids. He turned to face the crooked smile of this little fat tyrannosaur. He raised his brow, not wishing to speak to Felch.

"Our *nihonjin* brethren are asking us to be here Saturday morning.... well, not all of us, just two of us. Anyway, I thought you could be one."

"Who's the other?"

"Mr. Flattery."

"And then you woke up." Warren turned away. Felch got conciliatory:

"Aww, now, come on Warren...everyone else has something going on, and Mrs. Bloom is only part time and not part of the intake department. It's just you and Flattery."

"And you, Felch-o? What about your cottage cheesed ass? What do you have going on?"

"Me and the Mrs. are going to Tokyo for a shopping tour, with lunch at the New Sanno Hotel. Remember, its some extra yen in your pocket."

"How come Serazowa didn't ask me himself? Are you the errand boy now?"

"Warren, Warren, Warren…the man is busy and this is *gaijin* stuff." Which translated to it was shit that Serazowa didn't want on his shoes.

"When?"

"They have some morning scheduled interviews for some big money admissions. They need the pros from the NS department." Warren hated when Felch mentioned professionals and himself in any context. He was the only person in the department who actually owned a teaching credential.

Interviews were very boring, and the contrast between an Asian face and a western speaking voice from either the UK or the southern United States lost its charm a long while ago. Now having a Japanese kid with a heavy Scottish accent was tedious. In the beginning he loved interviewing the kids that come back from abroad and asking them how it was being Japanese and living in Liverpool or Edinburgh, Calgary or NYC. Riordan still loved interviews but was lecturing in the Five Lakes District, always on the lookout for extra jobs that allowed him travel in Japan. The kids were never too excited returning to Japan. Some had never lived there growing up western in all aspects except traditional home life; home was as if it were a mission in a foreign capital, maintained as a slice of Japan. Either the parent home company the executive was attached to or the embassy for diplomatic corps sent even the basic foods from Japan, so a household could maintain its equilibrium. The kids of course fell in with the locals at either public or prep schools, some culturally open and some common hooligans and attempted to slip into the stream of daily life. Some ran afoul of the law and their parents as they were played by local kids and at times exploited. While the girls were in a far stricter environment than their male peers, one or two girls took a hiatus due to unexpected pregnancies. Warren remembered one returnee from the north of England, who when asked if he was happy to be back in Japan answered:

"Wha'? To be back 'ere with all these gobshyte rice eaters? I canna stan' the bahstads!" It was as if once they were off the farm and into the west, no one was going to reclaim their *nihonjin* souls.

Warren made sure *he* was enrolled in Flattery's classes. He lasted three months before his leather jacketed dyed blonde haired self was jailed for stealing from a Sapporo machine on a corner in Harajuku with some other young criminals. Early on, Warren would see him at the 7-11 where he obtained his daily bento across from Kin Tama reading pornographic manga in the mornings. He barely showed up for any of Flattery's classes. Many of the returnee boys had learned the value of truancy in their host countries. The girls were far better in all aspects; courtesy, academics, and attendance. They for the most part kept their uniforms tidy and while rolling their skirts up as Serazowa bemoaned, were for the most part involved in their academics. The boys tried desperately to emulate American clothing while in a school blazer, matching pants and white shirt by pulling down their pants and revealing underwear tops. Warren laughed as they resembled the surfers from Manhattan Beach to Santa Monica Beach in the 60's who pulled their levis down low to reveal their boxer tops, until he was told it was hip-hop influence. He felt very old in that minute. The boys all tried to give excuses as to why their ties were mysteriously misplaced. Warren personally didn't give a shit about the ties and uniform problems but Serazowa was on a mission. He one day chewed the ass out of a teacher whose male pupils in class were visibly pulling down their trousers and he had done nothing. Warren was glad that wasn't his lookout, as he just cared about them applying themselves in class. The boys were by far the biggest slackers. The kids who were mixed, with one European or American parent seemed to be overachievers straddling two cultures who needed to prove something to their pure blooded Japanese brothers and sisters.

The interviews…Warren knew it was more yen in his account but still didn't want to do it. And to be stuck with Flattery didn't help. Flattery was like a poison. A toadstool. A blowfly. His true feelings about the Japanese and the kids were always hidden until the sake or beer peeled off the veneer of his smiling luck o' the Irish bullshit to reveal his true inner feelings. The first time they drank together, Flattery, after three giant bottles of Asahi started calling them 'Japs' and 'zipperheads.' Warren grew up watching 1940's war movies on TV and was used to the terms and worse after his father, living thru night actions in the Pacific, never strayed too far from his old vernacular, but to hear someone use it in 1995 made him start to cringe; feel uneasy and embarrassed. Then after a few more beers in between rounds of food at the *izakaya* they were at they became 'Jap tossers' and 'Jap bastards.' Initially, Warren liked Flattery for his breezy way of talking, his mildly annoyed stance on all things American and 'yank' and his incredible knowledge in speaking and writing Japanese. Warren, after a lifetime in California, could only manage 7th grade level Spanish.

But Flattery's dark side ran deep. His Gaelic pride and hatred of the English surfaced as well after a few pints were drained. Warren started to think him a 'sugar coated turd' of just dark, stinking shit on the inside. He hadn't known much about Warren's history, other than reading his book and seeing him on TV once so Felch filled in the holes and offered some dirt up on him via Internet, which was a new playground for information.

One night while in the thick of Warren's first departmental party at a hotel, in a banquet room, Flattery who was well into his cups matter of factly asked him, "So, how was it when your bird's body was cut in half-like in yer car?" Warren was immobilized in body, shut down listening to him. His eyes glazed and his head started to move slowly as if he were telling someone 'no.' It frightened Flattery, who waved it off.

"Touchy, subject, eh? You tell me when you're up to it, lad." And moved away from him quickly.

Warren, heavily drunk, staggered out after leaving the group. Flattery exhuming Lise felt like he had his heart pulled out of his chest and leaving the hotel in a taxi, was quickly thrown out by the driver for loud and drunk talk. Stumbling, he disappeared behind a flat block of apartments and found an unlocked bike and somehow peddled his way to an *eki* so he could train back to his rooms. When Flattery and he were alone a few minutes the next day he flat out explained to Flattery that if he ever mentioned Lise again he would beat him senseless. Flattery just smiled.

"Warren, you're a wee bit older than I am and I differ on the belief you could do me bodily harm, but maybe one day, old fella, we can give it a go. Until then be a good Yank bastard and toss off."

So it was like that between them. He called Warren 'Haas-been' a few times, at Felch's urging, but it fell into a cool professional standoff most days.

And now stuck together for the interviews.

Serazowa arrived early Saturday, the first hint of a fine autumn in the air. Warren was already at his desk gazing out the window from the third floor native speakers department drinking coffee. Flattery yet to

The Deep Slumber of Dogs

arrive, was chronically tardy.

"*Ohayo gozaimus,* Hass-sensei." Serazowa said quietly. Warren returned the greeting, bowing his head ever so slightly to the department head.

"*Ohayo gozaimus. Ii otenki-deska?*"

"Yes, a fine day, sensei," Serazowa smiled, "Are you ready for today? We have six. One is very, how you say…sensitive? I want you to handle, yes?" Warren took it to mean literally, you have it, Haas-sensei.

"Okay. Any thing I should know about?"

Serazowa seemed to strain to find the words. Then in a lower voice than usual, "He, the boy, was in America a very long time and I feel he would be better suited to your background. I know at times Flattery-sensei displays a dim view of America, neh? And this boy I think needs to speak to an American. It is for all intents and purposes, his native country. This is his first time back here living permanently. There are…issues."

"You can rely on me, Serazowa-san." Warren noticed the problem Serazowa had in word choice, and also was a little concerned he did not elaborate on the issues.

Flattery rolled in and appeared to be under the weather. Warren noticed he didn't ride his bike, which meant he trained in and was probably hung over or lamentating spending money in a Soapland massage and haggling over prices to reach 'a happy ending.' Warren allowed himself some proximity to his colleague and smelling the alcohol laughed.

In his best fake brogue Warren said, " We're a bit of hangover are we, shirt lifter? Fall into a pint, boyo?" Here he paused, Flattery ignoring him. "Better shape up, asshat, as Serazowa is here this morning."

At the mention of Serazowa, Flattery perked up, and opening his desk grabbed a bottle of mouthwash, and strode off to the men's room.

Warren smiled ruefully, knowing full well it was a shock to Flattery's system to know Serazowa was in the house. He was in fact in the head master's office discussing the interviews that were to begin in the morning.

Kitihara, the headmaster, was admiring the feel of his new suit. He recently made holiday during the summer break to visit Thailand and had three suits made for what would have been the price of pants in Tokyo. His wife did not accompany him, and that was for the better. He took the advice of another headmaster he knew in Chiba who spoke highly of the middle level massage businesses. They were up to his colleague's recommendations. He was thinking of these things when Serazowa entered the room, and bowed deeply.

"Kitihara-san, good morning." He said quietly.

Kitihara disliked and distrusted Serazowa. Since his appointment as headmaster, Serazowa was like the shark...at the edge of his vision, a shadow on the periphery. He was quiet in his manner and seemed never to expend any energy with exception to when he felt there was something wrong with how someone acted or misspoke, then with a thrust of his tail, was quick to take that person or student in his jaws. His whole demeanor put Kitihara in distress, and his arousal at his memories of Bangkok dissipated like so much smoke at the sound of his voice.

"Yes yes...good morning, Serazowa-san. " He could not keep the annoyance from his voice, and inwardly, Serazowa smiled knowing the effect on his headmaster, for whom he had zero respect yet for all who watched cultivated nothing but respect for Kitihara. "Have we the needed *sensei* for the interviews?"

"*Hai!* This morning we have Flattery and Haas-sensei's for the interviews. I have given Haas-sensei the interview with Moritani Yukio." Serazowa paused here. He still felt difficult emotions after the meeting with the boy's parents after they returned to Japan. They chose Kin Tama due to its reputation of having outstanding students who were returnees and how well they performed in the Ginza Speech Contests and admission exams for university. The Moritanis lived in the States for 16 of Yukio's 17 years and while they took trips back to Japan over the years, Yukio never bonded well with his native country and identified American. His language skills were poor in his native tongue, and when speaking English had no accent at all and while the Moritani's kept the inside of their home in suburban Connecticut Japanese, they had no control over his lifestyle at the prep schools he attended, and the Americanization of his character. There were no Hongwaji school teaching Buddhist values like in Hawaii, where the father tried to get posted. Regardless of his misgivings the Moritanis were very well endowed with money, and Kitihara looked no farther than the generous gift they offered to Kin Tama. Where Serazowa was a purist, Kitihara was a politician and a reason to promote Kin Tama was always in the best interest of himself and the board. He laughed thinking of Serazowa having the where-with-all in making money decisions and allowance of registration for those he considered undesirables. The board would be apoplectic.

"That's fine, fine. Haas-sensei has some knowledge of the boy?"

Serazowa left out the foundation of the *issue*. "Yes, some knowledge."

Kitihara waved him off, "Please, I am about to compose a letter for the board and I shall need my secretary. Thank you, Serazowa-san. That is all"

Serazowa, backed up a foot, bowed at the waist and then quietly exited the office, on his way out thrust his jaw out to the secretary who was not happy at working on a Saturday, as he strode out, his shoes silent on the carpet.

His face was like a mask; smooth, innate and cool. It rejected reality and used its artificial pallor to guard against any intrusion. Though small and seemingly fragile, its tensile strength was like wire rope, ready to unravel wildly if too much pressure was applied. So, this mask used back roads and alleys in life to make its transit. Daily, Yukio donned this for school, for his life. Warren wondered if he wore a separate mask for home, for friends, for everyone else. Maybe, they did specifically on the trains. It seemed everyone wore one on the trains with the exception of the blonde dyed youths who dressed in skater fashion and strap hung, dancing to music on their Walkman's.

Warren tried every means to penetrate that tired looking facade; the stark dead whiteness. He failed every time, so decided to allow the owner to cut him a husk. Yukio could resemble a snowstorm caught as if it were a still photograph. He could be that silent. After a few minutes he looked Warren in the eyes.

"I look like a dead fish has washed up on my face, do I not, sensei?"

"You look like a 17 year old." Warren said matter of factly.

Yukio smiled.

They conducted the interview from that point on.

Chapter 7

True Finery had taken off and Warren was in it up to his neck. It was as if a spoon was surgically attached to his nose and it was always full. Abundance and celebrity fit him as well as a monkey trying to fuck a football. Lise was also very busy with another writer since the book was published and back to doing some mandatory PR work as well. The publishing house she worked for dithered in offering a contract that she deserved as she unfortunately gave birth to a couple of ill-timed *faux pas* in front of the senior editor and also one of the partners at various parties and one book convention. Warren, when out on the book-signing trail for *An Unworthy Tree* needed her when feeling insecure, out of his depth and filled in the spaces with a pick up here and there. He made a fool of himself on some local morning talk show in Ft. Worth after a night of debauchery with a Cowboys cheerleader he met at a Borders book signing. He felt better when Lise was around, using her as a sexual backstop or sounding board but lately she became increasingly remote to him. On the show, he was asked some personal questions about his life and some greasy legman did his homework. This was near the tag end of his tour, and things were going extremely well; sales were brisk at first, carried on the fumes of his first book, he was 'A-listed' for some events and invited to places and houses he only saw on television shows. Up to this point, no one dug up his yard [illegible] only focused on the book, and not on [illegible] his press released story which focused on his teaching at a small community college in Santa Monica and then writing his book in his spare time, and its whirlwind printing and explosive sales. There was even talk of a [illegible]s he allowed his work to be optioned.

[illegible]s mother, when alive, had been a member of A.A. [illegible] mazement, Big Dutch had a DUI in [illegible] as blindsided and didn't know how to handle this [illegible] was smiling as he delivered this information [illegible] asked Warren how he felt about [illegible] he was apologizing, mugging for the audience about having one too many at a party the night before, and now with this revelation maybe that's why, and then this klieg light of National Enquirer headlines gossip! The host could see Warren was slyly digging out and getting the audience on his side…how dare they throw his deceased mother up on stage, and betray her supposed anonymity in AA. They could weather the father's DUI, because hey, they were in Texas. The host, his face hanging frozen like Cheshire Cat then asked Warren another question before the coup de grace.

"So…you're of Dutch heritage yes?"

Warren figured this was the host's way of digging himself out from the statements about his parents…maybe talk about the Netherlands and his family background. How wrong he was.

"Yes, my family's all from Einschede before they emigrated."

"And because of its proximity to Germany…is that the reason your great uncle Jann Haas joined the Waffen SS?" There was a distinct change in air pressure in the studio. Warren was hearing his words over and over in his head, and he knew his face must have reflected total confusion as well as hatred for this man in that microcosm of the moment. Warren became snow-blind in that instance; a white blur of lights and people melting in the studio and the audience. Then he registered the gasps and low murmuring voices and he could hear distinctly the word *nazi*. He thought of Lise's speech in describing her Jewish family's take on all things Aryan tainted. He wanted to tell the host, but hey, I'm *shtupping* a Jewish girl, I'm good, man. But after a long pregnant pause, and after the host, still smiling, said cheerily, its time for a commercial, and we'll get back to Warren Haas and his national bestseller *An Unworthy Tree*. Warren stood up, pulled his mike off, and leaning down into a cringing hosts face called him a cocksucker, and walked off the stage. Next day there was a minor stir in the *LA Times* 'View' section and the local Texas station's feed was being replayed all over the country. Even *ET* jumped all over it. His agent, Stanford Morris, who was Jewish called him and asked him point blank about Jann. He couldn't lie. Yes, Jann joined the SS, and was killed in Bastogne. And so? Stanford said he was cool with it, and let it go. The publishing house called Stanford and asked about damage control. He told them he advised Warren to just admit to the truth; Jann had his own politics, ties to Germany (his wife) and was basically ostracized by the entire Haas clan. Warren's own father, Gus Haas served in the Pacific in *USS San Francisco* at Guadalcanal, and awarded a purple heart. The worst part of it was his dad's phone call at his hotel in Texas after the show aired, and the news broke. How could this buried secret get out? How could this little Texas cocksucker drag his wife thru the mud?

It was a bad week.

"Nothing but class," Lise laughed on the phone. "You called him a cocksucker? Yea, he was, but you have to hand it to them…due diligence.

They did their homework."

"Jesus H. Christ, Lise, my dad is livid. He's like this big pissed off pitbull. Thanked me for kicking shit all over my mother."

"Can't choose family. You should see some of the maniacs in my brood. Wanna come to NYC? Bring your *nazi* cock?" She laughed.

"You at the Royalton? I am an ouch cube of spent nerves." He sighed, sitting on the bed in the Westin, DFW Airport.

"Yah…its warm here, so bring some snow."

There were phone calls from local news people and reporters that he avoided. The PR guy who was his contact there also tried to get a hold of him, as they were supposed to drive south to Austin for the next show. Warren told him to go fuck himself, and booking his flight, went to NYC.

Back then it was easy to fly with coke, weapons, sex toys. He would at times fly to meet her or she to him, sometimes with a ¼ of an ounce of coke and they would cavort like Caligula; snorting to *Aladdin Sane* or *The Man Who Sold The World* Lise would make herself speedballs with heroin, and coaxed Warren into trying it at least once. It was hard for him to take that extra step but languishing in a steaming tub at the Royalton in NY, they made slow, nodding love to the guitars. That was being too deep in Lise's world. He even escorted her to Compton to cop, and after a couple of runs couldn't hang with that anymore. This upper middle class chick that never knew any deprivation mingled so easily with her dealers; verbally sparring and dropping sexual innuendos that Warren couldn't handle. Lise would smile and play them; cozying up and slipping out of their grasp. He refused to go with her again. He hated her using heroin, and he was scared of it too. He knew once hooked he would never kick, too weak to even think about it. Lise never even appeared to be addicted, just took it in stride like she was buying cantaloupes at Toluca

Market. No big deal; just more speedballs, 'Heroes' on the cassette player, deep within her. He felt hypocritical in many ways after writing *True Finery* with its rolling lead character Mick Hatcher's easy usage of people and narcotics, and Warren pretty much a Walter Mitty, just dreaming this guy up. Lise was more of a basis for Mick, as her male alter self; Lise with a sex change. Loren saw thru it all. He dubbed himself and Warren 'the two moths.' He was right. Right up into the moment Warren hit that light pole, the metaphor for the flame, and his life and career imploded.

Everyone took Mick Hatcher to be a thinly disguised Warren. This led him to act, post Jann, like Mick in public, and contribute to his decline in character and degrade his book sales for *An Unworthy Tree*. Acting like Mick in interviews and public also created some places people could use to attack him. He gave himself over and wore Mick's mask until it became his face like that *Twilight Zone* episode of the creepy family whose faces became the masks they wore in correspondence to their disgusting character traits. Lise allowed him to carry out this charade. She had bigger fish to fry professionally and she didn't really need people to know she was actually part of the composite for this addictive poseur. She made her own mistakes, and digging out by editing this success was her means for redemption. This book was her ticket and she saw it as a means to level the playing field between her and Loren. Loren had it all…the public eye and adoration, access, respect. She despised being Mrs. Oppenheimer and insisted on being Ms. Dreyfus and *True Finery* did that in her circle; enabled her to have that identity. She hadn't told Warren he was basically yesterday's paper after the success of his book. She had more kites to fly than to worry about his next project. The imprinters wanted her to stay with him, work as a team for his next endeavor but she wriggled out of it, secretly predicting him a one book wonder and used the opportunity to fully embellish her work for the next move.

Warren was just cruising thru celebrity now and worked hard on his follow up and while she gave him minimal help she felt that well was dry even though this second work of Warren's seemed more relaxed and expansive; mature. Loren asked her what Warren's next book would be about and she simply smiled and said 'Irrelevance.' He just took her to mean the theme of the story, not a prophecy. Neither man knew that she welcomed a new lover; the agent for her current author. They returned to the scene of many a Lise-Warren crime and consummated the thirty-minute courtship at the Sunset Towers and if Warren knew, his own sense of irony would have appreciated the betrayal, the style and cold-bloodedness. Loren and Warren shared far more in common than being the 'moths' than they realized. Both were cuckolds and brothers-in-arms now and both soon to be widowers. Had she been around to see them in that state, she would have enjoyed a grand laugh.

Warren needed her far more than her husband. He felt her help in her ability to worm more from him in regards to his writing that it gave him an edge. When he was developing the white trash protagonist for *Finery* she could cajole him psychologically to dig deeper, think harder, understand perspective in a 360' sense. He actually did, in some sense, become Mick Hatcher and during sex she once called him 'Mick', slapping his shoulders and face when he went down on her. Some nights they were so drugged, no one could perform, another part of the book and Hatcher's character.

"Can't stick it...lick it..." She would growl with the utmost depravity.

And he would. Obeying like her dog.

Chapter 8

In Japan he could count on two fingers the times he had been half as stupid as those days in Los Angeles. He kept remembering Zevon's "I'll Sleep When I'm Dead" and knew he was finally out of that playbook. No more nights where he was pimp flush and cruising in the silver and black bathtub at high speeds and low drag. Laughing, the bicycle he motored around on now was a far cry from the salad days. Peddling to the *eki*, locking it, taking the train places when it rained…the trains… packed already at 6:45; Tokyo riders. Strap hangers with vacant stares avoiding eye contact; the aroma of fish, rice and cigarettes permeating the car. Sitting passengers in that Neverland they went to. Warren looked down at the tops of their heads. The halo of light on the exposed black hair from the dome lights; the youth with their dyed red or blonde hair. The youth. They rode the trains tuned into whatever their discman's secretly transmitted to their ears. They were detached and unconcerned. Dressed in already untidy school uniforms travelling the city all day. To school, to *juku*, to home, back to school. They could be seen in the stations all day eating snacks, smoking or flirting with each other, eye sockets deep in manga porn or comix; families incommunicado. Micro cellphones with secret numbers tuned to the older salary men calling their teen aged jump-offs, reservations at love hotels for assignations after compiling shopping lists for gifts; the men who could afford the 'Hello Kitty' shit and gifts of clothing, candy and yen. Marlowe gave him the low down on all this. Warren knew it was there but didn't have a grip on the Japanese. He didn't understand the norm, so its deviations were for him invisible. The drunks returning from the *izikayas* and brothels in Soapland behaved as their brethren from all over the world, but it was the voyeuristic, non-involved deals he was ignorant of till Marlowe set him straight. The guides to 'peeping' and voyeuristic behaviors he read of in Mishima novels but didn't really believe; the angles of the *benjos* or bathrooms in the station houses that afforded a slight view of the occupants. One of the best places to go at night under guise of walking your dog was 'American Village' outside Tachikawa that housed American service personnel and their families who were either permanent or awaiting base housing. The guide said the *gaijin* conduct business with shades up in the evenings or late at night.

They were discussing a young woman Warren had in his speech class that was a chronic truant even though Warren saw her daily near the *eki* on her new cell phone, in her school uniform that looked tailor made and quite spruce, all business.

"She's a tart," Mused Flattery. "Probably has an old fella, like, makin' a fool of himself over her and spending a lot of yen."

Marlowe pulled a face in Flattery's direction but turned to Warren and said that he was probably right. The year before Warren arrived at Kin Tama three girls were arrested for prostitution. All were 15-year-old 10th graders. Warren's student, Yuki, was 15. Kitihara deployed a full court press with local journalists to keep Kin Tama out of the papers. Reluctantly they just described it as a 'local school of good repute.'

Not two weeks after his chat with Marlowe, he caught sight of her in Roppongi, notorious area of nightlife and foreigners one night he was bar hopping. She was on the arm of a squat gray haired man whose face was very stern. Warren at first took him for an irate dad or a pissed off grandfather catching his daughter in a dangerous place. But on closer inspection he saw the old bastard feeling her ass in her short school skirt.

Warren caught Yuki's eye and seeing the horror in hers found he was walking up towards her. She was pulling her escort away and he was not pleased to be moving, crablike in the crowd. Warren caught up to them and then he greeted the old bastard.

"*Watachi wa Haas-sensei. Sensei!*"

The older man's face didn't flinch. Yuki nervously giggled. The man pulled her away ignoring Warren, who shook his head and wondered why he even given a shit. Why was he trying to bust this older guy's balls over his 'tart'?

He found he was constantly butting his head up against the changes, and needed to finally just tell himself to relax, watch, observe. Let guys like Marlowe lay down the tempo and go with it. It was all so different and yet so familiar that it was almost as if one were inside a dream, in a deep sleep knowing one was dreaming all along yet unable to transit away from it. The land and colors were familiar but the shapes and feelings one took from the landscape were foreign. Once, when hurtling downtown on the train with Marlowe, the first time he visited his small metro flat, he sat in wonder at the massive buildings, office windows visible to the passing trains and freeway drivers, as the train wove its way thru them like a long steel snake.

"It's pretty preposterous, isn't it?" Marlowe inquired. "It's like the UK stacked on New York and then there's this Asian twist to it. Nothing like it really."

Warren agreed. It was daunting in its presentation. Some people in one building were at the windows watching them as they whizzed by, Warren wondering their thoughts.

"Just start relaxing. Take a day trip. Tell the staff you need a cultural day, and take the train somewhere. Yes…go to Kamakura. If you told Serazowa you needed to see the Buddha, he would agree. You'll be blown away."

And so Warren had visited Kamakura, and Marlowe was right. For some reason, the enormity, the serenity surrounding it, calmed him. Stepping off the bus, he walked to the ticket offices, trees surrounding it from behind and then he made his way on the path. Turning one more corner it appeared suddenly in the distance, enormous and in that moment as it was revealed to him he stopped breathing. He never felt such serenity ever in his entire life. It was as if he took an emotional tonic. He vaguely remembered the train back, or walking back to the station from the Buddha's resting place; sitting lotus fashion its hands meeting on its lap deep in meditation. For him it was a turning point in many ways. He felt, had he not experienced this visit, he might have just quit his job in Japan and taken anything back on the mainland U.S. He been suffering under a delusion he was a misfit here and the inner office politics and bullshit were about to make him implode. It all seemed feeble to him now and he knew it was his ego. All of it. He, Warren Haas, chased out of town, like that varmint so long ago when he was ready to snuff himself in Hollywood at the El Norte, and now a teacher abroad, unable to keep down a job in his own country; all of it his ego, nothing more. He seemed drained of it as he sat in Kamakura, and burned incense.

So he returned to his rooms in Kin Tama and slept soundly. For the first night since it happened, he did not dream of Lise. He woke with a resolve to continue and, whatever the abuse or politics, to weather it all. He got here on his own and would take the ownership of his situation.

Chapter 9

Mari Kawakami started watching Warren in the *Eigo*-Native Speakers department rooms when to save costs they merged the two departments, Serazowa feeling that it would also create *espirit de corps* and comradeship. Of course he himself worked in an almost private cubicle so as to maintain his positional authority. She was at first taken aback that Haas-sensei cleaned his area, not allowing the elder Mrs. Fukuda, who worked part time, to do that work. But then she came to believe that although an idiosyncrasy of his, she accepted it, not as failing but as typical *gaijin* confusion. She started to study him slowly, measuring his actions considering his movements. Naturally she compared him to Japanese men and her ex-husband who left her for an 18-year-old graduate of the last school she had worked at.

Her husband. They taught alongside each other at their last school and she never knew what was happening, even that close up. This was one of the reasons she took to studying Warren so closely. She already decided if she were to take a *gaijin* lover it would be him. She was 34 and her chances for marriage were a diminishing return, daily. She harbored no illusions on that score. She recalled her husband apologizing as he packed his shirts and doing it so poorly, she stepped in and helped him pack. He said that he was sorry that at her age she would probably not have much of a chance to find another husband. Honestly, he said, who would want a woman in her thirties? Silently, she agreed. Who indeed would?

So now she decided to take some turns out of the mainstream. One of her colleagues from the public school they worked at was actually dating a Nigerian! Scandalous. Yet she accepted these changes stoically. Since Occupation, miscegenation, so silently frowned on in Japan even after decades of Americans of all races, but such a huge influx of African *gaijin* she felt perhaps it was her turn to take a step out of the circle. But it would be Haas-sensei, if anyone.

So, she watched Haas-sensei when he arrived in the morning during the summer and early fall on his bicycle and changed his clothes in the small teacher's closet. She had taken notice of what time he rode in and would be in the shared spaces sipping green tea and reading. She knew he was 40 or thereabouts and admired that he rode his bike and stayed in shape. She overheard Felch and Flattery-sensei's discussing his past notoriety and denigrate him mercilessly. She secretly read a used copy of *True Finery* and an article he wrote for *Vanity Fair* before he was in a disastrous car wreck that killed a woman. After that going into rehab and attempting suicide, and while still a stigma in America, she accepted his decision and took it in stride. We all have many lives, Mari thought. She was happy she did not know him then. She admired more his capacity for survival than his reckless past or his suicidal gesture of atonement. He was functioning now after his low times and she herself felt they shared this as she was surviving too. She also felt him as stronger that he was in a totally foreign environment doing it. From her seat in the department, taken just for the view of the small closet and Haas-sensei, she was content.

It had been two years since her husband left and in that time she took one lover. He was a friend of her husband's who escorted her out to a sushi-ya and tried to *explain* things to her. Even thought he knew what her husband was doing, it wasn't his place to intervene. But...since her husband explained how *devastated* she was he needed to console her. She was humorously taken by his words, not feeling devastated in the least. Her husband overstated his importance to his friend and Mari almost laughed out loud. They went back to the flat she kept after her husband left, and when the friend started to become amorous she just allowed it to happen, knowing the friend would not keep a secret from her husband. It was quick, and she refused to kiss him, as she could still smell the roe on his breath from dinner. She felt in her acquiescence to his friend she had rid herself and the flat of her husband's lingering spirit, and his memory. When she felt her husband's friend orgasm the thought foremost in her mind was that 18 year old girls these days didn't even know how to cook; eschewing most older traditions.

Two months later, after summer break, her husband returned to the flat and she knew the affair was over. He tried explaining it all as a mistake; growing pains on his part, a natural occurrence for a man. It allowed him to appreciate her and he forgave her all her faults. Things could be better and they could resume life. She already knew through school gossip that the immediate supervisor of the Japanese-English department unfolded the affair on the desk of the school's principal and headmaster, who was outraged and taken aback. Of course the girl already graduated but it was obvious they carried on while she was still attending school and under his tutelage. Perhaps the parents will complain? Perhaps she is pregnant? What's the world coming to? They called him in and advised him his contract was voided and would not receive a letter. Mari's husband returned to the small rooms he shared with his young love to discover her watching game shows with three other girls who had dropped out. He knew a couple were seeing older businessmen who bought them new boots and their hair shone brilliantly blonde in the dim, small flat. Whereas he and Mari enjoyed a small inner courtyard they could look at and refresh themselves from the long academic day but this new place was cheap, flat blocks all one on top of the other and no sunlight penetrated this gloom. Arriving home, he needed to hold her, alone, and try and wash away his guilt feelings as well as the dishonor the principal heaped on him. But she ignored him while they all discussed shopping in Harajuku, and clubbing in Roppongi or Ikebukuro. One of the girls was set up in a small flat in Hiroo so her lover endured only a two-block stroll from his work to see her. When could she get new boots? When could she go to Harajuku and stroll the boulevard window shopping and meeting her friends for teas and western desserts?

Mari could envision it all as he related it. When she looked at him he appeared very old, very small. His admission of wrongdoing and that he was apologetic made him seem to start withering before her eyes. A husband, jilting her and explaining it was all for the best in her eyes held some stature, but this melting invertebrate trying to weasel his way back into a dead marriage displayed none at all. She knew the school did not renew his contract and she already interviewed at Kin Tama as to start afresh. She told him as well. That it had hardly taken any strength at all to push him back out through the door amazed her. That she smiled when she closed it filled her with the greatest joy. Truly she experienced a metamorphosis in that moment. Molted her old skin, arose from her chrysalis and let her wings dry brilliantly in the sun.

Her husband's family was from the south, near Hiroshima. After he returned there he attempted to obtain work. He worked in the public school system in Akashima-shi for almost ten years and now took no letter of reference or recommendation, nor would his old principal accept calls on his behalf. Mari heard he stole pills from a terminally ill aunt and suicided, alone, at a love hotel with a picture of his 18-year-old lover next to him. When she heard the news, she only felt better. And her new job was beginning at Kin Tama. Life truly had many journeys and incarnations inside it. One needed patience.

Chapter 10

He found himself sitting on the lanai at The Old World restaurant where Holloway intersected Sunset Blvd. with Loren. The rounded pie angle of the building allowed them to see the traffic on both sides and Warren was looking at the hand painted larger than life album covers on the outer walls of Tower Records. Having extra money he would fall in and out of there on buying binges. The parking there was a madhouse.

Loren pushed his spoon around in his tea, a mischievous look on his face. Warren figured something was afoot. Were they really waiting for Lise or was this a set up? She was never on time, so he couldn't be sure, but Loren was calmer than usual, which was close to death and seemed at peace. They pushed their meal dishes aside.

"What's up Loren?" He asked lighting a cigarette.

He took some time to answer, contemplating the cars streaming by and letting his eyes and head follow a statuesque woman who crossed Sunset. When he turned back to Warren, he seemed almost calmer.

"There are levels of her lunacy you have yet to see Warren."

Warren laughed, "She's not *that* crazed. She's just a brat. And you enable her"

"You have yet to peel that onion."

"Yes, I have heard that, but the thing is…" Warren didn't wish to but he started to sound annoyed, "no matter how many layers, there's nothing in the middle but more onion."

Loren gave a small smile, "Yes, but until you discover it, getting to that nothing still keeps you crying."

"Where are we going with this? Sort of late in the game for recriminations, eh old sport?"

"She's dropped you. She's done with your book, and thinks you've half-assed this new one. She's already working Tim Simonson's manuscript…old sport…and fucking his agent."

Warren had to take a minute. He wondered about the long time in between their discussions of work and if it were the heroin or a combination of things. Simonson was a good writer. His new work, based on the time he was in and out of Folsom was supposed to be amazingly funny and well written. His previous book of poetry was well received and the literati, who loved ex cons, circled the wagons around him. This news, along with Loren's obvious Zen joy in telling him made him break into a quick sweat, his shirt slightly sticking to his flanks.

"Oh? You didn't know?" Loren smiled. " Yes…she may be mad, and have no center, but she has the instincts to know when to jump ship when she senses it grounding."

Calling her a rat by any other name? Warren was thinking of leaving, just throwing money on the table but asked Loren a question.

"So why is it she jumps from your bed, or ship, to so many others, but then returns? And why, pray tell, old man, do you allow her back? Maybe you should have this conversation with Simonson's agent as my sheets have been cool and clean lately."

Loren blinked, his calm finally punctured, and started to speak.

Warren cut him off; snapping at him, "Shut the fuck up!" He picked up the check and dropped it in front of Loren. " Here…pay the tab. Drop me a line when Simonson isn't useful anymore. Maybe I can make a referral."

His silver and black Porsche was around the corner, and when he pulled around the horn of the Old World, he made sure Loren shared the exhaust with his tea.

Chapter 11

When he first arrived in Tokyo he stayed at a hotel the school used on retainer for its guest speakers while work papers, bank accounts and contracts were finalized, as was his direct deposit of pay which to him was very cool not having to deal with a bank, just going to the post office ATM for money was easy. Warren enjoyed embarking on day trips and riding the trains when he wasn't busy. Into Tokyo, out of Tokyo, through Tokyo he was like a kid riding the Matterhorn at Disneyland. He would imagine he was a small cell, passing thru an arterial highway; Tokyo a huge fourth dimensional heart, a vast conglomerate of mixed Asian and western structures. Before he even met Marlowe he was blown away by the cultural mashing he viewed. The main train station, the giant central *eki* was a redbrick image of an elaborate Victorian English Station. Other major stations were housed in the lower levels of huge department stores, some towering at ten stories above the tracks. He loved the idea of the main hubs in the outlying cities and districts being self-contained with restaurants, bars, noodle shops and bakeries. He wished Los Angeles was this smart. He found in Kichioji a small tobacconist to indulge himself with a true Cuban or ride out to Kawagoe where there was a shrine bazaar and swap meet. He met westerners there and was able to strike up conversations and maybe share chai or coffee at a local café, swapping ex pat stories but avoiding who he was as a writer. Many were military, hoping to find a souvenir or some décor for their homes like a *ranma* or step *tansu*. The phony *samurai* swords or *kokechi* dolls were also big draws for the *gaijin*.

He would travel the trains on the weekends before he made friends to spend time with; the air force guys and shady civilians he played golf with after introductions from Marlowe, or his cultural sessions watching him cook and describe what he was making and how he was doing it in his flat in Ebisu.

When he was new and allowed to get his footing, Warren lived in the ancient, unused rooms attached to the school that had housed monks during the war when the school grounds in those days was home to a shrine and a monastery. Now they housed bachelor expats and an occasional foreign student who could not obtain housing with a host family. It was a small depressing domicile with no AC, no insulation, and seemed to attract every mosquito on the Kanto Plain. It was in Warren's mind, some sort of comic penance staying in the euphemistically named *visitor hospitality center*. But it was also convenient. He didn't have to awake at some ungodly hour like Marlowe and ride the train in from Tokyo to make it to the Native Speakers Department in the Arts & English Bldg. He would go to the athletic building to shower and shave. Warren maintained a locker there where he stowed his toiletries. He needed to use the showers early so as not to draw attention as he made the mistake of showering when students were in the building and discovered many watching him that became embarrassed when he looked up out of the soap suds and caught them. In Warren's wild time he endured the placement of a large Chinese dragon on his right upper bicep, at the shoulder, hidden by short sleeves but not a tank top, or nude of course. He came to understand this was a matter of much gossip and conversation. Only gangsters or military were tattooed, and as a finale, Kitihara took him aside and asked that he always made sure to cover it up. Warren did so and now made sure when it was exposed he was quite alone when in the locker room, until he eventually found a flat and moved out. Marlowe laughed and called him *Yakuza-sensei*. Jesus, Warren sighed, it isn't all over my body for fuck's sake! Flattery asked why he didn't have a pin-up done. By then he learned to avoid inquiries the Irishman made knowing they were loaded, and had ulterior motives.

"You coulda paraded a Betty Page-like portrait on yourself, Warren-boy. Black bangs, big teats…advertise all your latent tendencies with that one, eh?" He smiled.

"Why excite you?" Warren asked, annoyance in his voice.

"You're such a silly wank, Warren-boy. How is it you ever wrote a book people actually read? Oh yea…that was the *one* book of yours they read. They didn't read the other one after you re-habbed or they discovered your uncle was Hitler." Always smiling, always Barry Fitzgerald.

"Your mother read it one handed as she wanked me off."

"Imagine that! And then used it to wipe her arse after a grand evacuation, no doubt." Warren felt he would never get to Flattery in reciprocal taunts. There was no way to wipe that beautiful smile off his face.

Chapter 12

In regards to this new student Yukio, he labored while at home; how could he break through? He went to a search engine and started to plug in different pedagogies, theories. Is there an experience I can build on or do I just come at him as a Japanese since he was already saturated in Americana. He lit a cigarette and lay back on his futon, blowing rings at the ceiling.

Warren had always played with the idea of showing *Roshomon* in class, but felt hypocritical as he always dogged Felch for his movie theater style of teaching. *Roshomon* spoke to Warren on many levels, and to a lot of different things in his life in the different versions everyone witnessed, and perhaps he could interest Yukio on some different level, but strictly Japanese. Laughing, he wondered if he should show *Rodan* or *Mothra*! He looked at his watch and saw it was just after eleven. Since moving off campus months ago, life become more relaxed, and there was a regular bar, the Mifuku, he hung at.

The bar was no more than a space in between two buildings and was like an entryway into where they stow the trash bins, but the door of the establishment was well known to locals and always sported an eclectic crowd. They were all very young and the head bartender Warren called

Steve-orino for Steve Allen because of his little black pompadour and oversized black glasses. The rotating barmaids wore leis and cheap boardshorts and threw *shakas* at guests Hawaiian style and would always say to Warren with his blonde hair 'Suff's up!' Warren would counter with 'Kowabunga!'

So much about living there blew his mind. Just the differences; whether they were like loud grinding gears or a subtle whisper. He recalled when he walked inadvertently into a terse conversation between Felch and Serazowa in regards to movies Felch could show and those he could not. Felch had a soft spot for Deborah Kerr and wanted to show *Heaven Knows, Mr. Allison* about a nun and a marine marooned on a Japanese held island in the war. Serazowa, in a very quiet yet firm voice, eyes on Warren with his face to Felch, that *never* was there to be any movies, shows or musicals depicting the Pacific War. Warren saw a VHS tape of *South Pacific* on Felch's desk. Felch didn't back down.

In a slightly patronizing tone he answered, " Serazowa-sensei.... the kids know all about the outcome of the war. That *airbase* reminds them everyday. This movie has...historical value." Warren saw the skin tighten to the sides of Serazowa's eyes, and in doing so his ears pulled back slowly like a pissed off cat. Finally Felch took heed of this look, feeling it more than actually seeing it, and nodding his head forward, almost invisibly, begged off the issue. When the discussion was over, the room seemed frostier.

Warren looked into his beer and wondered how many Americans needed to remind the Japanese of the war? Felch was correct in his description of present day Nippon, but he also missed the impact of his history lesson. They all knew we fucking won.

"Suff's up, Haas-san!" One of the little barmaids giggled.

His mind went back to the problem he was having in his flat concerning Yukio, as he listened to the music Steve Allen played behind the bar. There was nothing but LP's that he spun on an old Panasonic turntable accompanied by ancient Maxell speakers. No one in the U.S. would bother with a turntable nowadays. It would all be CD's. The Lively Ones were playing *Surf Rider* and when he spun this, the girls would do an impromptu beach blanket bingo ass shaker dance, and everyone who was in the bar would raise their drinks and shout '*kampei*!'

So Bizarro world! On his way to the men's *benjo* he saw a small post card advertisement stuck on the wall next to other promotions for bands and movies. It was a black and white chiaroscuro of the writer Yukio Mishima with a headband, muscles flexed and bulging holding a *katana* or a *kendo* sword with some *kanji* characters over him and an address in *katakana* under his belt. After pissing, he tore it off the wall and asked Steve Allen, who spoke a modicum of accented English, what it was all about. He strained for the words, as much as Steve did in explanation.

"Hmmm...this ceeneema of Mishima Yukio's rife." He said using the proper Japanese format of last names first. " It praying in Ikebukuro. You know him?"

"Indeed." Warren knew him as a brilliant writer and read most of his works printed in the West and could recall vividly the memory of going to the Village Theater in Westwood to see *The Sailor Who Fell from Grace from The Sea* and the need to read the book. Yukio Mishima. He felt he found a key to open the door to his student. Rounding up some of the books may be hard, as Warren had only *The Temple of the Golden Pavilion* and a collection of short stories, he traveled pretty light from Hawaii, chucking a lot of his stuff that was in storage. It was a start and could work on lesson plans and Xeroxing chapters for the seniors, as there were only14 enrolled in this one class. He ordered another beer, excited at the prospect of teaching Japanese kids a Japanese author. Steve Allen brought it out to him, the girls dancing to another surf tune. Warren held it up.

"Suff's up, Steve-orino" He smiled.

"*Kampei!*" Steve-orino replied.

Chapter 13

Flattery was an ass and panty man and long ago resigned himself to the slim pickings of Japan in the posterior department. While the majority of women didn't have flat books for asses, nor did they have the expansive hips and Rubenesque lines stretching a pair of panties that he craved. When his fellow classmates in London took sex trips to Thailand and the Philippines, to Flattery those women were like boys so he went to Rota, Spain in search of thick blondes sunning from Germany. One night after drinking in Shibuya district, he was fooled when thinking he had at long last found a well-rounded Japanese arse but that it was actually an ass falsie the woman strapped on to give her figure a more ample western look. They met in a bar and when well into their cups, once outside he pushed her against a wall outside the *eki* on the way to her place. Smiling, he ran his hands behind her to find the foam rubber coating of the falsie in between his fingers that gave rise to stark horror and a harsh 'the fuckissis?' He found better luck when meeting Americans, European or Canadian girls on vacation and then taking a nice long shower at their hotels making sure to borrow all the toilet kit items. He knew they all brought their own hair shyte and wouldn't be hard up for the shampoos and conditioners and the like he pinched.

He especially enjoyed a visit to the airbase at Yokota because he knew there would be some buxom wide hipped cowgirls with panties that looked like stretched silk in a parachute riggers dream. He knew a couple of the current residents there who also hustled English teaching jobs on the side when not executing their civilian DoD duties. Flattery's name was handed down when some transferred out to those coming in as he was the 'go-to' guy for translations or lessons. He even found some side employment as a go-between at antique bazaars, haggling prices down.

He would fall for the large assed women who looked thick in their fatigue uniforms, which were none too flattering as it was, knowing if they looked big in their kit, they were what the Yanks called *The Real McCoy's*. The problem was that as charming and Blarney Irish Flattery could be, once he went that one drink south, he became a very ass-holish Blarney Irish who when he went there couldn't get laid in the proverbial cathouse with a fistful of fifties. His whole persona shifted to belligerent misogynist and was once escorted off base. Another time, so inebriated, opening his eyes to realize his nose was inside the mouth of the hairy-legged Polish linguist, who like Flattery ingratiated her way onto the base until she inevitably drank too much vodka and became as amorous as Flattery was angry. She lived in Fussa, near the 'gut' as it was called where the bars formed a wagon train from one block to the next, housing discos, pachinko parlors, strip joints and noodle shacks. To everyone's knowledge she had slept with every junior officer and airman on the base. Flattery was reminded of Europe when with her and actually felt comfortable even though she never shaved or plucked one hair on her body, and like Flattery, showered when she absolutely had to. Her 'call sign' to the military guys was 'Wodkah' which she would bellow when drunk in her thick Krakow accent, by then holding the bottle between her teeth, throwing her head back and drinking hands free. The moniker 'Wodkah' stuck when 'Sasquatch' in honor of her legs and armpits didn't seem to have staying power. The female officers who attended the parties and most of their civilian counterparts despised her. They would start taking odds as to which new guy would end up with her. Most of the guys who were residents on base awhile in their tours had already been there and done that, picked off one by one as they rotated in, and once done, to a man, none ever made that perilous journey again and they too would watch and bet on who would be the sacrificial penis among the newbies. And at every soiree there were new guys, if not air force or from the small naval detachment, they were civilian contractors.

And so the cycle would continue. Only Flattery slept with her more than once, at times feeling her a kindred soul lost in this obtuse country and surrounded by fucking yanks…so it wouldn't amaze him to awaken in her small flat near the train station next to the strip club and the Red Rooster Bar, hung over hard and pissing in her sink as the toilet always seemed to have issues, his body and head trapped in the rain forest of her hanging wash drying from the rafters of the *benjo*. He would steal away, her snoring covering any loud stumbling things he did in making his escape. If there were any loose yen on the countertops of her vanity he would liberate them and feel entitled as a repeat customer.

Doc Krinberg

Chapter 14

Warren looked out of the Native Speakers department windows only to find drizzle falling outside. He came from one of the conversational classes that were mandatory for all Native Speakers alongside the literature and English comps. It was a windowless class full of boisterous and obnoxious 10th graders who could give a flying fuck about learning conversational English. He caught a quick sad glimpse of his visage in the glass. He was working on a lesson plan consisting of Bloom's Taxonomical skills pertaining to parts of the saga concerning Mishima's *Sea and Sunset*. It was for Yukio's senior class.

It was the last week of September, and the second trimester had just gotten underway three weeks after summer holiday. Warren went nowhere in August. On a couple of steamy nights that ended in tropical drizzle he made his way downtown to the lights of the city, pressed against masses of people in the crosswalks, the bars and trains. One night, too drunk to make it home, he discovered he was a block from Marlowe's and attempted to stay there only to be rebuffed as Marlowe, hiding behind the door said he was with a woman. He ended up staying at a capsule hotel, sleeping it off in one of the small pods. Waking and cursing the tobacco stench in his clothes he returned in the humid dawn, swiping at the mosquitos resting on his door and staggered into the sweet damp cold of his small place in Kunitachi.

And now the term was underway and he was working late, the only one in the Native Speakers Department still there. Even all his Japanese counterparts were gone as well, so the office was quite silent. He looked at the office since Serazowa consolidated it. It consisted of rows of desks with two sets facing each other. In the formation, the Native Speaker teachers faced each other and the Japanese teachers faced each other as if there were a Pacific separating the two worlds. Warren looked at that gulf and sighed. It would never get smaller, the desks never closer.

Warren felt like he hadn't meshed with the world anyway and was on a chronic collision course with everything on the planet; not tethered. He reached into his desk drawer and pulled out a cassette and put on some Beethoven piano concertos, immediately losing steam on his lesson plans. His thoughts wandered to *Bunkasai,* cultural week which they were entering. A full week of games, food sales, cultural exhibits and the dreaded visit from the odd parent there for the festivities. On the holidays the chance of a parent showing up was elevated from nil to possibility. *Bunkasai...*

Warren drifted. In the middle of the week was the Autumnal Equinox day Holiday. It would be then officially be autumn. He looked forward to the mornings shaking off their humid, foul smelling shrouds. He would see less roaches in his pantry and would glimpse Fuji-san in the distance, a feat unheard of in the hazy summers. Summers like in Los Angeles. He remembered them easily with the L.A. sunrise like a flashlight in a swamp; just waking up, front seat of the Porsche full of empty bottles and Lise's scent.

Chapter 15

"This is a great system they have set up—all the computers networked. How in heck did Kin Tama get around the usual conformity and consensus to achieve this?" Warren asked Marlowe after logging on and reading about the NFL season.

"Serazowa, under cover from Kitihara, who if he had his wishes we would all be using brushes and writing in *kanji*. He recruited an engineering student from Rutgers who he met in California on some boondoggle deal to Silicon Valley. She was working some shoestring computer set up operation after quitting at Hewlett-Packard…just four to five techies and her who were branching off but underfinanced and a few of them too fond of pot. Anyway, he offered her a contract to come over here and take a look at Kin Tama's set up. We were just starting to buy computers en masse from an endowment offered to us by an old graduate from the salad days. This was back when I was only here for a couple of years."

"That's sort of ahead of the power curve." Warren was impressed. "What happened to the woman who set it up?"

"Well, she came over and she had a room downtown at a mid level hotel that Kin Tama maintained and was probably the same place you landed in when you first got here, nothing five star—but a suite and she would train in everyday. This was before they started wiring everything together. She said 'modem' and people said 'huh?' And she was fine too, Jenny from Parsippany, New Jersey; athletic build, a looker. And that's what the problem was."

"Howso?"

"Serazowa is seriously old school, as you have noticed. Women need to walk behind men sort of stuff...she was pretty much ram-rodding the modernization and she was innovative too. Read the blueprints for the school—electrical systems and started talking 'servers' and all this other high tech language. Serazowa was smitten yet at the same time he was Serazowa. He asked her to create a plan and a booklet out of it. He also tried to make her."

"Ah-ha...and that was that? Did she balk?"

"Most definitely. She was all about the work and having her way with it. It was the old, 'irresistible force meeting the immovable object' paradigm. He hired her to do it, so let her do it. And in her Jersey way told him, hey, I don't shit where I sleep or eat." Marlowe laughed at the memory. "If she wasn't so adamant about doing the work, she might've strung him along a bit, but as it was she was blunt and for him, after being turned down, too outspoken."

"And?"

"So the day she turned in the plan book, he said she violated her contract and fired her. It was pretty ugly. I've never heard a woman call a man names like that. I had the pleasure of hearing it all while in Kitihara's office. But he just sort of calmly said she didn't have a leg to stand on and his lawyers were already ready to go to war. Jersey!"

"So what happened to the plan book?"

"Serazowa handed it to Flattery and told him to translate it to Japanese, and he called in a group of young computer guys …all pretty good but nowhere close to Jenny."

"What happened to her?"

"Umm…I introduced her to a couple of people I knew and now she's in between South Korea and DC a lot."

"Serazowa, he's a piece of work. Sometimes he can be a bit scary. So she was hot?"

"Finer than the frog hair of legend, as they say. Very brunette, olive skinned and the most beautiful green eyes. Not like bright green, like emerald green you get with a redhead but more like jade---and against her hair and skin they were devastating. And I must admit stacked too." He pulled at his chin. "Serazowa…his father was what was termed *Yoharen*. He was in high school and passed exams to become a navy pilot and went through what can only be described as hell; cold water immersions, calisthenics in full flight suits, hung up by one arm and left to hang for hours. It was like SEAL Team hell week for months to include beatings from upper classmen. So he earned his wings and served in China cutting his teeth-flying escort to bombers, and then Battle of the Coral Sea. He wasn't at Pearl Harbor from all I know"

"Wow...how in the hell do you know all this?"

"Oh, this guy I knew at USFJ, U.S. Forces Japan was a historian. Let me know all this stuff and Serazowa being local, his dad was sort of famous." Warren turned up his brows. "He survived Midway and Guadalcanal too, and after one last visit to Serazowa's mom in 1944 was shot down in the Marianas. Serazowa was born in 1945."

"Jesus, that's wild."

"He was raised by his mother's family and then she remarried a guy who did really well in transistors. He's a throwback. Jenny can attest to that!"

"She sounds like she could hold her own."

"She also told Flattery to, and I shit you not, 'save his pencil dicked blarney and shove it up his ass sideways'."

"I like her!"

Chapter 16

Mari Kawakami experienced a serendipitous moment when she arrived early and taking her tea sat quietly at her desk. It had been raining hard and many of the staff had missed trains or were caught in traffic. Warren rode his bike through the squall and upon reaching Kin Tama was soaked to the skin, his clothes hanging off him as if they were melting. He came up the old forgotten back steps the janitorial staff used to use before renovations and entered the area he employed to change clothes now instead of the trek to the gym. Mari heard the door on the other side of the locker room open and suspected it was Flattery-sensei, early because of the weather, and would be walking in, dripping and smelly to brew some coffee to use the time before classes to translate some work he did as a freelance, but otherwise he would be a chronic tardy. Warren coughed as he started pulling his wet clothes off, shivering from the cold. Hearing his cough, Mari knew Warren was inside, and in the absence of any verbal intercourse, knew he was alone. She pulled her feet from her work slippers and silently glided to the door to the make shift locker room and bending, peered thru the small aperture built into the door near the latch handle.

Warren was half undressed, toweling his hair, half bent over, then rubbing his torso vigorously. He still wore his soaked lycra biking shorts, a second skin from waist to mid thigh. Mari automatically stood, turned around with a quick movement making sure she was still alone and the department was empty. Then she again silently returned to her place of viewing and watched as Warren rolled the shorts down, awkwardly removing the wet garment. Mari studied his genitals as he hobbled and lifted one foot, then the other to remove his shorts. She stoically watched with great intent now, as he was totally nude. He again used the towel and she could actually hear his teeth chattering as he was warming himself. As she was about to stand and return to her desk, feeling she was in peril of being found out, she stopped. Warren finished toweling and started stretching, lifting his arms to the ceiling and arching his back. Mari's eyes were on his body, and the thought in her head was that the intensity of her gaze made him aware he was being watched and this made her face feel flushed. She took one last look at his genitals then hastily returned to her desk; feeling warmed all over.

Warren continued stretching until the door opened and Flattery, looking as if he swam in, cursed the rain. Warren dragged the towel quickly between his asscheeks and tossed it to him. Flattery thanked him, as he did not maintain a towel at work, and smiling, Warren told him to keep it.

Mari, hearing Flattery, was thankful she left when she did. She discovered she was in a high state of arousal. A few minutes later Warren emerged in slacks, an old blue Van Heusen shirt and dark navy tie. All Mari could see were his genitals dancing in her memory of him removing his wet shorts. He turned to her after pouring some coffee from the pot she brewed for he and Flattery.

"*Ohayo gozaimus,* Kawakami-sensei" He said smiling.

"*Domo arigato,* Haas-sensei." She smiled, and excusing herself went to the ladies room. Warren wondered why she was thanking him.

Chapter 17

During that one fast frame time when he was riding high he would sit in the chair near the window and smoke watching the traffic lights well below him from that hill on Sunset Boulevard like waves of light rioting on the long streets. Lise, after sex, would just detach from him physically, like a spider that has just mated and either intends to leave or just eat her mate. She sat in bed reading or getting high again, and complaining about Loren. Warren would just detach in his own way and try and fly out over the lights all the way to Baldwin Hills. Just imagining looking down into the cars at people, see what they're doing, thinking. Were they also involved in sordid back room peccadillos with someone's spouse such as he? He felt insignificant, and in that moment very stupid. He recalled looking at Lise on the bed, her knees up and parted, shaved vagina exposed. His first thought was no child would ever know that as a means of egress. This was not mommy material. Transported by so much in his memory to moments with her, and so many strange interludes, the waters were muddied when he tried to accurately pinpoint the moment he entered her web, and couldn't find it.

Loren Oppenheimer, who didn't deserve to be a cuckold, even if he played the part as graciously if he were Ronald Colman, made Warren never really shrug off his guilt even when he lost respect for him. He was convinced he and Lise were just rats far below Loren's station. He was however, fucked up and hung up, as Lise described him as a spouse, even if a good guy. Warren's values, based on Big Dutch Haas reminded him to still respect 'good guys' even if stupidly betrothed to human piranha. She looked up at him, her nonexistent iris like a comic book zombie and she smiled that mischievous smile of hers...the one of untold humor that frightened him.

"Eh?" She inquired as if reading his thoughts.

"Just thinking...ever compare the constant traffic patterns down there to our lovemaking here?" He lied smiling.

"Don't be an idiot, Warren. You don't have to be the literary marvel with me when we're getting high and fucking." Shaking her head.

He hated being caught in the headlights when he was daydreaming. Like being busted by a teacher in algebra when the weather was changing and he was staring out the window thinking of the beach, Lise would hamstring him, catching him dozing and give him a verbal switch across his ass. Funny, he thought, about how he implemented that as a teaching tool now at Kin Tama. How easy it was to identify the moment when a kid's needle slipped out of the groove She would laugh seeing him now. He could hear the laugh it would be too.

He thought of her daily. He had no control over it, sometimes in the thousands, his memory a card deck in the hands of a magician; all motion and subterfuge. Her face, her opaque eyes, her laugh, the sex...and the end result in his car. She haunted him everywhere he went and sometimes found himself talking to her not only in his head but out loud and he shuddered to think perhaps he was slipping into some form of dementia.

Perhaps he was suffering from a living moment of *sonam*. Lise explained it to him one night when they were talking about fucking, fate and death. Reincarnation came up with the usual idiotic anecdotes about what they would come back as. Warren's default went to comical wishing he could be a penguin, and so dressed up forever with no place to go. She told him about *samsara,* and rebirth. Her ideal rebirth was to be a man. She decided it was too much trouble being a woman and living in the shadow of men. Warren took it to be another bump in her long road of angst being Loren's 'wife' and not Lise Dreyfus. *Sonam,* on the other hand, spoke to events in one's life that were so catastrophic in repayment of deeds that you are relegated to an eternity of suffering. When she talked about it, a night where she uncharacteristically lay with a leg over his hips post coitus, she actually made his skin crawl it frightened him so much. He knew what he was doing at that exact moment was part of the package for *that* place. He felt a fleeting, moronic desire to contact a Buddhist priest and try and talk his way out. Happily, he decided against it. Lise was quick to add that of course *she* was a prominent candidate for that. But the talk had the effect of killing whatever buzz was felt. Warren became circumspect and went into himself, and Lise being Lise was only too happy to retain possession of her leg again.

    He asked Marlowe, who lived in the east for a long time about *samsara* as he came to understand it. He often wondered if he were a continuation of someone in his family or from someplace totally different. Marlowe, being in a festive mood, wasn't having any of it and dismissed Warren on the subject. Don't worry about all this rebirth hooey he laughed. It was before a school trip, right after his first *Bunkasai,* and Marlowe wasn't attending as he planned what he termed a 'solitary' weekend. Warren never liked the chaperone jobs at Kin Tama his first year. He helped the soccer team his first year and also La Crosse. The trip to the shrine and Kyoto were awful. The hotels they stayed at were small, and

The Deep Slumber of Dogs

everyone was on a plan, which meant they starved or used yen from their own pockets to cover the hunger. The kids spent all night in pajamas going from room-to-room, chatting and listening to music. There were never any drug or booze problems or even sex for that matter but they made a racket on their floors and the next day all were flagged from all their nocturnal ramblings. Flattery would hold up in his room, usually shared with Felch and drink till he passed out, never minding the kids. Once Mrs. Bloom came, and she and Marlowe stayed up almost night with the kids, telling them stories. The one trip, which Marlowe missed, was one Warren really enjoyed. The trip was to Kamakura. He could visit there every day if he could. No matter what he did during the day, he would think of being in front of the immense bronze statue and lighting a joss stick, then sitting quietly on the side. He would feel like *Anri*, the old European man of *Sea and Sunset* whose journeys finally landed him in Kamakura in the 13th century as the caretaker of the shrine; sold into slavery chasing a vision and finally redeemed from slavery by a Buddhist monk who took him east. Warren, leaving the group for a bit, crossed the road and tried to find the place in the hills where Anri told his tale to the deaf child while waiting for the sunset on the sea's horizon. Finding a spot, he couldn't see the water but it filled him with an immense pleasure. He knew he had to get back, as the other teachers were covering for him, he felt like he needed a nap and he knew if he dreamed Lise would not appear. He decided he would definitely use the story in class.

As if spoken easily his entire life, he remembered the last line of Kipling's poem of the Buddha:

But when the morning prayer is prayed,
Think, ere ye pass to strife and trade,
Is God in human image made

No nearer than Kamakura?

Like Anri, Warren believed many things in his youth that drove him. Even things he held in almost religious remembrance. His father's work ethic embedded with Protestant dogma; the obsession with obtaining property and displaying the fruits of all that hard work. The meaning of responsibility and seeing how true responsibility made a person obtain respect, credibility, and a position of good standing with his family and neighbors. All the things Big Dutch emphasized in his young life. But Warren, succumbing to the sixties, looked at the underside of all of Dutch's lectures. He saw too much weight under that lofty title and felt it more a hairshirt, a penance to be paid just to have that title of 'responsible guy' to have standing with some people he could give a shit about. Did he even keep in touch with anyone from school? Warren saw obtainment of his dream and vision in literature as his religious pursuit. Dutch's 6 a.m. to 5 p.m. workdays showed Warren one thing; the Haas' had stamina. Warren's vision, like Anri's drove him to a decision that changed everything. Like Dutch's decision to work his ass off and, build a solid home, smoke his pipe and his Camels and drink beer, occasionally put his foot up his son's ass while warning him about girls, his foot up his daughter's ass reminding her about boys, and reinforce in so many variations *The Ant and the Grasshopper*. The 60's were a strange and strong lure as Warren weighed his options. And while he did finish his schools and actually get a teaching credential, he knew he would never be Big Dutch who obviously had a pituitary disorder of an overabundance of responsibility that didn't leach down to Warren, in his estimate.

Yukio was following his vision too. Sitting in Warren's Appreciation of Literature class he listened intently to *Sea and Sunset* and secretly he knew more about Mishima and his failed attempt against the

JDF. What true budding nationalist didn't know of his actions and *seppuku?* Before this he never even heard of Mishima, and here, after *16 years in America*, this ex-patriot *gaijin* was exciting him with this story of another *gaijin* who believed as a child he had a vision of the Christian God only to be enslaved by it and sold into servitude almost his entire life. Did his God trick him? This set many ideas in motion for Yukio who wondered if his vision of Japan for himself was a doomsday tragedy like that for Anri? And what of Haas-sensei's personal wraith that ruined him and pushed him to Kin Tama? How fortuitous was this sensei's fall so he could introduce me to these works, he thought. He knew all about Warren from reading of him on the internet; book reviews, story reviews, his arrests, infamous auto wreck, and his slide into obscurity and alcohol. Haas-sensei, he laughed, was an open book, but his discussions and questions about Mishima inspired him. He would talk to Haas-sensei, during his office hours and feel him out about more things, have safe discussions, but he would procure more works by the author in the meantime. It was good that Haas-sensei had been damaged. It made him far more human.

Chapter 18

The lesson plans were easy enough and Mrs. Fukuda helped him make whatever copies he needed as she insisted the copy machine, like the broom closet, was part of *her* domain.

Mrs. Fukuda's husband was a very successful banker and they met when attending university together. They married and she bore him a daughter who in turn had two children with her husband who worked as an executive for Takashimaya. Mr. Fukuda, for many years, kept a succession of mistresses that Mrs. Fukuda was well aware of. She dutifully turned her eye away and filled her time with attendance to operas, concerts, museums, and various ladies clubs, extended English studies and as of late, more time with her grandchildren.

Mr. Fukuda was also a published economist and the two of them had traveled abroad for conferences in Los Angeles, New York and Hong Kong. As Mr. Fukuda gave the school a fine endowment, Mrs. Fukuda was a revered member of the faculty. She spoke beautiful English as well as French.

Privately, she was disgusted and repulsed by Flattery and Felch. She once spoke, from her position as a concerned teacher to Serazowa-san concerning these two men to whom he replied his hands were tied as they were hired by Kitihara-san and were to be tolerated. She realized the politics of his problem immediately and never mentioned them again. She held a soft spot for the one she called *higeki* 'the tragedy;' Haas-sensei. Kawakami-sensei informed her of Haas' past; his success and failure and the death of some woman. She also thought him silly and so western in his desire to clean the office. She imagined him using the copier and had to intervene. She would take charge and allow him to direct her in what he needed.

At first she was surprised at his choice of Mishima-san, remembering well the 1970 Incident. But she also knew his work was transferable to westernized versions, such as his novel about the sailor. She then thought to herself when reading about his suicide, while looking across the table at her philandering husband that men were such idiots. So, she helped Haas-sensei and made sure his novel chapters and short stories were neat and bundled well. Kawakami-sensei asked Mrs. Fukuda her opinion of Haas-sensei as a man, in the physical sense and Mrs. Fukuda giggled, holding her hand in front of her mouth, trying to think of him that way.

"While of a fine shape, he is too pretty in my eyes," she said and then added, "and blonde!"

Mari tried to make a joke of her question, "He is what the Americans would call a '*gaijin* poster-boy." They laughed. Mari hid her inner feelings concerning Warren. Mrs. Fukuda was very classy, and also very old school and would not condone a romance between faculty members, let alone this white foreigner.

Some things needed to stay secrets. Blonde hair didn't bother her unless it was a *nihonjin* who bleached theirs. She did remember his torso and stomach were free of blonde hair with the exception of a golden trail that rain from his pubic hair to his navel.

Chapter 19

They had kept their meeting place an absolute secret. It was a coffee shop at the Kichioji *eki* across from the cigar and tobacco shop run by the two sisters. Her *juku,* cram school, was in the same neighborhood, so they could meet late and her parents never thought it out of the ordinary. Conveniently there was also a love hotel down the street that they used in the past. Ai was the one to suggest it, Riordan still feeling more secure when they were at his flat, but he lived in Higashi-Nakano and it was too far to travel to during weeknights when she was studying at her *juku* until 9:30. She would present her envelope with the payment along with the small box holding a pastry as a gift to her tutor who was prepping her for the university boards and then take her leave. The streets were usually teeming at this hour with students coming and going from cram schools to home or mischief. She would tell her parents that two other girls would meet her at the Italian restaurant there and over a snack continue to grill each other about the testing they faced.

Riordan would be waiting for her drinking coffee, killing time. He had arrived this night earlier than usual so he could relax and finish his book of Flannery O'Connor stories before Ai arrived in her heavy white sox, grey mini with matching blazer and white uniform blouse. No matter how many times he saw her dressed that way at school or here in Kichioji at night she excited him. The Japanese porn industry also understood the point of the uniform, featuring it as much as possible in attracting the salary men who eye-fucked the girls in the *ekis,* trains and department stores. Those uniforms reached deep inside a man, Riordan laughed, only too aware of its lure for him.

Before going to the hotel, she would change out of her socks which were a dead giveaway for 'student', and don a non school jacket, so Riordan wouldn't look so *skebbe* with an obvious underage girl on his foreign arm. It would also diminish a bit of the stares of disgust she received from other girls her age, let alone the men. He realized he needed cigarettes and so got up and walked to the tobacco stand that was open until 10 p.m. After some light banter with the sisters in Japanese, he strolled over to the coffee shop to take up his seat and await Ai's arrival. They would repair to the love hotel and tonight take a full hour. In his briefcase was a thermos of green tea, some cakes and a present of chocolate for Ai; her weakness after living in New Zealand a number of years. He couldn't stop smiling as he entered the coffee shop.

Warren had turned the corner to the tobacco stand coming back from Ebisu and drinking scotch with Marlowe taking another language lesson. He caught sight of Riordan's back, recognizing him immediately as he came up the street. He saw him enter the coffee shop and decided to say hello and grab a cup after buying his cigars, the two sisters supplying him his Havana's on the cheap.

"*Haje mimashte!*" The sisters greeted him in unison. Warren, who jokingly to himself considered them to be the singing sisters in *Mothra* in old age, went through his usual embarrassing *gaijin* act that the sisters still laughed at. He made his purchase and bidding them goodnight in his awful Japanese, they reciprocated in English just as poor, giggling like schoolgirls.

Warren left the store and waiting on some traffic was going to cross and ambush Riordan in the coffee shop. When the traffic cleared and Warren had an unobstructed view of the coffee house window, he saw Riordan and Ai, whom he recognized by her thick side parted hair. They were seated together and in their attitude it was not hard to see they were a couple. Warren backed up into the cigar store, and turning asked the one sister to cut one of his cigars so he could smoke it now, thanked her and returned to the street. He espied Riordan and Ai, who fatefully finished *juku* early, walking up to the love hotel. Under his breath Warren was pleading, 'don't go there man, don't…' to no avail. With his arm around her waist, her school socks and blazer in her oversized bag, she looked like a college girl with her *gaijin* boyfriend. Warren stood in the street smoking, feeling weird with this newly acquired knowledge; a secret sharer in Riordan's private life. How long had it gone on, he wondered, and was Ai the only one? The scandal that occurred the term before he started, of Hanako Inuye, the 15 year old being found working as a prostitute in Shinjuku was still a fresh wound at Kin Tama. She even made an *avi girl* loop wearing her Kin Tama athletic jersey cut to display her ample underboobs, the school crest highly noticeable! Tumbling onto Riordan's secret made Warren nervous. As that thought exited, the fact that it was he and *not* Flattery who made this discovery, while making him feel good, also in turn made him queasy. If *that* shitheel knew, he would blow the whistle like Cousin Sid. Nothing would make Flattery happier than to hang Riordan to dry, regardless of the collateral damage. He would request a private meeting with the headmaster, jumping Serazowa completely and in his flawless Japanese explain that he wished to get ahead of any scandal and make sure Riordan was taken care of by Kin Tama and not the poor girl's parents or Buddha forbid, a call from a police box in regards to underage girl at squalid love hotel with a *gaijin*. Yea, Flattery would paint the frame perfectly and Riordan would be banished, never to teach again anywhere in Japan; painted forever as a filthy *skebbe* bastard. Flattery would then, when alone, cut the lock on Riordan's locker and help himself to whatever was there. Warren saw the whole grim tableau in his mind and winced. The cigar tasted like it was dipped in battery acid and he felt exhausted just thinking of Flattery.

As he smoked, Warren started recalling things he had blown off before in the past. Little hints and clues that he was either too preoccupied or oblivious to. He ran it back like badly edited TV repeats; Riordan's longing looks at Ai as she sat in Warren's class when they did team teaching with him earlier in the term. His poetry that he needed help with that was always speaking to a secret lover. The flower petals that appeared on Riordan's desk mysteriously, cards in the teachers' mailboxes for him with no stamps or addresses. And Ai…her body language when speaking to Flattery or Marlowe, or any of the Japanese English teachers as compared to her relaxed and smiling affect when with Riordan. He was having his 'ah-ha' moment. He watched them disappear into the love hotel and so he stood on the street outside as vigilant as a lamppost, the need to speak to Riordan this night or he would let it go, he knew, tomorrow. The words he had were for now, so he loitered outside like a stone in the middle of a stream as students and night lifers took paths around him as they came and went from the *eki* to the coffee house or the *izikayas* up the road. Warren was resolute.

At a few minutes after eleven, he saw Ai exit the hotel, her non-school blazer pulled tight around her. Under the streetlamps she did not look seventeen. She looked older and very confident. As she walked alone to the trains, she checked her little phone with the Hello Kitty fob and then she disappeared into the crowd going up the steps to the train platforms and ticket kiosks. Warren turned to see Riordan quit the hotel, and lighting a cigarette, he took a long pull. Letting out the lungful of smoke he had a wistful smile as he walked slowly to the trains. Warren intercepted him as he passed on the opposite side of the street.

"Riordan!" He hailed him, and hearing his name turned a guilty, surprised look at Warren.

"Haas? What're you doing here?"

"I buy my cigars at that tobacconists. Tell me what you're doing here?" Warren's schoolhouse rhetorical tone wasn't lost on Riordan.

Riordan looked away, took a deep drag off his cigarette and then flipped it hard on the pavement. "None of your fucking business. I'm going home."

Warren touched Riordan's shoulder lightly as he passed him, "Don't shit where you eat. Don't do things that'll result in disaster. I'm your friend, man, I always have been and lucky for you only I saw you tonight. Think…if I was Flattery?"

Riordan was adamant, his *wa,* his harmony, violated by Warren. His anger almost had him shaking, "Leave me alone. My business is my business."

Warren just looked at him vacantly, turned and walked away. He said his piece and that was that. Riordan was on his own. Warren would neither reveal or help him and felt better just in voicing his disapproval. Warren was 40 now. He had been 31 when *True Finery* was published. He was 33 when his not so well received follow up novel came out and he immolated in the public eye, almost invisible by 34. He burned out his welcome and the media helped opening the door that he jumped through headfirst. Having a great uncle in the Waffen SS was one thing, sawing a woman in half when not being a magician was quite another. He would find himself reflecting again and again on that time of white heat, in between *True Finery* and Lise's death and wished someone told him 'No,' or 'Stop.' He knew why Loren didn't as he wished for whatever perverse reason to watch Lise and Warren play their reindeer games and go up in flames. And they did, far beyond expectations. Warren was turning up the volume to *Good Day in Hell* for a reason when he lost control of the car. Always, he was nauseous at the memory. The one he replayed day after day. The image. He had thought, in that moment of first seeing her when the blood was out of his eyes of the biology teacher telling him in 10th grade that intestine, when laid out, were the length of a tennis court.

    He found he was crying as he stood in the street watching Riordan disappear and remembering her eyes. In all that she just endured; the whiplash speed of the crash and her crude vivisection…the eyes just said "really?' Then blinked and left them open, like a doll on its back, staring at the ceiling. He shivered at the memory. His agent, Stanford Morris supplied him with coke afterwards so not a lot of guidance there. After Stanford quit him, his second agent, Donny Shapiro, worked hard but the damage had been done and no matter how much Shapiro worked the publishers and PR folks, Warren's goose was cooked. Looking up to see a train leaving the station, he felt a premonition that Riordan's goose wasn't long until serving time.

Chapter 20

The next day in school Riordan avoided Warren, and he was all the more happy to oblige him. It seemed as if everyone survived a flat evening, with the exceptions of Marlowe and Mrs. Bloom, who herself was very cheerful. Warren commented on her disposition.

"Mrs. Bloom, you seem to be in fine fettle this morning, " He joked.

"Warren, I am. There I was at the main gate on Rt. 16, waiting for my ride, when who should pull up in a borrowed car but Mr. Marlowe. And we had a delightful ride in, even stopping for coffee." She said still smiling. Mrs. Bloom, on her days of work, rode in with another military dependent that worked at a school near Kin Tama as a math/English tutor.

Flattery snorted, "Me mother rode her bike to work every day for 23 years, rain or shine."

"Did she take it out on you?" Warren said to himself. "Or just happy to have something between her legs that lasted longer than 30 seconds?"

"There now, Warren boy, let's not go down a trail you don't know how to find your way back on, eh?"

And so the morning went, as they all left the office for their

The Deep Slumber of Dogs

respective classes, and duties. Riordan said nothing all morning to anyone, and tossed a student out who had come to ask a question about a forthcoming quiz, which was against his grain, usually bending over backwards to accommodate all his students. At lunch, Warren braced him and asked him what the hell?

"Don't talk to me. " Riordan said weakly, sulking.

Warren almost laughed out loud, "You fucking kidding me? Because I happened onto your little affair, somehow I'm like cancer of the rectum? This is your deal, not mine. I just saw it; I'm not fucking living it. If you hadn't noticed there's a star on the boulevard of fuck-ups with my name on it, so please, go ahead and find a spot for yourself." He said with more sadness than anger.

Riordan hung his head, fiddling with a book on his desk. "Haas, you know what I mean, I mean I don't even know what I mean. I'm just pissed at being caught. We took like every precaution."

Warren laughed, "That's what people who used condoms and had kids said too."

Riordan, still looking down, shook his head. "I love her, Warren."

"For fucks sake, Riordan, she's 17."

" Jesus Christ, I'm 25! It's not like I'm...you!" He argued. Warren saw his point without being hurt or offended. It was what it was, and he wasn't all that much older than her, but it had the ethical cloud hanging over it.

"Ok...then why not just go to her parents and come clean?"

Riordan's eyes opened wide, "Fucking crazy? They'd probably kill me."

Mrs. Bloom, Marlowe and Flattery returned from lunch, as well as their *nihonjin* department mates, Ms. Tanaka, Mr. Yamato and Ms. Wada.

Warren was studying Marlowe, and his body language. He started stealthily watching him when composing his short stories of "Turner", an ex-pat who lived in Japan. Today he was very different, and Warren couldn't figure it out until after lunch when he arrived with Mrs. Bloom. Felch, out of the office that day, was accompanying his wife on a field trip her class at Yokota was taking to Landmark Tower in Yokohama.

Riordan gave Warren a look of mild desperation when the others walked in, and he scooped up some notebooks and went out of class. Flattery paid him little notice.

Marlowe. With his murky past and omniscient knowledge of all things trivial and bizarre, was still a puzzle to him. If a conversation involved the Middle East, Marlowe described the way the gas stations had amazingly high overheads. If penguins were mentioned, he would look pensive then smile and laugh about how at a distance Emperors looked like fat men waddling around in overcoats. Flattery would have a quizzical look and after Marlowe would leave the room ask why Marlowe was in Antarctica? Like the Hank William's song, Marlowe had been everywhere. He would never make some self-serving story or explain what he was doing, but comments ranged from El Yunque in Puerto Rico, to Elbow Beach in Bermuda, or Somalia and the amount of sharks at Mogadishu. The U.K, Greenland, the Māori culture and Hawaiian petroglyphs, the Battery's at Gibraltar. He would just quietly insinuate his reflections into the general conversation, and then retreat as quietly as a tide on the ebb. Once Flattery called Marlowe out on a comment made regarding the ferry in Fishguard, Wales to Ireland. Marlowe had looked at him and his eyes flattened and every bit of the considerable warmth that lived there seemed to dissipate. Marlowe looked at Flattery for what felt like a year until the Irishman mumbled under his breath and left the room. Indeed, Marlowe

The Deep Slumber of Dogs

was a mystery to all, and as much time as Warren spent with him; he was still the Shroud of Turin at Kin Tama School.

Marlowe was an E-coupon attraction at Yokota Air Base. The ventures to the officer's club and a sort of home cooked meal were a fun break. Warren did some networking and met a few single officers who still treated the military as an extension of their frat or sorority houses in the barracks, or 'O' country as they called it. Warren attended a couple of the parties, thankfully without the presence of Flattery whom he heard also fell in there once in awhile. Once, to his horror, he found a worn copy of *True Finery* and departed the bookcase back to the keg offered in the kitchen.

There were also women, both military and civilian. The civilians held DoD jobs either as teachers, or fulfilling a role as contractors as the base could not hire local Japanese for certain work due to security reasons. Many were also spouses of men stationed there who either accompanied their husbands to the parties or came stag. Sleepovers at the base were normal as the parties lasted too long into the night and the local train line, the Ome, shut down early not being a major artery. He would wake up either on a couch or a well-worn rug under his coat or if lucky one of the many women who attended. He was older but still not over the hill since he scotched pharmaceuticals and the Walker Bros as sources of vitamins and nourishment. He knew where he was sleeping when he heard the usual refrains:

'I'm tired of immature guys...' 'My first lover was a friend of my dad's...' 'In your 40's? No way...shut up!' 'Oooh, so someone said you were a writer?'

But some nights he just left early to ride the train back to Tachikowa, and connect to go home to Kunitachi. Sometimes he would just laugh out loud remembering the stories the airmen would tell. At the parties, the pilots held sway over all the other non-flying AF people. One such character was Mervis. Short, hard built, wide shouldered he flew C-130's, what the pilots called 'garbage haulers'. He looked like a strange oversized kid, always managing a mischievous smile that either ingratiated you to him in a second or repelled as quickly as a spider landing on your arm. His eyes could go from twinkle and laughter to cold-blooded murder as he recounted some adventure. Warren saw a lot of this at Yokota, and wondered if this manic behavior was a prerequisite to military service. But Mervis always entertained him, Warren admiring his prowess at telling a story, and one night in particular he was telling one about a layover his plane had at some base in Oklahoma.

"We had to stay out in town and get a room, as the base was under renovations and the O quarters were being rebuilt. There were only the crew so we doubled up which was no big deal, the skipper getting his own room, and since we were deadheading we didn't have anyone hopping with us. I bunked with the 'gator while the enlisted guys went out to find liquor. Bought a case of Bud and like 23 bags of Cheetos. Shit, after that you knew their fingers would smell like the creases in a fat man's ass. Skipper, 'gator and me went to a local bar next to this beat down Ramada we were staying at. There were some good looking local gals, not like some of these hogs you see here," he laughed winking, crinkling his eyes, and shining brightly. "Anyway, we ate and I went up to them after the meal and was bullshitting and making headway. Since the place was right outside the base, and you know how fucking lax the AF is, we were still in our bags so we looked important. These chicks were impressed and after a few drinks I was in the Jar-man zone. Then, someone bought a round of Jaegers and I was in ready mode! That fucking Jaegermeister…now that shit is brewed in the kettle those witches from *Macbeth* used. Anyway, I'm short on cash as we weren't ready for this layover and I blew off the ATM...fucking 130's...had some weird electrical problem that worried the skipper. Me and the 'gator were like No, dude, lets just fucking fly." He paused to drink his beer before he continued. "Anyway, I remember this story a navy guy told me once about how he scored drinks for free in like Jacksonville or in some other shithole the Navy owns...before I down my full shot I went off to the latrine and stripped my bag down. I took my left forefinger and ran it up my asscrack, nice and sweaty, a few lint balls, cling-ons...whatever...so, when I looked at my finger it looked normal but smelled like *balut*! I went back to the bar, tossed my drink down with my right hand and then made a huge noise as if someone had sprayed me with shitmist, and everyone shut up and you could hear the needle scratching across the record and the girls asked 'what's wrong, honey?' feigning total umbrage I started screaming.

"Hey!" I raised my voice, 'Do you guys wash your glasses with shit?' That Okie barkeep came over slow like, because you know we're in fucking Oklahoma, and he says, 'do what?' I says, 'hey pal, here I am minding my own business, fighting for my country, tossing a few back with these fine ladies----baby, I was in that Jaeger-grandiose scheme of things---- and I have a drink that not only smells like shit but tastes like shit!' I hold up the shot glass between forefinger and thumb and hold it under the guys nose, forefinger being the one that took a ride thru my Crack-a-saurus rex (Mervis then demonstrates on a guy next to him, who backs up as if there *were* ass residue on his finger) and the guy's head jerks like I just Bruce Lee'd him on the chin! He lets out a huge 'whewww' and I demand a full round for myself and the ladies, and then I extend it to the whole bar, I mean why the fuck not as I added some muttering about the Board of Health."

Mervis pauses here, watching his audience. Then slowly he says, "Man…that was one goddamn good round of booze. I just drank with my other hand after that."

"Did you get any pussy, Major?' A junior officer asked him.

"Pussy? Who gave a shit about pussy after that beautiful scam?"

That was Mervis.

There was an odd assortment of people Warren met with Marlowe's off base contacts. Most were 'corporate' guys who worked in Tokyo and were in and out of the country a lot. They all gave him a card but he never called anybody. They all said they could use a guy like him, but they never did. His contact with Marlowe was enough. He had bigger problems in deciding what he was going to do for the rest of his life. He was only 40.

So he watched Marlowe in the NS Dept. offices and was curious as to his nonverbal sharing with Mrs. Bloom. And how in the hell had he been to so many places?

Chapter 21

The week of *Bunkasai* started as a clusterfuck for Warren. Serazowa assigned him to create a cultural table for himself and the other western teachers.

"Like in what way do you mean, Serazowa-san?" He inquired carefully from his department head.

Serazowa looked through him and said evenly, " While many feel the west is void of any cultural statements or practices, I have been there and have actually viewed some vestiges of them. So, please head a table to showcase…something…perhaps Mrs. Bloom can contribute some desserts, or you can contribute some art…something? Please be sure to be representative of America or Europe?" Then he walked away, not waiting for Warren's acquiescence or protests. Warren, staring at his back had a brief flash of a small bronze reproduction of the flag raising on Iwo Jima that they sold at Yokota base in the Xchange that he could adorn the table with, then felt immediately disgusted with himself as he figured Felch would probably buy them to sell at *Bunkasai*.

And so he told the NS Dept. about Serazowa's order, knowing full well Felch and Flattery would blow him off.

Seeing Felch shaking his head 'no' as he spoke, he just told him, "

Felch, don't worry…I know you have the cultural values of a iguana."

Felch, always smiling, straightened his clip on tie, " Well Mr. Haas-been, you could set up a table with all the unsold copies of your second book."

Warren shook his head, "Jesus, Felch, say something surprising and fresh for once, eh? You're a one trick pony of Haas-isms."

"But he's fucking honest, you shirt lifting wank."

Marlowe asked Flattery why he hadn't found some excuse to leave already, in a calm yet firm voice.

"I need to do a bit of shopping at that." Flattery smiled.

"Remember bath soap this time, ok?" Marlowe said to his back, as Flattery floated a bird over his shoulder on his way out.

Felch hadn't moved. He watched Flattery walk out, but didn't join him.

Warren turned back to him, confused.

"Hey Chet, your ride just left."

"I don't agree with Mr. Flattery. The boss asked us to do this, and I will follow orders." He said quietly.

Warren was ready to laugh until he realized Felch wasn't kidding.

"You do realize I am in charge, right?"

"Charge on, Mr. Haas."

Riordan and Mrs. Bloom signed on immediately. She felt like she could probably manage some kuchen or beignet, buying the supplies at the base commissary. Riordan offered hotdogs, asking what could be more American? Flattery walked back in to get something he forgot out of his desk, and laughingly offered a fifth of Jameson's. Warren told him he was excused to whatever cultural Siberia he inhabited. Marlowe asked to pitch in and with his access to the base offered to help Mrs. Bloom, and Warren thankful for any help, felt indebted most of the time to Marlowe; his help in getting acclimated to Japan and his friendship. They weren't soul mates but Marlowe appreciated the fires that Warren walked through and that in spite of it all, he kept walking forward. There was, he told Warren, something Nietzschean about his life in that way. Warren accepted the sentence he was given, and serving out the time, looked forward to that life after to begin. He just never knew when *that* would happen, or if it already begun.

So they fielded a table with Mrs. Bloom's desserts from Missouri and New Orleans and they were very popular. A few of the middle-schoolers suffered through accompaniment of their parents, some with both and others with a single parent, the looks on their faces mirroring every teenager in the world at their respective situation. Warren met a few, meeting them with small bows of the head, learning long ago never offer an outstretched hand as it will stay in space alone and silly, and met the bows with formal greetings in English, and stiff postures.

Serazowa again had an idea. For the mid-week holiday they were to help their *nihonjin* counterparts and also learn more about Japan. Warren was informed Ms. Kawakami would be his partner. Warren, by now impervious to whatever whim Serazowa kept in store for him, just shook his head. Kawakami? He could've done worse.

Tanaka was like a Yule log. Wada-sensei's teeth were so poorly arranged they seemed to resemble a stack of cordwood blown over by a storm. Warren remembered Lise telling him about her cousin who grew up on a kibbutz whose crooked teeth could, in her words, eat corn through a picket fence. That was Ms. Wada, so Kawakami-sensei was fine by him. He actually started taking into account her compact, athletic figure, with exception of bigger breasts since the warm weather months and her style of dress allowed them to be more obvious. He walked up to her at the 11th grade table where they were pounding *mochi*. She caught him coming towards their table out of the corner of her eye. Tall and blonde, Warren stood out against the multitude of shorter dark haired kids and staff. She brushed a lock of hair out of her eye and stood up. He was smiling as he met her gaze.

"Kawakami-sensei, *genki deska?*"

"Hai, *genki des*. Do you know of being my team mate?" Warren almost laughed hearing the term 'teammate.'

"*Hai*, Teammates." He never really engaged her in any conversation other than greetings, asking as to her health or curriculum and student matters at joint departmental meetings. "So, what do you have in store for me?"

She didn't understand his question when he said 'in store.' What store? Warren caught the quizzical look and realized he needed to talk in a more direct way and avoid idioms, "What do you wish to do tomorrow?"

"Ah so…Have you been to Yoyogi Park?" He had, actually, to visit the Meiji Shrine, but the park was one of the biggest in Tokyo, so there were vast areas he hadn't seen.

"I look forward to it, and if you can recommend a place to get a very Japanese lunch, it is my treat." She smiled at him, wondering why he would do such a thing, and just letting it go. She did not wish to make him obligated in their coupling by Serazowa.

They decided to meet at the *eki* and proceed from there, but the weather had turned on them and into Harajuku and an *izakaya* they fled chased by the rain of a large, end of summer thunderstorm. Luckily they beat many others in their dash out of the rain and from their seats saw many people standing, soaked to the skin.

"We got in, as you would say, ahead of the rush, neh? Mari said, using her hand towel to cleanse her wet fingers. Her hair was damp and lank, and her white cotton blouse pressed against her breasts from the mad run in the sheets of water. Warren's hair too was wet, a few strands thrust out over his forehead like a crashing gold wave. Mari reached over the hibachi in the table between them, holding her hands over it, the waiter having lit it when he came over. She then half stood, and reaching towards Warren, pushed his hair back and to the sides as Warren noticed the material strain against her, wet and semi transparent, her slightly visible brown nipple tight against her top. He turned his eyes away, so as not to be caught taking advantage of his view, and in doing so, make Kawakami-sensei self-conscious.

She sat back after brushing his hair off of his forehead and looked at him again. His tanned face, lined deeply on either side of his nose and mouth and corners of his eyes, the high cheekbones look weathered and yet he still had a vestige of energetic youth. It was his eyes, Mari thought, they always seemed on the verge of laughter. The small flame in the hibachi illuminated his irises, even in the dark of the pub. She had been excited to learn that Haas-sensei would be her companion for the day and feeling giddy even tried on several different blouses before her final decision. She felt silly in her behavior, as if she was a girl, but that also thrilled her to feel that. She kept thinking of him changing in the small locker room, his body. She had no idea why she reached over to brush his hair back in a gesture so aligned with intimacy. She never before felt anything of this type of emotion with her husband or the two lovers who came before him. The desire to touch them, or even want to, and now she felt that brushing this *gaijin's* hair off his forehead was so natural. When she did it, she noticed his eyes looking at her body, then pulling them back to meet hers, and smiling, just pulling the corners of his mouth slightly.

They ordered a *set-to,* a predesigned meal combining meats and vegetables with marinades and spices to lie on the small grill in between them, the heat felt on both sides. Warren also ordered beer and sake. He preferred it cold, but ordered it warm as they were still somewhat damp from their dash in the storm, and Mari was appreciative. The waitress brought the sake out first and it gave her nice inner warmth to offset the sexual heat she was feeling since they sat down. Warren was enjoying himself and actually admitted it was the first 'date' he been on in years. Yes, there were lovers since Lise, and the few he bedded from Yokota base, but he never really had a day to meet and hang out, the reality being almost all the others were drunken hook-ups on Nuuanu Street bars, Duke's or if he were really desperate, some wild girl at Moose McGillicuddy's. Before he left California, and resigned from Santa Monica College while on probation, he barely socialized in fear of some asshat popping up out of the woodwork to ask again about Lise, his Uncle Jann or why he was such a miserable loser. He couldn't remember even just talking to a woman on the phone since Lise and having just a general conversation. He also reminded himself that he and Mari worked together, so whatever horns he started growing in the dimness of the *izikaya* had better start shrinking. While Warren viewed these thoughts, Mari again returned to her marriage and reflected on the sterility; living together as if brother and sister even after the honeymoon they had taken to Okinawa. Did they both contribute to allowing it to atrophy? She could barely remember him now, his features a blur. She could only think of Haas, nude, and in front of her. And she needed to stop those thoughts.

They cooked their meal, and shared in it, making small talk about California and Hawaii, and how she wished to see more of Hawaii, only going once during Golden Week holiday when in college. Warren was conscious about his meal consumption, not wishing to take anything off her plate and being a typical *gaijin;* overeating. He was learning to temper his behaviors; anger, drinking, eating. So he paused himself during the course of the meal and conversation. He watched as Mari ate with her chopsticks and daintily drank her sake. Lise would have just grabbed the tumbler and pounded it, and he found himself smiling at the memory. They talked about possible other places to visit in a *cultural* way and she was surprised when he put so much emphasis on his visits to Kamakura and other shrines and the effect on him. Warren explained that he felt absolute peace when there and he was even surprised he told her, but found he was comfortable.

"Have you climbed Fujiyama, Haas-san?" He didn't mind her calling him Haas, as he knew it was far easier than the double r's in Warren.

He had not, and as of yet not planned on it. He knew many took it upon themselves to see the sunrise from the summit, the rim of the old volcano; young and old carrying their walking sticks bought at the Fifth Station with the old rising sun battle flag attached to the top. There were anywhere from eight to ten active small stations where hikers could stay, drink hot tea and eat and with another small fee get brands from that elevation in their sticks.

"Perhaps we can find a suitable day to do that," she said, actually picturing the two of them heading up the steep volcanic rock switchbacks. Warren knew from people on the air base that a trek up Fuji was a summer venture and that he and Mari were, while sitting in that restaurant, on the equinox itself, almost into October. Neither owned a car so they would have to train out and take a bus to the highest place to start their ascent.

Warren thought about his wardrobe, and realized that since he left Hawaii he hadn't even a pair of hiking shoes anymore. This would take planning.

He was starting to become aware that Mari changed during the course of the meal, and the beer and sake. She was less formal and her body language more relaxed. She stopped covering her mouth to smile or laugh as she did in the NS Dept. When conversing with Mrs. Fukuda or Ms. Wada, the three would hold a hand over their mouths when laughing. Warren was just used to it. Her teeth, while not as disastrous as Ms. Wada's were also a bit jangled up.

"Do you know what *Tanabata* is?" She asked him.

"No, is it another holiday?"

"Like *Bunkasai,* a festival. But it means the 'evening of the 7th.' It is a *star* festival, originating in China. It is for lovers. The story is about two stars that are kept apart by the Milky Way and they meet only once a year, on July 7th. In Kanagawa is the big festival. We shall have to wait until next year. Do you think it is still raining?"

"Probably not," He ventured and wondered about her story.

"So," she continued, "this is your cultural lesson of the day," and she laughed lightly, her hand rising to her mouth from out of habit. Warren was glad as he hadn't stopped looking at her teeth, and while very white just sadly crooked. His inner voice told him to just stop; stop thinking and judging, and oddly he started to feel more attracted to her as a result of her teeth.

Warren ordered more drinks, and so they sat, post meal, making more small talk. He discovered she was from the south, near Iwakuni, where she met her husband. She told him of the famous Kintai Bridge, and living so close to Hiroshima. He learned about her teaching position before Kin Tama, omitting the saga of her husband, his infidelity and subsequent

The Deep Slumber of Dogs

suicide, so sorry. He told her about becoming a teacher again in California and then getting an offer to move to Hawaii and teach at UH in the English department then relegation to adjunct status, and that he again had worn out his welcome.

She was quiet for a bit, sipping her beer, then excused herself to attend the ladies room. Warren picked at his napkin, and drank his beer still not sure of what he was feeling and disgusted with his analyzing, just admitted he was enjoying himself. When Mari returned, she looked refreshed after brushing her hair. She had worn no makeup.

"When I was younger and immersed in English, " she started, " I read much Fitzgerald and I remember him saying in America, there are no second acts, like in a play. Do you feel this is so?"

Warren thought about that one, "Hmmm…back in his time, anything could ruin you; an affair, drunken behavior, a financial disaster, a suicide in your family. But nowadays everybody seems to get a second or third, even if they were caught in some transgression in public…things have slacked off a bit and anyway, everybody loves a winner or a loser."

She asked him slowly, "Do you believe in reinvention of one's self?" She found herself wanting badly to talk to him about his past life, but abstained out of courtesy.

Again he had to think, so he drank more Sapporo and tried to find his words.

" Yes, I suppose, but some people are past that. They just crash and burn. Immolate, professionally and personally, and that's that." And then he was quiet for a minute, peeling the label off his beer bottle before he began again, " I crashed and burned, and I guess Fitzgerald was speaking to me as I did not have a second act. I broke too many laws…and people. Sorry, Kawakami, I didn't mean to go all melancholy on you."

"Please, I enjoy when you call me Mari-san."

"Mari-san. I cannot go into all that stuff that has happened to me."

"I understand, and I respect your wishes."

He felt an enormous sadness envelop him because as he looked at her brushed straight black hair he realized she cut it in the style Lise did and found he just missed her, even when she was acting like Margaret Hamilton. He could hear Lise laugh and tell him she was his Dickensian lover; the best of times and the worst of times. Mari saw this look come into his eyes, as if he were seeing something else, a *yurei* or spirit.

Seeing she was finished with her beer, Warren asked, "Are we ready? Let me visit the *benjo* and then I'll get the check."

She nodded her head slightly and started to gather her things.

They had lost track of time, spending so much inside the pub, so that when they emerged it was into a throng of people, off work and going places for the autumnal holiday either converging or exiting the *eki*. They drew closer together in the crowd, instinctively creating their own little herd caught up in the busy pushing throngs.

Warren's hand sought her forearm, not wishing to impose intimacy by clutching her hand, but when she felt his fingertips on her arm, she pulled up and took his hand in hers. Warren was surprised. Did she feel an urgency to touch him? Was she attracted to him?

The closer they got to the station, the going was tougher, and as if they were in slow motion it was so crowded. He turned to look at her as she increased the pressure of her hand in his, as well as pressing closer to him in body. He found he was fantasizing her...in his small flat, the shabby futon smelling of sweat and cigarettes. He envisioned her there with her crooked teeth and found he was aroused. But he couldn't have her there in that dump. He would have to take her to a love hotel, not his private flat, his laundry a symbol of procrastinated bachelor laziness. He wanted her more than he realized as his arm brushed the side of her breast in the crush of the crowd. As if it were signal, a silent cue, she pushed back on him and again increased the pressure in which she held his hand, pulling it closer to her to her and then pinning it on her hip. Warren started to erect, feeling her hip shift under her skirt as they walked thru the *eki* and thankful she couldn't see him so aroused as they came to the kiosks, pushing their way to the ticket machines.

    Mari finally got to the front of a machine and dropping yen coins into the slot to get her ticket, she turned towards him and looking down saw his fly protruding and averted her eyes, paying Warren the respect of not being embarrassed, but seeing him so aroused caused her two separate reactions. The first was her dismay at possibly making him feel self-conscious by letting him know she was aware. This would cause him to stress and lose face in not controlling his emotions. The second was purely selfish. Her womanhood long invalidated and this helped her esteem, and in turn it aroused her as well, remembering him naked, and how intense her reaction was then. She gracefully turned to face him as she decided to bid him goodbye. There was something she felt, an inner voice whispering to her that this wasn't the right time, and perhaps it would never be right. Warren weighed this elegance of her body in turning towards him against the shambles of his emotions and started losing his hard on. A moment and a feeling had passed, and it was gone, as surely as a train bulleting by on the tracks. He smiled at her and taking her hand said thank you, for a wonderful day. And he lifted it and kissed the top of her hand.

    "Thank you, Haas-san. It was an enjoyable afternoon, even if we did not venture into Yoyogi Park. I think we met Serazowa-san's threshold of success," and at this she giggled. He laughed too. She turned and walked into the crowd, her track opposite of his so they would use different stairs. Almost immediately, the crowd swallowed her and he turned to buy his own ticket.

It was not the *evening of the seventh* and the Milky Way of Kin Tama was thick and filled with dangers; impenetrable in its mere existence.

Back on the train, no seats so he was a straphanger, again towering over his fellow riders staring at scalps and hats. Sometimes he felt as if his time in Japan had become one train sequence after another; a somnambulist riding from one life to another. School, home, eat, drink, train, one station to the next. It allowed Warren to dream, to travel inside himself as the images of the fleeting landscape outside reached into the cellular levels; again thinking of himself inside the veins and arteries of a vast network of concrete and steel physiology. His eyes, skipping like speeded up film from the montage of travel, and then back into the car he was in, staring at oiled hair and glimpses of white scalps.

Station to station. He thought of his room at Kin Tama when he first arrived and his train ventures, thrilled and frightened by them simultaneously. Outside, in the summer night surrounded by nothing but crickets. The nocturnal chirping on the semi forested grounds where the old building sat gave him bad feelings. He hated hearing them as a child, when staying up late playing in the yard with his sister Maud on warm summer nights when Big Dutch and his mom smoked and drank Heinekens on the back porch. When finally in bed, he could hear them outside the screen, windows wide open for the heat of the night. His room fan ran slow and quiet so the crickets could be heard easily. He never slept well on those nights. So he would lay in the room of the only building at Kin Tama to survive the war, on an old musty futon that held a strange and piquant odor to it and would listen to the crickets, feeling like that little boy who couldn't sleep. He took to riding the trains the third night.

He arrived at his flat, made himself a coffee and lit a cigarette, and he thought of those crickets again, and wondered if there were crickets outside the bedroom window of Mari Kawakami.

Chapter 22

To Yukio's parent's surprise, he started to open up after returning to Japan. His face, usually a solemn idol of stone softened and he would actually talk in his American accented Japanese more fluently. He had joined the Kin Tama soccer team having played at the prep school and American travel leagues when in Connecticut.

His parents contacted Serazowa after a month of school passed to discover his classes were going well, his workouts with the team fulfilling and that he appeared a normal seventeen year old. Satisfied they fatefully turned their eyes away from him as his progress report allowed them a parental respite and security.

Yukio found that immersing himself in school was a good policy. Out on the soccer pitch he left his anger defeated; a dead foe extinct and cold on the grass. He played an aggressive style his coach was pleased with. When at various schools he always played, eschewing the traditional baseball. He attended special camps as well, and a coveted summer clinic at the U.S. Naval Academy. His father had pulled a few strings for that. His play, forged at times by playing with boys much larger physically and fast that during practices at Kin Tama he shredded defenses and setting up his kick or a cross to a teammate enjoyed the fear he saw in the defender's

The Deep Slumber of Dogs

eyes.

He also met Tomoko.

She had lived abroad in Seattle and Los Angeles. Her father was an executive with a financial firm who also invested in shipping and containers. Dutifully she attended her American schools and while never totally mastering her English was an energetic mathematician who wished to study engineering when she graduated Kin Tama. They lived abroad for five years and upon return had been accepted to Kin Tama in the 10th grade. Her parents hoped for her to compete in the Ginza Speech Contest in the 'returnee' category but shy and without the confidence in her English, she withdrew during her rehearsals. She was taken by her first look at Yukio with whom she shared Haas-sensei's Lit class. The first day of school he resembled a white, expressionless *Noh* mask; inscrutable and closed. He was cold and remote as if he were a distant star remorseless and without life. But for some reason, he was also attractive to her, and like the other returnees, he was a boy who shared her experience and so shared a common bond. Tomoko had been back in Japan for two years and decided to break the ice with Yukio. In algebra, with their *nihonjin* teachers she sat to his right, one seat behind. She noticed when he opened his notebook he did not have a protractor, and having at least three in her pencil kit, offered him. Thankful, he accepted with the slight bow of his head. Later at lunch, in English he thanked her.

"I left mine at home on my work desk from doing the homework." Usually, so solemn looking, he allowed a small smile.

"No problem," she smiled and in speaking English, a couple of non-English speaking students looked at the two with distrust.

They spoke about their time in America and where they lived. Each successive lunch they traded more stories, and his on each of these occasions seemed to reanimate in small ways to her. His eyes filled with light, his mouth more mobile and sensual. It was as if every moment spent with Tomoko, his blood flowed warmer, his senses more acute.

His changes weren't lost on faculty or his parents. It was one of the reasons nobody knew about his absorption and collection of the works of Yukio Mishima. He found copies of his best-known works at the Anglo-Japanese bookstore. His mind was a kaleidoscope of new images, new feelings and that of a new Japan. He started noticing how the West was *everywhere*. It was as if a fine dust of western architecture and culture had permeated every pore, every area of the skin of Japan. He and Tomoko walked to the *eki* after school and taking a side street they found themselves in front of a KFC. The small, stout and pink-faced Colonel statue stood in front, his glasses intact and white Southern long coat shining. Seeing this upset Yukio, and he felt an anger he hadn't before and said aloud to Tomoko, in a voice that startled her:

"Even the fucking Americans don't have a statue of this in front of their restaurants, as it would be vandalized in a vulgar manner, yet these fools are out here daily cleaning it and polishing it as if it were part of a shrine!" He caught the look on Tomoko's face, and embarrassed, apologized.

"*Gomen nasai,* Tomoko-san."

She laughed it off, "Too much time in America for you! We have to Japanize you." Using the common *Japlish* term bridging the two cultures. "Now, let me take you to Burger King, so you can have it *your way!*" Yukio finally smiled and laughed, "I hated eating there in America, I cannot imagine it here."

Tomoko thought a minute, "Actually, we make it better here." She rubbed the top of the Colonel's head. The statue wasn't very tall, so she leaned on its shoulders. She smiled at Yukio.

"Its finger lickin' good, "she said in her best southern accent.

Yukio laughed, "Okay, redneck, let's go to the soba stand near the station entrance."

They stood in the hut behind the tarp that acted as a wall at a tall standing table they rested their bowls on.

"So, now that you have been here a bit, how do you like Kin Tama?" Tomoko asked as she slurped some noodles off her sticks.

He thought, "It's okay. I think, as a high school some of the standards are actually below my school is America. But, its okay."

"Best class?"

"I'm enjoying this literature class with the writer, Haas-sensei."

"Writer?" She looked at him with that news.

"Yes, he wrote a bestseller, then became eccentric and got into trouble. But I am enjoying reading Japanese authors, even if in English." He in turn slurped his noodles, watching her closely.

"That's strange about Haas-sensei. I did not know about his past. He just came last year and a half. I do hear from other students who have had him that he is not a bad teacher."

"Ah so? So he is as much a stranger to Japan as I am." But *I am a Japanese,* he said inside, as he smiled outside.

Tomoko felt good seeing him smile, and felt a rush inside her.

Chapter 23

In the time in between *True Finery* and *An Unworthy Tree,* Warren wrote short stories and some prose. He had no idea where it all ended up since he became pretty much a soup sandwich in that time period. He started a series of what he termed 'Los Angeles' stories. They all dealt with people and issues in L.A. and Warren, like Bukowski, was a creature of the city and he knew it well even driving a cab when he was in college. When he read Chandler or watched *noir* movies, he knew every street and every building mentioned, and showed many to Lise, who was turned on by that.

In his spare time, of which he had eons, he stayed in his small little flat and secretly wrote continuously, only now they were a series of stories in Japan. Marlowe became his protagonist in his 'Turner' series. He saved the work meticulously on floppy discs and stored them with care. He wrote twenty stories in his Japanese series and just finished his last and titled it *The Deep Slumber of Dogs,* and it was based on a conversation one night of drinking with Marlowe after a night at the Garlic Restaurant back in his flat. Marlowe loved to wax eloquent about Japan and his love for his adopted country, in all its quirkiness for Westerners. They talked about the serin gas attacks in the subways, and Marlowe had known someone who was hurt and hospitalized. This segued into mass transit and about the new laws against men who felt women up on the trains, or read porno *manga* in front of them.

It was now fall, and outside the wind could be heard as it twisted and squeezed between the buildings, complaining in its familiar whine in its turns. He was staring at his computer screen, and wondered where he was going with all this, if anything would reach fruition. He felt it was necessary to base his character off someone he knew and could invest more in. When he created Mick Hatcher around Lise and himself, he didn't have trouble in truly defining him in a physical sense. Half the time he almost wanted to change Mick into a woman, but in the case of Turner, he was firmly grounded in the physical footprint of Marlowe. Each story about Turner was told from someone's standpoint he was either involved with as a friend, a lover or student. Turner never has control over his stories or life as he is rendered *Roshoman*-like with each different perspective, and the story revealed as much about the person involved with Turner as it did Turner himself. He read through it one more time.

The Deep Slumber of Dogs
(Kieran's Story)

Warren Haas

He arrived home around nine p.m. when Hana, the institute's secretary, called and explained briefly in her singsong English that Turner had an accident, was dead, and the funeral would be taken care of by his family in Oregon, so sorry.

Kieran was in shock or what he felt shock should be. Are numbness and disbelief symptoms, he wondered? Or is that the literary or

Hollywood version? Whatever the motivation he didn't remember falling asleep in his clothes the next morning. He didn't have to be at work until four p.m. when he had a scheduled class and was relieved for the time off in the face of the news last night. He rang Turner's flat and got the cheerful faux-hangover voice on the machine in both English and Japanese. He called work and finally reached an English speaker in Rossiter, one of the directors of the Native Speakers Department.

"You can imagine that we're just ass over tits here, Kieran. This is a mess. What? No! No accident, he killed himself. The company line is accident...did you know about any problems he might've had?"

"None, none to my knowledge. How?"

"Japanese style---like right out of 'Shogun.' Stay loose...we may need to talk later."

Hollywood style, you mean, Kieran said to himself with disgust after hanging up. How many times had he and Turner said 'Kill me now' after a brutal, headache-inducing day with English beginners? They taught conversational English at the Tawa Corporation with branches in America, Great Britain and South Africa. It was an easy job but at times frustrating and sometimes boring; a bad duo. Keiran had run into the same duo years ago when teaching high school and meeting head on the phonetic nightmares of 'whole language' and video and gamer apathy. There were just not enough students who cared for Hemingway or Fitzgerald and too many who after never passing a test or turning in an assignment asked why, quite rudely over the top of their Oakley's, they deserved to flunk? He then moved to Hawaii after getting a job at a college there and tried to make a fresh start, but again, the familiar slackers were hiding even in Paradise. He was asked to substitute some of the dead 'haoles' or famous white guys for local authors who were genuinely

Hawaiian, so he included some local authors in the course and even had one short story writer in the pipeline for a guest appearance and Q&A, but the same students who protested the dead white guys never showed up for the seminar or with the live Hawaiian writers. In the end, he was just labeled as another ginger haole trying to impress the wahines for a piece of local ass. His frustration just simmered, a slow burning stew of unrequited education blues.

He started dating a Japanese woman who worked in Honolulu for a major concern in Tokyo. Her English, while not Bryn Mawr quality (and whose was?) was very good. She explained how she learned grammar and structure at school, but no real conversation. Her company gave her private lessons with native speakers whom they retained from English Language Institutes in Japan. She said they made very good money and also allowed housing allowances in some cases, and the students were very motivated, very eager to excel and master the language. Also, Keiran-san, with your advanced degree, you should qualify easily.

He couldn't see another year at his college, and so interviewed with a company after floating a resume. He put in his papers, cut the rope and after a crash course on Berlitz, moved to Japan and became an ex-pat. It was here he met Turner.

Turner was one of the many ex-pats at the Institute, another 'gaijin' who went 'native.' He lived Japanese in his modest flat in Ebisu near the Anglo-European-Japanese bookstore, in his kimonos or yukata, his house slippers and Japanese cooking utensils. There were no Western chairs in his house. Turner explained to him how he had come to pull up chocks and repaired to become an exile. The scenario was familiar, with the exception that Turner wasn't running away to come here, he was on track to arrive, and when he would he was never sure but was going to make it here all the same. His students loved his style and his genuine warmth, the fact he knew so many good restaurants and that he took a few onto the US military golf courses on the cheap, where he was sponsored. He told great stories and never dated any of the staff, all of which were serious eye candy. Kieran teased him about his romantic ideas about life in the orient. 'If they still wore kepis,' he would tease Turner, 'you would've joined the Foreign Legion instead.' They become fast friends and Kieran dearly needed a friend early on. But even as they joked, he saw some things in Turner's life that were out of kilter with Western thinking. There was a suicide on the Chuo Line that shut it down temporarily and they just hung out at the bar in Lumine. Kieran was still too Catholic to shrug it off, while Turner embraced the idea. Why not he said? Kieran had to admit, who was he to say what was right? He, an Irish-American who taught English in Japan, his framed Bird jersey, 'his shrine' in contrast to the Shinto altar in Turner's flat...who was right by definition? So he didn't think anymore about Turner's becoming Japanese. He concentrated on his becoming Kieran, whoever the fuck that was.

Turner had an Air Force buddy on tap at Yokota and they would golf at Tama Hills. He many times took Kieran along for these outings to round out a foursome. On spring and fall days, one can see from certain fairways Mt. Fuji as well as Tokyo. Turner would expand sometimes while they pulled their carts up and down the hills.

"I enjoy all the idiosyncrasies, or what Westerners perceive as idiosyncrasies and the duplicity of life here. The politeness followed by extreme rudeness---I know you've been hip-checked going into a train, even by grannies. The mania for cleanliness, 'maskos' for germs, don't lick fingers in public, yet let's all take baths in the same water at the bathhouses. The suppression of sex, yet the obvious flowering of it

The Deep Slumber of Dogs

everywhere, from the hiked up skirts of girls' school uniforms to the raw porno read on the trains by businessmen," Turner was matter of fact as he took a practice swing from the tee box. He took the life here easily, total acceptance of his host country and all she was. Rossiter, in the Native Speakers Dept. was on the other end of the spectrum; loathed his job and his wife's forays into the shopping districts. Without his little tootsie on the side and the cash, he would be sweating it in an assistant principal's office in Bumfuck, Iowa. Turner would laugh when Kieran dissed Rossiter. He would talk more as they golfed.

"Another thing, have you noticed, Kieran, is the way some pretend to sleep while riding the trains? Like at work when they take their power naps, the inemuri, to impress their employers" Kieran had said, yes, he noticed that too, the evasion of making eye contact or to give up more privacy in that crowded space. He watched how the women bowed their heads deeply, tuning the men out, black scalps haloed by the overhead lights. The men on the other hand, feigned sleep and caught furtive glances of a leg here, a crotch there. Kieran saw the scam right away and the men never gave their seats up.

Turner saw him smiling, "Yea, you've seen that on the trains. It would drive me nuts watching. I became the guy watching the voyeurs 'voy!' That act...not the deep slumber of dogs. Only dogs reach that true deep place, when they twitch and not even the refrigerator door opening stirs them. Or maybe people when they're comatose."

"Or dead," Kieran added.

"Or dead," Turner agreed, smiling. Kieran turned and looked at Fuji-san and heard Turner's swing as if far away.

The next morning, after the news, he received a call from a man who explained he was Turner's uncle from Portland and that Rossiter had *recommended him. The uncle was in Turner's flat and needed help sorting out all this 'Japanese shit,' the police having done a cursory walk through, no evidence of a note there. Turner had saved the integrity of his flat, his shrine, by taking a hotel room, which was also very Japanese in its application. Kieran agreed to meet him there. No hurry, said the uncle, suffering jet lag as it was.*

In the station, the music heralded the arrival of the train. A short ride to Kawagoe station and transfer there to Ebisu. The train was packed, everyone headed to the department stores surrounding the various stations. Kieran was a straphanger and started people gazing. He watched the people sitting, their heads dipped as if in deep trance. A haiku spontaneously came to him:

> The space between things
> A dreamland not unlike the
> Deep slumber of dogs

The announcement of arrival at the next station made them miraculously pop up as if a magic wand had touched the tops of their heads. After the straphangers filled the vacant seats they too succumbed to the trance, faces gone. Not the deep slumber of dogs, Kieran reflected, hearing Turner's golf swing.

Who was Turner really? He wrote about him through many different sets of eyes, and he also did the same thing years ago using Lise as a mainstay character. He named her 'Analise,' a riff on *analyze* because in each successive story, a different character, based on a real person was peering into her mind, and no clue where they ended up or even if they were still in existence. Was Turner a metaphor for his own inner self, using Marlowe as a physical base? He had no idea, but if nothing came of it, he enjoyed writing the stories.

This was his second autumn in Japan, and it was his favorite season. Last year, the excitement of his first snowfall was short-lived when he realized he owned zero warm clothes and hit a local outfitter to get some appropriate apparel. Marlowe, thankfully, loaned an extra wool greatcoat and items to help him out.

"Did you think you were in Southern Cal, dude?" He laughed.

"For real? I've been in Hawaii for years. Sun and alcohol have thinned my blood!"

But autumn filled him with tranquility---the temperature lower, the air breathable and the trees turning. He didn't mind the shorter days at all. He enjoyed seeing the fall fashion changes in the older women on the trains, in the stores; wool suits and smart matching handbags. He would sit back in the bakery coffee shop at the Lumine department store at Tachikowa *eki* and admire their style as the crowds pressed thru. He was in no hurry; no one was waiting for him.

His relationship with Kawakami-sensei was static. Something inside him desired her, yet her proximity and their professional relationship precluded any tomfoolery he thought of, and she was of exactly the same mind, unbeknownst to him. It wasn't once that she used his memory of changing clothes as she lay in the room of the house she shared with her mother, listening to the rain, her hand stirring under her blankets. Warren felt she was keenly aware of his feelings that day, and he had felt the pressure of her hand, her hips shifting under their clinch though they parted as just friends, boundaries invisibly falling into place. In the office, while they spoke to each other more directly, it was of school issues or local educational and cultural events. They never returned to that moment of spark each looking out their respective windows at Kin Tama seeing the trees turn orange, crimson and brown. He didn't count the time he pulled one of the 'Suff's up!' barmaids out of the dive and woke up regretting it, forgetting his lecture to Riordan about not shitting where one ate. His only joy in that she wasn't a student, but it killed his attendance at the bar.

Riordan, in the meantime became far stealthier in is trysts with Ai. They stopped their meetings at the coffee shop, *never* telling her the true reason, just saying he saw some Kin Tama students from school there in the neighborhood of the station after she boarded the train. They moved their meetings two stations closer to Ai's residence as there was a hotel there as well. They also become more circumspect in their behavior at school. No more rose petals, poems and little notes. They saved their feelings, bottled like a fine wine that they could share and drink together when intimate; a special toast for lovers. Ai did not question him about the change in behavior and felt secure that he knew best in protecting them.

They started months ago, in the last term; she was having problems with an assignment in Flattery's class. Her personal abhorrence of Flattery-sensei came from his insistence of sitting in front of the class in lieu of standing at the podium afforded all sensei. He seemed to wish to be at level to look at the girls' legs in class and finding his eyes on her a time or two made her feel somewhat discomfited. He also kept a large book on his lap, that while it had a bulge inside of it as if there was a thick bookmark, it was never opened, and she wondered why. She saw Riordan-sensei, whose name was at times impossible for the other students to pronounce, sitting at his desk when she entered the NSD and felt relieved Flattery was not present. He looked up from his work and saw her there, lithe, tall and framed in the entryway. She stood still, as none of the students were allowed entry without permission. He waved her in, and he smiled. Ai never engaged him in any conversation before and had never really been this close to him, although she saw him of course at school, but she did not realize how young he was. And the color of his eyes caught her off balance; inside the iris an orange band circumnavigated his pupil inside the blue oceans of color.

"Can I help you?" he asked.

"Yes, sensei, I have a question about something from *Frankenstein*. Most exhausting." This told Riordan she was Flattery's student as he was the only teacher who used Shelley's novel. Marlowe, Haas and Felch didn't; the latter due to the fact he was incapable of teaching a novel of any complexity.

"Mr. Flattery isn't in." Riordan told her.

"Yes, " she said quickly, "that is okay. May I ask you?" She asked expectantly.

Riordan looked up from his desk gain, taking in the New Zealand accent of her voice. Ai was standing at his desk, her crisp white blouse revealed by her open blazer and unlike so many of the students who allowed or wore their uniforms poorly on purpose, hers was sharp and spruce. His eyes met hers and he felt that first flutter of feeling; a signal from eye to heart. He swallowed and said thickly, sitting up:

"Yes, please sit down." He motioned to the chair next to the desk, and she smiled and brushed her thick hair to the side of her face.

Riordan was thinking of that time and more; small intense memories of lovemaking and moments together. He started taking more precautions and his paranoia at being discovered after his run in with Warren had him at tweak on the stress meter. He even burned all his saved letters at home that Ai left for him at school, but while he was imploding inside, nothing changed between them, and if anything things became more intense. Ai told him she was thinking of applying to a couple of schools in the United States as well as in Japan. Her parents felt perhaps, Stanford, Berkeley and MIT were a better path in her pursuit of a chemical engineering degree. Her five years in New Zealand allowed for an extremely high understanding of English.

This excited him, his skin breaking into goose bumps when she explained it to him as it meant if she were accepted and left for America, he could just break his contract at Kin Tama, fly home and find work. With her eighteenth birthday in May they could live together. His fear, while agonizing, was manageable when he pictured them together, far from Japan.

The night Haas called his name after meeting Ai was as if he were a snake in a frying pan; he writhed the rest of the night in pain and heat. Sleepless he tossed on his futon sweating hearing Haas' words, '…what if it were Flattery?' and it scared his shit white. He understood what Haas said and he wasn't so much angry as frightened of the outcome from that bastard.

Ai…if only they could make it to graduation and her eighteenth birthday, he could die happy. He kept away from Haas, but realized after thinking it thru that he was an ally, and not the enemy. He knew *who* they were. Even Felch would turn on him in a New York minute. Ai asked why he seemed thinner, his abdominal muscles exposed like brick pavers and he just said he changed his diet, not that stress was eating a hole in is body.

Chapter 24

November was cold and every morning since midmonth had Warren cursing and missing Hawaii and California. He didn't mind it crisp, but when he could feel his bones he wasn't happy. Was this what 40 was about? October was a beautiful interlude; the leaves softening and changing colors, falling on the sidewalks and the parks full of people celebrating the freshness of the air and rejoicing in seeing Fuji-san on the horizon.

He started a 'fall cleansing' in his flat and started feathering his nest. He bought a couple of pieces from a shrine bazaar, and more cooking utensils. He chucked his frat house brick bookcase. The little waitress from his surfer/dive bar returned one night and with her some cleaning supplies she had taken from work. Standing there in shorts and a George Blanda jersey, he just watched her walk in and go straight to his kitchen. He followed her and she handed him a sponge. They hadn't said two words to each other, but they scrubbed, mopped and shined his small eating area. She opened her backpack, pulled out a bottle of sake and two joints and smiled. She took her hair out of her ponytail and shook it briskly.

"Suff's up," she said to him. Warren laughed.

"No shit…"

Later, after they had shared a bath and shower rinse, he finally learned her name was Aiko, and he stopped calling her 'Surfah Girl." He started returning to the bar and his first night Steve-erino poured him a 22-ounce Sapporo and welcomed him back. He discovered thru Aiko that his blonde California look also gave the bar some 'surfer cred' and he wondered if Steve-erino sent her on a mission to bring him back after he disappeared over an entire month.

Warren started relaxing more inside and as the days chilled around him it felt as if he were adapting to the cool air with his core settling. He was also secure in his work at Kin Tama and while he still felt it would take longer to fully understand Japan, he was feeling it more and more. He stopped sweating the pissants when the elephants were coming through the jungle, and while Lise, in true Shakespearian form still appeared before him daily and whispered 'Really?' she was starting to blur at the edges; bleed into the world that swerved as her borders. He could live with that. He could accept that she will never disappear but fade like ink in a years old ledger. He knew he owed something in that ledger too; but didn't need to live inside of it. She could. He recognized that when he started to attend to his flat and make it more than a cubicle from work. He was changing. He had never settled into Hawaii for all the years he lived there, some boxes never coming out of storage, a suitcase never opened. He didn't mind Aiko showing up when her shift was over as her train ride was long and the nights were so cold; her body a brisk, cool application to his warm futon waking him and turning his body towards her, bringing giggles.

His attraction to Mari diminished along with Lise's apparition. It wasn't Aiko's nocturnal forays as he realized that was just a reciprocal booty call; comfort and security in the dark of night. He thought of his day with Mari when they met at Yoyogi Park and shared that brief moment.

Truly, there was a spark and had they not been workmates, perhaps a different ending. What was this part of his life about? Would he ever connect with anyone, be so in tune as it once was with Lise? Even then it was a hit and miss drug and alcohol induced crapshoot. There was never a future there. At one time there was a pipe dream they would work together and turn out enough books so he could have some security and they could perhaps be together but that was so much smoke. He would feel embarrassed going back over that ground and reigniting those feelings and images. He would picture Lise and Loren amusing themselves at his expense, never fully knowing what contempt they felt for him, so to wean himself off those emotions was a healthy outlook. After those moments of self-flagellation he felt hollow, and knew it was useless to ever go there, but in the past was unable to stop. Now he at least limited his visitation rights.

Thanksgiving came and went, not accepting Marlowe's invitation to go to a dinner at NAS Atsugi and do up a real turkey as he was invited by a squadron commander he knew and tried to coax Warren who just wasn't feeling it. The following Friday Marlowe talked to Mrs. Bloom in the office, the two of them sharing food stories. Mrs. Bloom had attended a 'mandatory fun' dinner at her husband's commanding officer's house on base in 'Colonel's Row.' He invited her husband and one other senior NCO as well as his exec and principals, and one other colonel who was at Yokota on temporarily assigned duty. She related how boring it was as her husband and the other Sargent Major couldn't relax all night around so many senior officers and Mrs. Bloom felt no interest in the topics the wives discussed. Her fellow enlisted wife was busy kissing ass all night and politicking for her husband, while Mrs. Bloom wished she could just drink until she was numb from the boredom. Marlowe on the other hand enjoyed a raucous evening with his buddy and his wife along with some single junior officers they invited, all homesick and thankful to be taken in. The evening ended with drinking games and Pictionary. Mrs. Bloom was jealous, and then turned to Warren.

"How was your Thanksgiving, Warren?"

He thought for a minute, having spent it at his bar and singing drunken Beach Boys karaoke with the Surf's Up twins, culminating in Aiko staying over, just smiled and said to Mrs. Bloom it was truly a night to give thanks.

Felch, walking in injected himself into the conversation, as usual.

"The wife and I dined at the Officer's Club. We were blessed with a traditional dinner for a set price. We had our reservations in since before Halloween." Felch never used his wife's name; she was just 'the wife.'

Warren just found himself staring again at Felch. There was the stain of what looked like gravy on his clip on tie. His arms, small and thin, were held out as if relaxing on an invisible Barca lounger. Felch just always looked like a misshapen turd that refused to be flushed; the remnant left in the bowl that succeeded in cheating the drain and stared back at you in defiance. Just the thought of his name made Warren want to punch him in the forehead.

"The meal wasn't all that," he continued, "the turkey was a little dry, but the wife didn't feel like cooking."

"So, do you ever cook, Felch?" Warren asked, staring down so he didn't have to look at him.

Felch employed this tired affect when speaking to Warren, as if he were the exasperated principal who has a perennial troublemaker in his office again, "I'm old fashioned, Mr. Haas, and my place isn't in the kitchen. This is where I agree with my zipper headed *nihonjin* brethren in where a woman's place should be."

Marlowe looked up sharply, cut off by Mrs. Bloom who fairly snapped her neck she turned to Felch so quickly, "You wouldn't last very long in my house with that attitude, and how dare you refer to them with that horrible name!"

"Mrs. Bloom, excuse me, but you're not really my type, so I doubt it." He smiled at her with that same tired look he saved for Warren.

Marlowe touched her arm seeing her face flush. She turned to Marlowe who smiled the faintest of grins and nodded his head. She grabbed her purse and left the office in the direction of the lady's room. Felch, paid her no mind, humming to himself as he stacked papers for grading on his desk top.

"Felch," Marlowe said casually, "don't ever use *that* term in this office again. Ever."

Felch looked up. The little pale blue crabs of his iris' calm and serene, "And what term might that be, Mister Marlowe?" He smiled.

Marlowe said in an even voice that lacked any warmth or humanity, "You know fucking well, you fat lizard bastard."

Riordan walked in, breaking the pressure that shot up in the room. "Everyone have a good night? I actually had some great turkey with the University of Maryland people on base at Yokota. They said the Officer's Club dinner always sucks so they did one up on their own."

Warren got up and slapped him on the back, "Better timing than Henny Youngman, Phil."

Felch made good his escape, never turning around as he scurried out of the department. Warren turned to Marlowe, who still looked as cold as wet sand. He was about to speak, but then decided better to let those dogs lay for now. They all had classes to attend to.

Doc Krinberg

FUYU
(Winter)

Chapter 25

The first Saturday in December brought a huge snow shower. Warren was in Tokyo looking at some books to buy and while inside the Anglo-Japanese bookstore caught sight of the first flurries. Seeing the windblown snow was for him exciting. He barely paid attention to the weather and not owning a TV relied on word of mouth from either Riordan, who fancied himself a junior meteorologist or Felch, who complained of it nonstop. This day caught him off guard.

He was to meet Marlowe and go for a drink at some place he recommended, as he lived close by, and he looked forward to hanging out with him a bit. Warren felt he became, without a true social life and a schedule, the ultimate jellyfish, floating on life's indiscriminate tides. So Marlowe's company was welcome. He hadn't planned on going to Mifuku, as he didn't wish to see Aiko. He wasn't tired of her but there was the reality of missing parts: Conversation that wasn't part pantomime or a run to the translation book and he started to miss just talking. He cursed his poor command of the language and couldn't at all retain parts of it. In retrospect he hadn't even been able to fully communicate with the American women he met on base either! He made attempts at parties but was inundated with one way conversations of complaints about their seniors, subordinates, pushy civilians, pushy military, how much work sucked and they did most of it while others shirked their duties and couldn't wait until they rotated back to the States and in one case when a female major shook him awake in the middle of the night and asked, 'why are you still here?' Warren said nothing, just got out of bed, dressed and in the dead of night walked the empty main street of the air base. Finding the MAC Terminal, which was open 24/7, he stumbled in and found the coffee machine available and poured a cup from the spigot. At the counter, where a very serene looking Filipina manned the register, he pulled nothing out of his pockets except crumpled yen and Japanese coins.

"Only US Dollars, sar," she said calmly.

Warren shrugged his shoulders and apologizing, walked away, leaving the coffee.

"Sar," she called to his back, "you can take your coffee, but please next time remember to change your money before the flight. Ok, sar?"

Feeling like a hobo, Warren thanked the little woman, sitting with absolute peace in her blue frock and hairnet. He took his coffee and walked slowly over to the seating area. The Terminal was dead, obviously no flights coming in or leaving, a sign indicating there was a 0630 Showtime for a flight to Kadena. He sat in the cool AC of the empty seats and sipped his coffee.

He didn't even remember falling asleep, and was awakened by the noises of people queuing up for the Kadena flight. Warren got up, used the facilities and once off base walked through 'The Gut' to Fussa station, unknowingly passing 'Wodkah's' small flat.

Watching the snowfall and remembering that night in the terminal and the attendant's kindness, for some reason he felt a twinge of homesickness. He was holding open a dog-eared copy of *The Dain Curse* and was wondering how to work Hammett into a lesson plan for the future. He had wanted to incorporate some 'hard boiled' fiction and introduce the kids to that style. Maybe even Hemingway's *The Killers*. He looked up to see if there were any other Hammett titles and then saw *them*. The spines were well worn but he could tell one was a first edition paperback of *True Finery* while the other a dust-jacketless, beat down copy of *An Unworthy Tree,* by Warren Haas. It was as if he were looking into a grave and bidding someone he was acquainted with but didn't really know or understood very well a confused farewell. He felt embarrassed and started getting the warm skin feeling preceding a breaking sweat. He turned to go into the cool air outside the store when he smacked right into Marlowe, who came up behind him quietly.

"Hey Man!"

Marlowe laughed, "Is it that hot in here, old man? You're sweating."

"Yes, I'm warm…it's this fucking overcoat of yours." Warren pushed around him and Marlowe looking up saw the two books, side-by-side, silent witnesses to their creator's escape out the front door. Marlowe frowned and followed Warren out.

Once outside, his breath a huge plume of smoke as he hit the cold, Warren felt better. Marlowe stepped behind him pulling on his gloves.

"Let's go get that drink." Marlowe steered him to the jazz bar down two blocks from the bookstore. There was a small marquee with some *katakana* and musical notes surrounding the edges. They entered the foyer, which was quiet and very still. In the semi dark, Marlowe directed him to a booth and they both removed their overcoats. The bar was low lit with a row of blue lights ringing the room, facing the ceiling giving it an almost underground grotto look; as if one was submerged in icy cool water staring at a starless sky.

"So what do you think of my secret jazz club?" Marlowe asked.

"Secret? No one knows about it?" Warren smiled.

"Nobody. Its all mine." He looked around, as if taking it in for the first time, " It actually has very good music at night, and sometimes when jazzmen come from the States or Europe, they get up and play with the locals. There's this Japanese cat who comes in, Ken Saito, who blows a sax and if you closed your eyes you would swear 'Trane was in here. Sweet."

Warren tapped a cigarette out. He started smoking again after taking OP's at his little dive bar, and he had been pretty good about stopping for a few months. A cocktail waitress came over with a candle for the table on her round tray. She sported a silver beehive wig that shimmered softly in the low blue lights, and was drowned in their reflection. Lighting the candle she asked in her stilted English what they would like.

"I suppose it's too early for a gimlet," Warren said softly.

"A gimlet?"

Warren smiled, "Sorry, just a line from an old book that this place reminded me of. Two friends whose string had run out and they drank gimlets in a quiet, cool bar during the day much like this place. And one was named Marlowe"

Marlowe thought that over and the waitress stood bored, waiting. He turned to Warren and said to trust him. "Let's have two Stoli martinis, straight up, two olives each." He looked back to Warren, " The extra olive means I don't have to buy you dinner." Warren laughed appreciatively.

"You know a lot about literature. The rest of us run off of old lesson plans, *Cliff's Notes,* and stuff left behind by past teachers when Kin Tama was *truly* a prestigious school and academy…teachers who knew their shit. You're actually a published writer, not some *gaijin* with a business degree faking it. Jesus, do you know what my degree is in?"

Warren, feeling somewhat embarrassed at Marlowe's effusion, just nodded 'no.'

"Fucking Political Science, "he laughed, "Can you imagine teaching *that* at Kin Tama? No, you're the real deal. Even that prick Flattery envies you in some weird part of his twisted brain pan." He paused a second, his speaking tone almost one of reverence,

"Tell me what it's like to write a book, be famous." Warren saw that Marlowe was sincere.

He laughed nervously, " Famous for like 13 minutes on the Warhol Scale."

"Seriously, Haas, tell me."

There was an brief image in Warren's mind, riding the coat tails of Marlowe's words of him sitting by her pool, Lise chain smoking and picking his brain over some plot hooey he had laid out. She never wore a bathing suit, just stripping to her lingerie. He looked up into the dying blue light of the ceiling at Marlowe's jazz bar and then looked into his eyes.

"I wont bore you with the usual 'gee, it's like giving birth hooey.' It was exciting. It was like being in a movie and at times I got to watch myself, and that part was scary. I had a brilliant editor and friend who helped me tremendously, but I blew it…in the end I was just an impostor, a ne'er-doo-well, and my second novel crashed and burned. You know all that." Warren looked down. The girl came over with their drinks, and he took the end of the plastic spear the olives were skewered on and swirled them around in his drink. "I was white trash rich, I was popular and most of the time I was as high as Cooter Brown." He lifted his glass and took a long swallow. He put his glass down and opening his arms to signify abundance, "And here I am."

Warren finished his drink.

After a brief silence, Marlowe cleared his throat, "Did you meet a lot of famous people?"

Warren smiled, "I did. I met a few on the talk show circuit, guests who were on the same shows plugging their movies or products. We were all on this conveyor belt as a product for the shows, and we were hustling our shit at the same time…seriously symbiotic."

"You sound like a communist agitator!" Marlowe said with mock gravity.

"I guess so. Listen, I don't have any good memories of that certain period. I know I sound like a whiny crack…yea, money, prestige, celebrity…and also a great uncle in the Waffen SS…talk about a fucking deer in the headlights when he was outed! I was already on the skids, in over my head. Too much coke, smoke and I had *that* smell. So let's not talk about me anymore. I'm yesterdays paper."

Marlowe frowned, "Sorry, Haas. I feel like I turned over a bad penny there. I was just curious. I know you saw your books at the Anglo-Nippon store." He paused and sipped his drink. " They were mine. I donated them after reading them a number of times, so somebody else could enjoy them. I did."

Warren was again surprised. "Thanks. But the fact that there they are speaks to my forgotten genius"

"I liked them both. I think *An Unworthy Tree* got a bad rap. I was very satisfied with it and felt that it was more mature than *Finery*. Warren, you should write another book. That's my 2 cents. So there!"

"I wished you worked for the *NY Times* book review section, "Warren laughed, "they pretty much breech-loaded me without a reach around. That was a good drink." He flicked the edge of the martini glass with a finger and it chimed.

Marlowe looked around for the waitress, and catching her attention, held up two fingers.

"Now you tell me something, man." Marlowe looked at Warren suspiciously. "How in the hell and why in the hell do you know all these places, visited all these places? I know your dad was navy but he didn't go to all those places and sure as hell couldn't take you to most."

Pushing his napkin back and forth with his fingertips, Marlowe grew a small lopsided smile. "I just love to travel---and we had the money and means so I took advantage of it. Why, did you think I was a spy?" He laughed.

"Damn, when I was flush, the farthest I made it was the Bahamas for vacation and London for a show taping, and I was drunk almost 24/7. I'm so provincial. Being here is probably biggest move I ever made in my entire life. I told myself when I had cash I was going to see the Taj Mahal and the Eiffel Tower, Pyramids and Angkor Wat. Does Kamakura count?"

"Yea, but you accomplished a lot, Warren, so stopped playing the damaged goods. You're here, you're intact and you're probably banging someone. Kawakami? I'm getting that vibe," he laughed.

Warren pulled his head back and pursed his lips. Where in the fuck did Marlowe pull that out of? "NO! We're just friends." He remembered her brown nipple, showing thru the wet, tight cotton shirt and thin bra. "Well, there was an interlude, a moment. We had a connection during that lame *nihonjin-gaijin* intellectual fest Serazowa cooked up, during a conversation but we both shut it off before it went somewhere. And that's that."

"Hmmm…I thought there might be more. I have caught her

looking at you when she didn't know I was looking. There were definitely some come-hither looks, old man." Marlowe said slyly.

The second round of drinks arrived. Warren felt as if he had been dancing to Marlowe's tune. "You mean the way Mrs. Bloom looks at you?"

Marlowe rolled that one over and paused before he answered. "Aha...the writer's studied eye. Sweet woman. But you know she's married." Warren caught something in his voice that told him a different answer. The waitress waved Marlowe off when he went to pay her.

"Ueda-san has bought your drinks."

"Buddy of yours?" Warren asked.

"She's an artist and likes martinis."

"Well, shoo her in, man."

Chapter 26

Yukio dropped the soccer club, abandoning the winter workouts, and instead joined a kendo academy. He had started feeling foolish in his long shorts and jersey modeled after a professional British team. Soccer. It was an Englishman's game and it was a *white* game. Kendo was Japanese. Kendo was pure. Kendo was martial; physical and spiritual combined. Mishima had been an accomplished kendo fighter.

His coach, Unimora-sensei, asked him why one of his best strikers was calling it quits and Yukio calmly replied to his confusion 'Because I am *nihonjin* and that is reason enough.' Unimora took back the jersey and watched the youth walk away, wondering whom he could play that could score like Yukio.

The books.

It was as if his eyelids had been pulled off and the naked sun seared into his sclera, infusing it with heat and light. He finished reading *Confessions of a Mask, The Palace of the Golden Pavilion* and a volume of short stories of which *Patriotism* and *Sand and Sea* were his favorites, and begun *The Sound of Waves*. He had three books of the final tetralogy and couldn't wait to start them. Why did a *gaijin* enlighten him to Mishima-san? Why was this rich heritage hidden from him and his new school not even advocating this treasure? Haas-sensei...a failed foreign writer had in one stroke given him a vision for his life; a manifest destiny and a pride in his total being like never before. It was fate and nothing else that brought Haas-sensei to Japan. To *him*.

He was been spending less time with Tomoko as he was busy at the academy. She in turn started studying hard for her entrance exams and thinking possibly of studying abroad, having discussed it with Ai, who was going to apply to colleges in the US. She had yet to discuss it with Yukio. She noticed a change in him as the days cooled and he dropped the soccer club. He was more introspective and seemed to carry himself more as a man, instead of the angry boy she met in the heat of summer; the cool air itself solidifying him in some way.

The winter festivities would start soon, and they would be on a small break. She missed the two to three week breaks she would have when living abroad during Christmas. And she missed the festive lights and change of mood with her classmates. She would stay at times over at their houses and join their culture, being lectured on how one needs to give themselves to Christ, and Tomoko had respectfully listened to them all, thanking Buddha for her patience. Her Caucasian girlfriends would sneak eggnog laced with rum or Kahlua into the bedroom after the parents were asleep and all guests gone. They would gossip about the boys in class, dish up the girls who weren't there. She didn't really have any friends in Japan who carried on like her old girlfriends, and she did miss them. Before she moving back to Japan they 'pinky shaked' and promised to write, and they were pretty good for the first six months and then slowly the communiqués trickled, and finally ended. Out of sight, out of mind, she knew. Ai, and a couple of the other girls who were exposed to western holidays, understood what she meant when they talked, but they did not reenact those times with each other. It was as if they needed that part of the formula the western girls gave the mix, and so there were no pajama parties and snuck drinks. No sex talk.

What would her western girlfriends think if they had to attend Kin Tama and wear a uniform like theirs? Would they sleep on the floor on a roll away futon? Could they use the metal footprints in the floor *benjo* in the subways? Her thoughts turned back to Yukio, and surprised she became excited by his memory, wishing she could just talk to him about of all things America.

Chapter 27

Warren woke up in a western style bed that felt like a five-star mattress in a room that was very white. Looking at the wall in the direction he faced was a large, beautiful reproduction of the carp streamers from Hiroshige's *Suidobashi Surugadai*. Turning his head he saw on the wall opposite the foot of the bed an extremely graphic *shunga* that opened his eyes wider; the exaggerated sex organs of the couple in it insanely grotesque to wake up to. He was alone in the bed and undressed and made an attempt to remember the circumstances that led to this moment, but clarity eluded him and he sat up and examined the rest of the white room.

Above his head was a plexiglass skylight that was full of beaded and splashing raindrops; a moving mosaic. The drops settled on the glass were pushed aside by those falling on top of those seated and were transformed from small shining spheres to rivulets of streaming quicksilver. The wall to his right held Hokusai's *Dream of the Fisherman's Wife* and studying it had to wonder about the inspiration. The position of the octupi struck a chord and he recalled how in a strange photo roll of memory, this somehow made sense. The rest of the room was barren of any furniture save a small nightstand with a lamp. He leaned over each side of the bed in search of his clothes but the white carpet just yawned back at him. Where the hell was he?

The Deep Slumber of Dogs

There was a small door in the corner of the room where the carps streamed in the wind, ancient Edo beneath them. Stretching and then out of bed and investigating, Warren found a small bathroom with a sink and a western toilet. Taking stock of his face, his bloodshot eyes didn't surprise him, nor the sinister aspect of his bedhead. He sat, pissing and scratching his arms. He tried to piece together the previous night, and after recalling meeting Ueda-san and then hearing some jazz and other people in and out at the table, pretty much drew a blank. Ueda. Where was she? And where was Marlowe? Strolling through this strange flat or house nude struck him as a bizarre journey with a mystery ending. But he was dressed for it, he imagined.

After flushing the toilet and washing his face, Warren decided to explore his white walled landscape. He went to what he figured was the door that issued out into the rest of the house, and coughing, as if to warn someone he was coming out, opened it slowly. He walked into a long passageway, its walls lined with framed art and photos and not feeling up to investing time on any of them, strolled down the plush carpet until he discovered a spiral staircase to a lower floor, and feeling like a Picasso, descended.

Sitting at a finger bar surrounded by breakfast items and a large pitcher of orange juice, Marlowe sat reading a *Japan Times* wearing a silk kimono of ivory and black. Looking up and seeing Warren, he smiled and motioned for him to come down and take a seat then started pouring a glass of juice into a small pony glass.

"Morning. How do you feel?"

"Naked and naked, other than that, not too bad. My head doesn't feel like a weather balloon, and much better to find you alive and here." Warren looked around. " Waiting room for admission to Hell?"

Marlowe laughed, "We're in Ueda's flat in Roppongi. Let me see if I can find another kimono. She probably has a few stashed here and there." He got up to check inside a hall closet as Warren sipped his juice. "No joy here. Let me check another room." And he sauntered down the hallway.

Warren found a croissant and started to nibble on it, looking around. There was a small sliding door to an equally small wooden deck that was stained dark by the rainfall. What happened to the snow? He lifted a small decanter and opening the top discovered it to hold coffee and poured himself a small cup from the service on the bar top. There was a large framed picture of a reclining nude, facing him, her long lacquered hair pulled up in a classic aristocratic style; pins intricately arranged. Her breasts were firm and prideful, as were the eyes. The slight swell of her hips held his eyes, and when he started to examine her legs Marlowe strolled in with a royal blue robe over one arm.

"This is the best I could do." He caught Warren's eyes turn to him from the painting. "That's our hostess…probably 35 or 40 years ago. Some food, eh."

Warren, sipping his coffee, raised his eyebrows, "Wow. And how. She has something, that's for sure. So what the hell happened last night? I can only remember the jazz starting and whistling loudly, and then I wake up naked as a baby in Roppongi."

"Well, we had a few hundred rounds, and you and Ueda-san got into a discussion about literature and impressionist art and you went into a detailed description of an art exhibit of Henry Miller's watercolors in Westwood you attended, then the jazzmen started playing and we entertained a lot of people at our table, on and off…some writers and artists, musicians and strippers and some gay men very interested in your blonde Freddy Blassy beauty. No recall?"

Warren pushed his hair back, "Noooo...I didn't do anything felonious did I?" Warren worried, aware of his excesses and effects of vodka.

"Not a thing. You were a pretty funny and decent gent from all accounts. Its how you ended up nude too. Hey, hand me that last croissant will you?"

"Where's Ueda? And so, you're just going to sit there eating a crescent and not tell me? I'm also curious as to how you know your way around here so easily" Warren shook his head.

"In due time, old man." He turned to the painting. "We only found one of your shoes though. Sorry. We did look for a few minutes." He laughed.

"Fucker." Warren laughed. "I hope she has some shoes or slippers here I can steal. Or don't you have that information? So where is she?"

"Actually, arranging for your clothes from the cleaners. She has a service and they came and picked them up early and should be back soon."

"What time is it?"

Marlowe looked at his watch. "It's like almost 3 p.m."

Warren was in shock. He hadn't slept this late since his salad days as an author, and then afterwards when there were nights he couldn't sleep and slipped into a late awakening depression before his suicide attempt. Dry cleaning services that picked up at your house and delivered them back? He was duly impressed. He glanced back at his hostess's nude painting and sighed.

"Well, I feel like afterbirth here. Where's a bathroom with a shower? The little one in the room I woke up in has only a shitter."

There was some conversation in Japanese from down the hallway

Marlowe had disappeared to in search of his robe and a woman was telling someone something in a tone that said authority. Noriko Ueda and a small man holding some clothes swaddled in cellophane came into view. She looked at Warren and smiled, "Ahh so, Haas-san is awake. Did you sleep well?" She turned to the little man, and taking the wrapped clothes, shooed him off. He bowed at the waist ever so slightly and left.

Warren was looking at her, the portrait hanging behind her, trying to keep his eyes fixed on the living Ueda-san. "I slept like the veritable rock, thank you."

"Ahh good. *Genki-deska?*" She turned to Marlowe. "Do you need to leave or can you both stay for dinner?" She raised her eyebrows.

Marlowe cleared his throat, "I must beg off, Noriko, sorry. Previous engagements, so I wont speak for Warren." She turned to Warren, her eyebrows still up in questioning. Warren had absolutely no plans.

"I am totally free. And would be happy to have someone fill in the blanks for last night, thank you."

Ueda smiled. "*Hai!* Oh, here are your clothes. I have your wallet and belt in my room. You can use my *shisetsu* to shower in. Towels are in the cabinet, and the girl will show you all." She turned and in her authoritative voice called out. A maid appeared from a lower level in the flat, on the bottom part of the spiral stairs. Ueda gave her some instructions to which the maid dropped her head in quick successive bows whispering numerous *hais*. "She will take you, Haas-san. Her name is Megumi.

Marlowe stood, stretching, and slapped him on the back. "Take care, old man. See you on Monday." And he walked down the hallway Ueda and the man from the cleaners had come down. Megumi made a slight bow at her waist and motioned for Warren to follow her.

Warren, stood and loosening the chord to his robe followed her.

Chapter 28

Loren had kept the house in Beverly Hills after Lise died and having moved back into the main house, rented the small one in the rear to a painter/sculptor. Not much changed in the orbit of his life. And he was sad to discover how little he had figured in Lise's. He made a few discoveries in the hacienda when cleaning what at one time was their shared master bedroom that did not surprise him. He was glad he did not call in a cleaning crew or allow the police to search the house.

When Lise's tox-screen came back positive for opiates, cocaine and valium his lawyer was prompt to stall those actions while Loren collected, scrubbed and cleaned the house and her room in particular. There were marijuana seeds in the carpet, a few empty and some partially used small amber vials of what he figured were cocaine with tiny spoons attached to the caps you could purchase at any head shop and finally the small folded foil squares of brown powder that no doubt held heroin. Her coffin shaped box with syringe and a small folded and blackened spoon that he recognized from his grandmother's sterling collection were in a desk drawer that also housed scattered bills in small denominations, some semi rolled for snorting, others loose. He went through her clothing;

pockets and cuffs. Her purses were garbage cans for chewing gum wrappers, pens, empty pill bottles, roaches and matchbooks. There were uneaten Twix bars and one full sleeve of yellow Easter Peeps. In the nightstand was a jar of Vaseline, scented lubricant and a vibrator. Loren held the vibrator up and mentally measured it against himself. Slowly he brought it under his nose. It had the vague aroma of the scented lubricant he smelled upon discovery. Pulling more treasure from the vibrator drawer he found under a *Vanity Fair* a copy of *Blue Boy*.

After this devil's inventory, he carefully disposed of all the drugs in the toilet and taking the spoon on a long drive, made a gift of it to Santa Monica Bay via the pier. When he was convinced there were no more narcotics or incriminating items left in the house and a professional crew came in when he was ready for the police but by then they didn't care. Warren's tox screen had come back clean so it was a dead issue. Loren was so incensed towards Warren that even in his grief the driver needed to be punished and if Loren didn't have the law backing him up, would make him pay in a wrongful death suit at the very least, in any way he could.

In regards to Warren, he remained stoic. He watched as an entitled rubbernecker, Warren as a plane that had flown majestically high start spiraling to Earth and it's cartwheeling slowly in the last few hundred feet finally disintegrate as it crashed into the hard ground. That was how he viewed his rival's fall; at the end of it discovered he felt no satisfaction or sense of closure. Lise was gone and Warren for now was as good as dead professionally if not already personally. He reveled in watching the oft repeated daytime talk show where Warren was in Texas, relegated to the d-list local shows in half-assedly promoting his new book *An Unworthy Tree*. By then he was on the shoestring account and a long way from late night prime time. Loren had actually watched the slow motion destruction of the interview where his uncle was outed, and Warren wore that sick expression of a loss of words and then the photo appearing on the screen of his uncle in full black shirted SS glory, blonde hair shimmering silver in the black and white picture with the graphics underneath "Jann Haas, SS Sturmbanfuehrer." But as he sat in his studio about to tape a show he wondered why it ran on a continuous loop, again now two years later until he saw the screen switch to a live feed as a stretcher outside the El Norte was being loaded into an ambulance with the graphics switching to:

'...Novelist Warren Haas attempts suicide and is being taken to Cedars of Lebanon.'

Seeing him on the stretcher being loaded, as they repeated it at least fifteen times, did not fill him with any satisfaction. They showed a stock file picture of Warren from his heyday, his hair shorter and in a finely tailored suit, the woman on his arm blurred. It was Lise as Loren examined her dress and figure. Still he found no glee or amusement. Lise was long dead.

Loren had Lise cremated, against her family's wishes and she was interned at Hillside Memorial in a joint wall unit he bought after their marriage, and where he could be next to her for all time. But in the meantime he still watched Warren's fall and crash to earth. After cleaning her room and making those discoveries, and as time went by he started to feel as if he could not hold Warren accountable. Once the years passed he started replacing Warren with himself. He started to see where he was at fault and created certain scenarios; allowed for them and even helped orchestrate some. As his own culpability grew, Warren's crimes diminished until the point that when Loren thought of Lise and her death Warren was relegated to mere bystander status. But he continued to not communicate this to Warren, who still wore the hairshirt of her death.

Loren felt he needed to come to terms with Lise's death and that Warren do the same, on his own terms.

Lise kept all of her work in a filing cabinet. The edit works, the researched items that were catalogued on index cards, an unfinished dissertation prospectus she started when only 19 and had already earned her Masters in Lit…the volume of her work startled Loren. The numerous projects and people she had been in contact with dropped by the house when appropriate to inquire as to where she left off in their work and Loren would painstakingly assemble her notes and marks on their papers. The publishers were most adamant about where she was at on her current project for the convict's prose. He was surprised at the degree to which she conducted her business, as there was so much he didn't realize or was left out of conversations. This chimera he was married to with so much business on the backside of her life; the part she left him.

Another shock was her bankbook and safety deposit boxes. At her death, Lise had $48,000 in her savings and another $6,000 in a checking account he knew nothing about. There were beautiful Hopi and Zuni turquoise pieces, squash blossoms and rings and a beautiful Indian head nickel bracelet, in the safety deposit box as well as childhood keepsakes and what looked like more brown heroin in small tin foil bindles. Staring at the jewelry and dope he was overwhelmed and outplayed. Her legion of work files were one thing, but her substantial secret stash was quite another.

Loren relegated the filing cabinet to the garage, and there it stood for more years. He finally called in a junk man to take it away along with some other items he wished to jettison and make some more room for storage of some of the sculptor's work. The truck pulled up and Loren took the man and his helper back to the garage, both looking around and admiring the house and the garden. When they were inside the garage he pointed out the items he wished to have taken. At one time Lise started collecting old iron gates and statues she found at garage sales and swap meets. He saw no need to hang onto the rusting inventory. It was very hot and he asked the men if they would enjoy a bottle of water. While walking back into the garage the truck owner, in his accented English asked what to do with the papers.

"What papers?" He asked.

The man held up a folder full of typed pages. " In the bottom, senor." He made a motion of something being pushed with his hands downward. He held them to Loren.

Taking them and understanding they had slipped into the bottom after the cabinet in which they were stored was shut, he looked at the title in tape across the top.

Lise in Repose/ Voor Lise

He remembered that she mentioned at times Warren would lapse into Dutch when he wrote to her, and turning the folder's cover page found a short note paper clipped to the copy:

Zevon said it best in 'Hasten Down the Wind'...you're so many women.

So I decided to write about them all. Ik houd van U!

Loren could easily translate the Dutch without too much thought. There were in the manuscripts 15 short stories about Lise, as seen by 15 different people. Holding the folder, he allowed the two men to finish their work and then alone with it, went back into the house to have a drink and read more. After the discovery he wondered if he could get past the dedication page and table of contents. As he sat, a gin and tonic sweated in his hand as he saw one story in particular was circled and had a note in

Lise's manic scribble, 'My fav!'

The story was written from Loren's perspective.

In Loren's voice, as written by Warren, he was sitting at the table and watching Lise read something she was working on, a cigarette in her hand and her glasses partially slid down her nose. Loren could see the crown of light in her hair like faint lights on dark water, or phosphorous in a crashing wave's recesses. He described her just as Loren had seen her so many times and as he watched said nothing, just admired her lithe compact frame and squared shoulders, her resolve in regards to the work and her focus. In the story she looked up once and catching her husband's eyes, smiled self-consciously like a beautiful child caught doing something good. She cocked her head and gave an appreciative laugh for his loving eyes and then just as promptly returned to her work. They said nothing to each other in the entire story but the mood captured transfixed Loren and sent him years back to the time before she left him in every sense but the physical. That Warren captured his thoughts and memories astonished him. He read all the stories.

There was one that was similar to his and yet different in that she never allowed that self-conscious moment to appear. Her only observance of the nameless man's presence was to lay back nude and lift a leg as if to say 'fetch, boy' and for that man in the story, Loren felt only profound sorrow.

Chapter 29

The many serving plates were either empty or close to it and Megumi was warming more sake for them. The meal had been a fine sample of Japanese cuisine from the miso soup and edamame, small talk over rice and fish followed by the tempura vegetables and sashimi and the choice of marinated meats over the hibachi. He felt his body relax and his soul expanding. It was a beautiful repast and he marveled at his hostesses' generosity and society, and felt honored to be a part of it. He felt so curious since waking in the strange white room, so different. It was as if his mind were muted in a sense; toned down to a place where he just felt a fluid inner warmth and a satisfaction that he couldn't understand. He allowed her to take the lead in the conversation and many questions she asked while calmly eating and taking on a glow from the beer and sake he consumed. The small dining area they sat in on cushions was cozy and low-lit, as the lights seemed to focus on their table alone while throwing a shadow on the rest of the room as a dark border. Megumi returned with more rice wine and smiling, Ueda thanked her. Bowing, Megumi started filling the empty tray with dishes and then kneeling, left the room by the *shoji* screen.

They raised their small porcelain tumblers and both said,

"*Kampei!*" After drinking them Ueda reclined to her side and leaning on an elbow in much the same attitude as her nude portrait and asked Warren if he wished to smoke, and if so, they could retire to a room where it was allowed, the rest of the house off limits. Warren at that moment was content and feeling tranquil, declined.

"So, Haas-san, did you admire my portrait in the breakfast bar area?" She inquired with a mischievous look.

"Yes, I did indeed." Warren wasn't surprised by her question after spending time with this woman, whose art seemed to also ask questions of her audience very straightforwardly.

She shifted on her elbow, "It was painted in 1956 when I was 26 years old. He was a very brilliant artist and I lived with him in Paris until the riots in 1968 and then returned to Japan. He became too dependent on alcohol and he viewed the students as left wing trash and communists. He became bitter in our relationship and I also didn't enjoy being addressed as his *petit bijou Japonais*. His politics took a sharp turn to the right, and he also fumed over the debacle in Algeria…almost flirting with fascism. By then his production and artistry dried up with help from the liquor. His sexuality also diminished and while he had never been a miraculous lover what little was there was not evident by that time. He died in 1970 of cirrhosis of the liver." Her tone and manner were matter of fact, the fires for this person having burned out long ago. Warren said nothing. She arched her back, and let out a breath.

"I'm glad Haas-san that you like the painting. I'm not above common exhibitionism and besides, at 26, one can be nude all they wish!" She laughed.

Warren smiled, "Did he do other paintings of you?"

"Yes, he did many more nude studies and a few which hang in

some prominent homes in France and abroad." She paused and poured them another round. "*Kampei!*"

Warren raised his tumbler, "*Kampei*, Noriko-san."

She cleared her throat after drinking her sake, "You talked extensively of Mishima at the club, when between sets we could have conversation. Do you recall that I told you I met him in Paris in 1966?"

"I don't recall too much of last night, "he apologized.

She rolled her eyes, "You can certainly hold your martinis but your memory seems to have been a collateral victim of your imbibing. Yes, I met him in Paris. There was a party and it was a to-do with some fashion thing that year. I also had a showing at a gallery of wood block carvings I accomplished in the manner of *Ukeyo-e*, but with contemporary Japanese men and women in western style clothes. I'm sorry, *Ukeyo-e* was a style from approximately 1600-1800's, and so I substitute the fierce samurai with milquetoast salary man and his hat and cheap briefcase and the classic geisha or lady in waiting with a woman sporting a huge beehive hairstyle and unglamorous house frock holding a duster." She laughed, "So sorry, the sake is leading me down different avenues. So, yes I met him. It was very awkward. I knew he was bisexual due to the circles we kept and while in separate ones we enjoyed mutual friends who walked into both of ours respectively. Imagine two permeable membranes with a few cells floating hither and yon, in and out. He was already very nationalistic and right wing and I was very apolitical and that bothered him. His writing was beautiful and for me as important as any painting or sculptor in the day for the statements he made. Hah! He paid more attention to my fading Frenchman as they shared such harsh views of the left. I was also very drawn to him physically as he was so well built from his bodybuilding and his devotion to martial arts, and in comparison, my poor Frenchman had gone to seed.

Hmmm, you seem to take care of yourself Haas-san. Both Marlowe and I admired your form when we put you to bed."

Blushing, Warren gave his eyes a vaudeville style of surprise and then they both laughed. "You have me at a disadvantage. Did he talk about his writing at all? He was neck deep in *The Sea of Fertility* tetralogy in that time period."

"No, as I say, it was a bit awkward. I started speaking French then switched to Japanese due to my feeling this way. Then out of the blue he told me in Japanese he thought my art a statement on the new decadence of Japan---it's westernized nightmare and said he was a secret fan and the fact I was *hibakusha*-- one who is affected by atomic bombing--endeared him to me on some level. And that was pretty much it. He killed himself four years later. Such a waste." She looked at Warren and he felt her eyes held many questions. "You attempted *seppuku* as well, neh? Please tell me if I am stepping over a boundary here, Haas-san. Please pardon my intrusion."

His mood was unaltered, neither put off nor surprised by her inquiry. "Yes, I did. Obviously not very good at it," and gave a small self-deprecating laugh.

Ueda made a sour face look with her lips, "Lucky you did not. You have much unfinished work left in you, very much. When we talked in the club, and with the other writers who came in, they also insisted you continue your work. Your first book was well received and in literary circles here *An Unworthy Tree* as well. I think in America it was misunderstood and overlooked for the potential it held and unfortunately your celebrity dominated its lifespan. Marlowe also speaks highly of you. Are you sure you don't wish to smoke? I myself take a cigarette now and again."

"I'll accompany you to your smoking lair," He said with mock resignation, "but I don't even know where my cigarettes are."

"I have English cigarettes; Silk Cut #5's and John Players, so no worries."

Ueda's flat, Warren discovered, was the entire top floor and roof garden of a building in Roppongi. The Mori Tower was visible from her enclosed roof top area. It was cooler in this room as it was so poorly insulated. In the corner was a standing fan, obviously for the summer when the AC could not beat back the merciless July and August sun.

The rain continued into the evening and so he listened to it while they quietly smoked. Ueda broke the silence.

"You do not inquire about others very much, but in that regard I also notice you observe many things and just store it away without verbally categorizing. I like how you just allow for flow."

Warren flicked the end of his cigarette into the ashtray, "I didn't always do that. Yes, I have always watched people and what they say, or how they react to things but I also used to intervene as well and insert myself into their lives for better or for worse and usually worse," he paused and continued with a rueful smile, "yea, definitely worse."

"Why have you not continued writing?"

"I have actually. I've written a collection of short stories and coincidentally I have used Marlowe as the main character. Seriously now, where did you meet Marlowe?" He had to understand her connection to him.

She looked out towards the lights over the district, "I met him at a gallery showing of my work in San Francisco while he was on vacation from teaching, so after some conversation about art, he said he would look me up in Tokyo when he arrived back. Usually such talk is just that, and while I found him attractive I did not believe I would see him again and yet the first week of his return he rang me up. He knows much about art, and literature. I was very impressed with his knowledge of Japanese woodworking as he collects *ranmas*."

"I think he's an international spy," Warren offered, "I can't figure him out."

Ueda pursed her lips in thought, "Perhaps he is." She stubbed out her cigarette. "Are you tired?"

"You know I must've slept damn good as I just feel rested and content. Total cliché but since I woke up I am a new man." And he did, since opening his eyes in the white room he felt different.

"Maybe Haas-san, you are reincarnated. Let's have a drink and I will show you my studio."

Chapter 30

Yukio detested the Christmas season and seeing it in Japan infuriated him even more. The store displays were an insult to his culture and use of a Christian holiday to boost sales in stores was nauseating. To make it worse, Tomoko celebrated the holiday from her time abroad and had persuaded him to accompany her shopping. There were some *gaijins* on the train, probably from Yokota Base who wore those idiotic elf hats and Santa beards, very talkative and loud and from what he could glean enroute to go shopping.

When in America he would never take part in any of his schools festivities or pageants come the Yule holidays. He would bow out and be excused based on his foreign standing and religious differences. His last year at his American prep introduced Mr. Burton as his counselor and academic advisor. This created a problem that eventually snowballed into a crisis during the last week prior to the Christmas break. The junior class had a planned excursion for caroling and a fundraiser for homeless families. Yukio bowed out of the caroling evolution but his family sent in a check as a pledge to support those families in need.

Mr. Burton, an evangelical, called Yukio into the academic advisory office and asked him why he wasn't going to carol with his classmates. Yukio was somewhat surprised by the question feeling that the answer was obvious, and being called out on the spot made him very nervous, and in turn silent. Burton asked if he were against Christian values in his host country, and if so, why? Again Yukio could not answer and fidgeting in his chair stared at the floor, his face donning the *Noh* mask to hide behind. Burton, feeling the silence as disrespectful and hostile to his position and values, notified the assistant boy's headmaster who was in charge of discipline. Arriving, the assistant, Mr. Gannon listened to Burton's report in regards to Yukio's behavior in light of not wishing to carol. Turning to Yukio, Mr. Gannon spoke in a very soft voice.

"Yukio, were you excused from caroling last year?"

Yukio, a fine sheen of sweat on his skin and feeling hot inside his school blazer, nodded yes, still looking at the floor. Gannon looked at Burton with an expression of 'why am I here?'

Burton couldn't let it go, "Regardless of last year, this year he shall accompany his class and join in the spirit." He exclaimed.

Gannon looked at Yukio and how miserable he looked. He took a small pre signed post-it from his pocket, and writing the time on it held it out to Yukio, "Return to class, Yukio."

Freed from Mr. Burton's grasp, Yukio could only bow his head, and standing, walked from the office with his shoulders pulled forward and his head down. He never knew what Gannon said to Burton, but it did not end there. Burton took his complaint to the headmaster who in turn counseled him on respecting other faiths as he wished his own be respected. Burton argued that Yukio, as a non-Christian should be exposed to Christ in the hopes of a transformation. The headmaster had warned Mr. Burton then to cease this train of thought and not to have any contact with Yukio, moving him to the sophomore academic advisor, Ms. Shepard in the meantime.

The last Thursday before the holiday break; Yukio took part in an indoor futsal tournament on the basketball court as the seniors played the juniors for bragging rights. In the locker room, sweating and shouting, the 30 odd boys were catcalling one another and shaming the losers, the juniors, who went down to defeat. In the midst of this din Mr. Burton, using a loud outdoor voice grabbed their attention by asking for quiet. There was a bit of tittering and shushing from the boys, as no one really knew what was up. They expected some academic news or an announcement for the holidays.

"Boys…I want to take this opportunity to ask you for a favor." He shouted over the remaining voices of those exiting the showers who did not hear him before. "I want you to take a moment and reflect on how good we have it and how God has provided. I also want you to bow your heads and pray for our Japanese friend, Yukio Moritani, who is not a Christian and needs the Lord's advice." Burton hung his head.

There was stunned silence in the locker room. Yukio, in his towel started turning red, and his just showered body again felt heat and broke a sweat. The boys looked at each other quizzically and some shrugged their shoulders in disbelief. Burton raised his head.

"I don't hear you…I shall lead."

"Mr. Burton?" Adam Norris, a senior from Pennsylvania spoke in the silence. "Mr. Burton…I'm not Christian either."

"Yea that's right!" another boy shouted, "Norris doesn't even have a foreskin!" And many of the boys broke out of their trance to laugh.

"Yea and his crank is so big he would need a fiveskin!" Another screamed.

Burton exploded, "This is not a laughing matter…we're talking about Shintoism, a religion that isn't recognized as such in our Christian country. Mr. Norris is at least a Hebrew."

Yukio was shrinking inside his towel, and his skin was shining in sweat. Adam Norris moved to where he was in between Mr. Burton and Yukio. "Mr. Burton, you are out of line and need to stop, sir." Yukio looked up and saw nothing but the legs and back of Adam, and then he saw nothing as falling back he had passed out and slid off the bench.

Later when he awoke on the cot in the coach's lounge, he discovered Adam Norris sitting across from him reading a magazine. He looked at Yukio and smiled.

"Hey man, your dad is on his way. It's all cool. Burton was taken away by Coach Bogen and the headmaster is outside getting statements."

Yukio shook his head as he listened. Norris was turning a page to his Sports Illustrated, "Why did Mr. Burton become so insistent?"

Adam Norris cocked his head to one side and looking around for the words, found he just didn't have the formula, and shrugging it off laughed, "It's America, Yukio. It's America."

That memory of only a year ago was in his mind as Tomoko rode the escalator ahead of him as they came down from the platform at the *eki*. They were in Shin-juku to shop at the name brand stores so she could find gifts for her family. The throngs were already thick, and people were bundled for the cold on this Sunday. The freak snowstorm had given way to rain late Friday and it was still a faint drizzle, just above freezing as they issued into the street.

Mr. Burton was fired, and his father threatened the school with legal action for the advisor's discriminatory act. The whole ordeal was a major embarrassment for the family in that they had to share their time and private lives over something that should never have occurred, yet for this man who insisted Yukio carol with his classmates. The grounds on which he insisted were hotly argued in the headmaster's office, and it included Adam Norris' father who was in town to pick up his son for the holiday break. After hearing how the episode rolled out, Yukio's father, following tradition, appreciated Adam's treatment of Yukio and the small protection he afforded him and handed Mr. Norris a small envelope as a gift.

"Reciprocity is a custom from my country, to give a gift to those who do service to us. Please accept it for your son's proper stance in light of this sad interlude, and allow him to benefit, please." Yukio's father looked up into the taller man's blue eyes, and in his eyes beseeched Adam's father to accept and not make a conversation of it, as he did when conducting business at work. Mr. Norris, seeing the resolve in the other man's eyes took the envelope and thanked him.

"Your son has courage and Yukio and his family extend our respect to him."

Yukio was proud of his father that day in the restraint he showed in dealing with the issue. Yes, he lost his temper when the headmaster repeatedly offered a defense for Burton's behavior after clearly stating Burton had no right to proselytize and verbally attack Yukio. But who would not in light of such an idiotic argument?

Adam Norris and Yukio were teammates on the varsity soccer team and in the spring became closer, and good friends, probably the only friend he could claim when in that school. He wrote Yukio twice from the university in Pennsylvania he attended but Yukio had not written him back. He decided to turn his back on that history of his life and to only look forward. Forward to Japan. Not receiving any reply, Adam stopped writing altogether, not even sure if he had the proper address. The entire episode was part of the determining factor for Yukio's father to obtain a position back in Japan, as they were abroad almost the entire length of his son's life.

"Buy me a coffee?" Tomoko grinned, breaking his memory. "There's a new coffee and espresso place there near The Gap." Her smile looked beautiful, lighting him up inside, exciting him.

"Only if you kiss me." He smiled back. Tomoko, turned her body to him and putting her hands on his arms, leaned in and lifting her head up kissed him full on the mouth.

In Japanese she told him, "It's about time you asked for one."

In his mind, he could hear Adam's voice saying in English, 'It's America.'

Chapter 31

Riordan took Warren's advice and while he still harbored bad feelings every time he remembered the lecture, he knew it was right. Ai asked a couple of questions about why they changed their schedule but Riordan just reassured her it was the best. They moved their rendezvous from the love hotel they frequented to another that was on a totally different train line. And at his insistence they cut back on lovemaking. They diffused their actions at school as well when in passing or when she was in the office. While he hated to not be able to he realized restraint was the best policy. It put a strain on his relationship with Warren, and that even though Riordan was the transgressor he hated Warren for finding them out; knowing their secret and passion. Warren, understanding the younger man's feelings just kept a professional distance and when Riordan came under fire from Flattery or Felch, he turned his head and didn't engage. Riordan was a big boy, and he figured he could start fighting his own battles even against the NS Department powers of darkness.

He had started putting out feelers in Northern California, convinced Ai would attend either Berkeley or Stanford, the west coast just that much closer to Japan and easy to fly from. Her mother and father already discussed the idea of perhaps meeting in Honolulu for a vacation and enjoying a family outing for her breaks, and the ease by which it would be for her fly from the Bay Area. Ai and Riordan, when together, discussed their future and how to break it to her parents. One scenario they always fell back on was the one where he always planned to leave Kin Tama, and serendipitously meeting Ai in either San Francisco or Berkeley, and finding each other had coffee, etc., and then things just happened. They could scarcely bring up an illicit affair between teacher and student and hope to build the foundation of a marriage on that.

They planned a two-day get-away over Christmas break as Kin Tama recognized the foreign students who were non-Buddhist and allowed them time to either fly home or receive family. Ai informed her parents that she was accompanying a group to Nagano for snow activities and the fact that a group from school was going gave her good cover. She and Riordan would be staying just outside Nagano at a chalet he reserved. His parents sent him an early gift of $2000 to spend on what they had been led to believe a 'cultural winter tour' of Hokkaido and Sapporo. He felt guilty until that next time Ai was next to him in bed and he explained the plan for Christmas break. He would wonder what his parents would say when he finally got to introduce Ai to them. He knew it was the 90's but there was some ingrained 1950's at home he thought he might have some problems with.

Ai looked forward to the holiday break, her natural and healthy vitality; this effervescence was right below the surface. Her stress in filling out the applications, helped by the dutiful Ms. Hyodo who worked in the International Studies Office, had almost dissipated, and upon finding out her SAT scores were at near perfect she met that hurdle and felt much better. This mental timeout afforded by her hard work gave her pause to actually reflect on the last semester since the end of summer. The last time she and Riordan met, he described to her their getaway vacation. He had actually rented a car so they would not have to utilize public transportation and perhaps run into anyone from Kin Tama enjoying the recreation at Nagano. She felt grownup and independent when he described the chalet and showed her a small brochure from a travel agency. He was holding the glossy picture of the cabin that appeared to be taken in the summer in one hand while his other was entwined in her thick mane, both of them propped up on the western style bed. They were quiet as they looked at the picture and then could hear someone in the throes of sexual ecstasy through the thin membranes between the rooms. They turned to each other and made a face of surprise, and when Ai started to giggle, Riordan shushed her, and they strained their ears to listen more. Riordan, erecting, pulled her head to him by her hair, and they kissed.

    She was daydreaming of that encounter, her excitement bristling, and she wrote a small note to him expressing her immediate lust for him and described an erotic encounter they could have at Kin Tama if they dared! Knowing this would make him think of her and also imagine the encounter as she described it, she sealed it in an envelope and made her way to the administration spaces. Finding the teachers' mailboxes deserted, she slipped it into the slot for him and returned quickly to the main area of offices to greet Ms. Hyodo and wish her good health.

    Flattery, having just turned the corner coming from the Japanese teachers' lounge had seen Ai place the envelope. Stopping so as not to be seen, he watched her leave quietly and looking about to see he was still alone, walked to Riordan's box and picked up the envelope. There was nothing written on it, and feeling that a letter with no address or name belonged to anybody; he placed it inside the pages of the book he carried and returned to the NS Office.

Chapter 32

Her studio was just below the deck they smoked on and the huge factory style windows commanded a dazzling view of the skyline.

"How many times in your youth did you see my city destroyed by giant moth wings, alien monsters or the breath of fire?" She laughed.

Warren let out a harsh, spontaneous laugh, "Oh God...about a jillion times! I must've watched every Japanese monster movie made, even the awful ones with the Smog Monster and Mecha-Godzilla. Oh, one of my favorites, even though Tokyo wasn't a part of it was 'Attack of the Mushroom People'...classic! I liked the early ones better. 'Rodan' was always a fave and of course the original 'Godzilla' with Raymond Burr, that towering thespian."

"Yes, I doubt we in Tokyo could ever recover from all those attacks! I found them amusing to watch. I was once almost commissioned by ToHo studios to do a poster but some suit from the PR offices discovered some of my more avant garde work at a gallery and it was too much for them, so I was dropped. At the time I had just finished some provocative pieces from a series of work I did concerning Hiroshima and Nagasaki."

Warren, as an American, a baby boomer, never quite knew how to deal with Hiroshima whenever its head appeared above the calm waters of aversion. He immediately pictured Big Dutch who to this day, after fighting in the Pacific and surviving Guadalcanal and numerous kamikaze attacks on his other ship would defend the use of the bomb to the point of violence. Warren cultivated mixed feelings having grown up post war; having Big Dutch on one side and his own pacifist feelings on the other side, not being drafted for Viet-Nam. He had yet to travel south to Hiroshima. Ueda noticed a change in his countenance at her mention of it.

"I can see you are conflicted Haas-san, by my mention of Hiroshima. We shant discuss the politics of 1945, neh? That was not my intention. I was born in Hiroshima in 1930, and so knew it well before its change." Warren, warming from the conversation needed to go back to the roof and smoke. But he spoke to her, this new friend with the voice he found on this strange day after waking in the white room.

"This day, this night, I feel open around you, Noriko-san. I don't feel the need to circumvent any conversations, however queasy it may make me feel. I just don't know about Hiroshima. I grew up with a father who fought in the Pacific and who lost a lot of friends. When he would wrap himself around a bottle of Old Forrester he would take me off to the side, away from my sister and mother and tell me about the war. How at Guadalcanal, parts of men littered the decks of his ship after a night action, and that many in the water were just taken, screaming by sharks. This makes an impression on a 19-year-old man fresh off the farm, so to say. He believed the bombing was the best thing that ever happened and no amount of argument can sway him. I grew up in a separate generation and I'm not so sure, and now here you are, a resident of this city; famous, prosperous and so creative. So I just don't go there. At Kin Tama, the Pacific War…see, even I am calling it that, is a moot point, and I am glad in a sense as it just makes all concerned so nervous. I'm nervous now, and I feel guilty in a sense, but that's actually a silly thing to feel. I know for you it is a daily, painful reminder, yes?" He shrugged his shoulders.

Ueda pulled out a sketchpad and while it balanced in her lap, she sharpened a thick black pencil, "I understand your father taking that position as a war fighter, a survivor. But remember Haas-san I am Japanese. For me, the bombing happened, yet I am here, but it greets me every morning. I imagine any person who has lived thru a catastrophe has much the same feelings when in reflection, as this is not exclusive to my experience. As the saying goes, this does not define me" Warren just turned away and looked out the window.

Sitting on a stool, she asked him to come over towards him and sit on a chair near her perch. "I like your profile and mean to make some sketches of you if you do not mind." He sat crossing his legs under the thick, long kimono and gave a theatrical smile.

"Ahh! Stop that horrible look. Just look that way towards my window, look at the skyline...see Godzilla walking by." She said as her hand moved rapidly on the paper. At the same time Warren wondered how much, under her kimono, she resembled her 1956 portrait. Her age meant nothing to him as he felt close to her soul and her years weren't a thing that mattered. Quietly she sketched and it allowed him time to think. He surmised she had been in Hiroshima August 6, 1945 and not evacuated somewhere prior. Was she wearing her navy jumper top with neckerchief and skirt or a kimono on that sunny morning? Was her family killed? He wished to ask but the more he thought about it, it became something he knew inside. Those flow of senses, as if she were sending a secret message to his heart. Of course he would never ask. He would settle and accept anything about it she wished to impart.

"There!" She said at last, holding up her sketchpad, Warren saw his profiled face drawn very well, even if his hair was exaggerated. She had given him the tresses of a Breck Shampoo Girl. "What do you think?"

"Wow...very good, but when did I grow all that hair?"

She pulled her chin in, her lips curled, "When I decided to draw it that way. Artist's prerogative. You don't have a lot of hair on your body Haas-san."

"We Haas men all boast hairless chests, "he joked to her, "Even the women."

"Are all your family blondes?"

"Immediate family yes, but I have a few brunette relatives and there's one redhead in the mix too."

There was a silence then and as it settled, he could hear the rain hit the windows and the faint din of traffic and again he felt an overwhelming peace. She turned to him.

"Do you have plans, Haas-san?"

"Nothing. I have never been so without plans in my entire life."

"So stay again tonight and I shall release you after breakfast. I shall attempt to find you a workable pair of shoes. I enjoy your company." Warren pictured the white room and the deep sleep he enjoyed in it.

"Thank you, I will."

"But...first more sketches and sake. I'll ring Megumi and we shall drink," then putting her sketchpad down, "or do you prefer martini? She makes a very good drink. I do not have Stolichnaya in the flat but I do believe we have Smirnoff. I used to have a connection in Marlowe for obtaining good liquor on the cheap from the military PX, but I stopped asking him."

"Sake is fine." He was glad they had changed course and did not mention Hiroshima again. Ueda went to a small intercom and buzzing it, spoke in rapid Japanese.

Turning back to him, "Are you going to continue your art, Haas-san?"

"Writing? Like I said, I still do but not another novel. I don't know if I have another one in me. I thought the second one would be a valediction, would speak to me as an author with more to come; established. But it was a disaster and the events surrounding it didn't help. I didn't help myself either. Old story. Old news." He pulled his kimono lapels closer as if he were cold.

There was urgency in her voice, " You must continue. You have been given another chance. It is why you are here. You have survived and I know teaching at Kin Tama is not the work you pursue for a lifetime. You have a gift, Haas-san. But for now I will immortalize you in *my art,* neh?" He closed his eyes and turning inward tried to tap that electricity he used to feel, feed on when with Lise. Maybe instead of pain inside when he envisioned her he could use it as a power source; his muse once again.

"Have you ever been an artists model?"

"Never."

"It is a thankless and boring occupation. When posing for my Frenchman, I would constantly have to break—to eat, go *shi-shi,* smoke and he would go off in a rage. I could never be the statue he demanded, so I teased him. Early on I could do that and break thru his crust, making him smile and throwing down pallet and brush, make love to me but later on, with his drink, not so much. He had lost that part of himself and he didn't realize how painful he was to be around. In telling you this, if you need to break your pose, please do so, I shall not cut my belly.

"But I need a spark and you have given me one so I must spend it while it still burns in me. I cannot leave it to go cold." She said with triumph in her voice.

Megumi knocked on the studio's western style door and entering carried a tray with a center carafe and the tumblers on each side. Pouring, she turned to her mistress and spoke softly, and answering her, Ueda said *hai* two times.

"So, to what do we toast?"

"Samsara." She said.

"*Kampei!*" They said together.

Chapter 33

"So you just left him there in a borrowed kimono?"

"Yes, it's a good place for him to hang. Get his juices flowing again. He's really very talented. Have you read his work?"

"Never. I'm more Scott Turow, John Grisham. I like that sort of stuff."

"Really? You never told me that before. But he has something. So I'm hoping she can jumpstart him. She's creative 24/7. Maybe he'll get sucked into her turbines there."

"How old did you say she was?"

"Like 65, I think. She has a nude portrait hanging on the wall in an informal dining area from when she was 26."

"Wow! Was she hot? Oh she must've been for that smile you have. Ha ha."

"Very! She is still very attractive. Not 26 hot but she is something. Her art keeps her young."

"Hmmm...so how about 39 hot?"

"You're 39 hot. Very hot."

"Did...did you ever sleep with her?"

"I did, yes, years ago after I met her at a gallery in San Francisco."

"Before you met me?"

"Before I met you."

"Was it good?"

"She was good, yes."

"Her body?"

"Not 26 but still pretty nice and fit."

"MMMMmmmm…that was a nice kiss. Was that a 'stop asking questions' kiss?"

"Sort of. Also sort of to make you do things to me kiss."

"Bad man. I do things to you I never did in my life before or dreamed before. If *he* had even tried those things with me I would've hit him with a pan. But you…you."

"Me?"

"Why yes, you. Oh, what's this?"

"Just something I want to give you"

"If only he could give *this*…well, it might be a different ballgame."

"You think?"

"Hmmm...not really. There's the body attached to it that really makes the difference. *Your* body."

"Thank you. Your hands feel wonderful, Mrs. Bloom."

"Thank you, Mr. Marlowe. Do you think Warren will write again?"

"Not sure—but after hearing him wax eloquent at the jazz club, man that guy has some knowledge. The best part was later."

"What happened?"

"It was snowing madly and there was a lot of slush too, I mean that storm was just insane, in the streets and gutters, and some drifts as well. We were a couple of blocks from the club looking for a cab to send Ueda home in when this big ass garbage hauler was rumbling up the road towards us. As it came up closer it started taking out a huge snow bank and slush in the gutter throwing up a wave and parallel to us were no parked cars for cover so Warren opens his coat like the Batman spreading his cape and yells 'Duck behind me!' so we do. He takes the full blast of dirty snow all over his front, and we didn't get a drop and then he starts chasing the garbage truck like a maniac, throwing a shoe in the process! We found him laying out in the middle of an intersection making snow angels!"

"Maniac!"

"Total maniac. So just then we saw a cab and we went to Ueda's so we could undress him and put him to bed. His clothes were soaked. He was whacked."

"You both undressed him? How did he look?"

"Why, Mrs. Bloom, I didn't have my ruler handy, ha ha."

"Oh stop."

"You would've enjoyed it. There's something comical about a man's genitals bouncing around when you're undressing him. Ueda even put it in her hand, like she was weighing it. Want more details?"

"No! Yes!"

"She said *ce est grand homme.*"

"Which means?"

"Basically, a man of substance. She was a bit fixated and for 40, Warren is in good shape. He must've been hell on the ladies back in his celebrity days."

"Hmm now you're making me curious about him."

"God, I couldn't wait to leave earlier to see you."

"You do say the right things, don't you?"

"Stop smiling you, and grab your knees like I like you to."

"Yes, a very bad man."

Chapter 34

"Do we really need to go over it?" Lise asked, not exasperated yet, but edging close. She was talking to Warren on the phone in her bedroom and was using one hand to shape her part in the mirror at the front of the bed. This was now exclusively her room as Loren moved out to the guest cottage in the last year.

Warren could tell he was skating on thin ice. He just wished to seek closure of some sort and also get a handle on his direction. His writing was sporadic and without any purpose, the sophomore book tanking in store sales. The story of his Uncle Jann wouldn't die. They even found a picture of him in full black dress SS uniform surrounded by what looked like dead civilians! Why weren't they also showing pictures of Big Dutch as a bluejacket in the South Pacific, awarded a Purple Heart at Guadalcanal?

"Pick me up and let's go to the Charthouse for dinner then. How's that?" She felt a tiny flicker of remorse. She had not given him his due or an explanation. He at least deserved that. There was never any definition of love in what they did but he did walk the walk with her, and his feet felt that fire. He was a companion through many fires. She looked outdoors and it was a beautiful evening; warm and swathed in Santa Ana winds. She would wear a skirt.

She knew Warren could never make a clean break of it. When he was involved with someone and things started going south he was unable to smoothly cut the rope, and instead he would initiate intrigues with whomever he felt attracted to and vice-versa. His affairs were never sprints; an explosion out of the blocks and a meteoric rush to a known termination point. Warren preferred to conduct his business of the heart as a long distance relay, a baton passed carefully in that grey area between runners. He would, like the baton itself, make sure his paramours both entered the handoff area even if it were painfully uncomfortable for both. At times the baton was dropped, all the players out of sync with Warren's poorly manipulated orchestration; the ensuing humiliation for the lover he just left to the one who just arrived. Not for Lise. Sadly, he had no idea of the untenable position positions he placed women in with the exception of her. She would never stand for it or allow herself to become the *last* or the *next* woman in his race. She would, intuitively, like a wild animal know a storm was inbound and where and when to obtain shelter. For others, she had wryly observed in the time she knew him, Warren was a lightning rod of amoral dysfunction they could not be allowed to escape from and retain any shred of dignity. His need to be touched by his outgoing lover made him feel secure while at the same time spineless. Lise, on the other hand, used surgical precision or heavy caliber verbal ammunition to excise herself from any and all entanglements with the exception of her husband Loren. Where Warren had some lopsided romantic fixation on how he ended and started his dalliances, Lise had no illusions nor had any need to put lipstick on her pigs and Loren knew full well what his bill of goods with the opaque eyes was all about, and she knew those eyes inflicted an ungodly amount of pain and remorse. For her this was part and parcel.

The Deep Slumber of Dogs

Warren just didn't know how to trade in this currency. Tonight she would put this to rest.

Warren's ride from the El Norte in Hollywood proper to Lise's house took him almost a half hour in the dry October evening traffic. Their house was on Rexford just north of Sunset, a two story Spanish affair with lots of white washed stucco and red tiles, bars across the windows Hacienda style. The garden was filled with hollyhocks and lilacs that fat lazy bees still bounced too and fro on in the heat of early evening time. He knew from experience that when he dropped her off later, the night blooming jasmine would be thick in the air.

It took a lot of juice to maintain that place, Warren mused and he knew Loren not only had money but he came from it too, as did Lise. Warren always felt like Nick Carroway in between the two of them. Big Dutch, his mom, Maud and he lived in a three-bedroom rambler in the blue-collar section of Manhattan Beach, off of Sepulveda. The house and garden off Sunset always amazed him. By the time he pulled into their driveway, the dry red wind pushed his blonde hair back and held it there, this dried frieze of bronze. He wore a black raw silk shirt and faded jeans, the same 501's he owned for years; definitely Manhattan Beach. Getting out of the Porsche he went to the door on the side of the house under a carport that protected against the endless Southern California sun; garage and guesthouse in the back. The door behind the screen was open. He knocked lightly on the door.

"Lise?" There was no answer, and because of her erratic behavior and hours they could never keep a domestic past sunset. He looked to the garage and didn't see Loren's car so he pushed the screen door and went inside. He could hear music from the house interior now and decided she couldn't hear him. As he moved through the kitchen to the den he could hear that she was listening to The Clash. He called her name louder.

Lise had just finished doing four lines; three coke and one of a brown heroin supposedly from Iran; Persian Brown her connection said, and Lise laughed that most likely the closest it ever got to Persia was the deserts of Sonora, so feeling guilty he dropped the price for her. She rubbed her nose and inhaled smartly, then giggled. Her brain felt warm and fine, a small fire inside her. She heard Warren call out to her.

"In here," she looked in the mirror and played with her part one last time, " I'm coming out."

Warren already issued into the hallway to her bedroom as she emerged. Lise was wearing a dark blue Chinese collared blouse and a black leather miniskirt. He saw her hair was longer when last they met as it had been awhile, just brushing past her shoulders, still bone straight with her trademark bangs. She put her hands out, palms towards him, bent at the knees and opened her eyes as wide as she could,

"How do you like me now?"

Warren always flushed seeing her. She brought some inner heat from him he never realized existed until her. "You look fine, Lise. Always fine."

She took him in, standing there in her hallway. Over thirty but still her beautiful Dutch boy with his deep tanned face from never putting his ragtop up to his sun lightened hair an inch off his shoulders. She did think him a beautiful lad even with the sad business at hand, and her current lover did not stack up as well against Warren. She felt a shiver go thru her looking at him in his old jeans and simple shirt.

"Hungry?" She asked.

"Yea, when you said Charthouse I immediately felt like a fine rare T-bone and a super dry Stoli straight up."

The lines had ignited her like a slow liquid fire; the flames rolling slowly over her, into her loins. "No baby, I meant *hungry,*" and she lifted her miniskirt over her panty crotch.

Warren was melting, "What the fuck, Lise...when's Loren coming home?"

Lise started pulling her panties up into her lips, "Doesn't matter. He doesn't live in this house anymore. My bed is *my bed.* I've missed it Dutch boy."

He couldn't see it happening, and hated when she called him that. Couldn't do this in her house, had *never* done this in her house regardless of where her husband slept; started backing down the hallway turning to exit into the living room and back to the kitchen. Lise, her eyes closed as she flushed in pure heat didn't realize he left. When she opened her eyes and focused she found she was alone, and laughed to herself, "Mad about the boy, but he aint mad about me!" She found him in the kitchen pouring a glass of water. "Come on, *Little* Dutch, let's drive to the ocean and eat. Obviously nothing on the bill of fare here has anyone's interest." She said flatly, walking by him towards the door.

The air was bone dry and desert hot. When Lise walked outside she put on her Dietrich accent, "Thees hot air ees like the dead ashes of love, eh bebe?" Opening the car door plopped into the seat. Headlights appeared in the dusk behind them, as Loren was coming up the single lane driveway. Warren, thinking it was prescient now not to have bitten at Lise's apple, didn't like how things were rolling. The act in the house, obvious she was higher than Hogan's Goat, and now Loren. The trifecta.

"Well hello, people," he said in a fatherly way. " It's been awhile Warren. Where are we off to?"

Lise leaned over, unlatched Warren's door and flung it open,

"Pedal to the metal, bub." She turned to Loren, "We're going to eat. Warren doesn't wanna fuck me anymore, so we decided to eat dinner instead." She rummaged thru her bag for cigarettes. "Come on, let's generate some wind, It's hotter than a chimp's ass here!"

Warren looked at her husband. The older man said nothing, and just turned to back his car out of the driveway. Warren got into the offered open door, sat down and helped Lise light her cigarette, then took one for him. The tobacco ignited and burned fast in the heat. He threw an arm over the back of the seat and turning his head, backed up. As they pulled out into the street, Lise threw a finger in the direction of the waiting car, and sitting so low in the Porsche, all Loren saw was a periscope of a forearm and a hand, finger extended. Shaking his head he watched the tail lights slip up the street towards Sunset.

She pushed the cassette tape in, turning the volume before the music even came on. Warren knew the drill and had even cued the tape for her. Steely Dan's 'Babylon Sisters' was just the speed for her now, with that punctuated horn section slow rolling building up to the vocal. Hearing it, Lise smiled and went inside herself and her world. He let her stay there as he shifted gears down Sunset to the sea, the song's lyrics almost guiding them there. Lise leaned over and touching his arm smiled at him and asked to tell her when they got close to the beach.

Past UCLA and the 405, he started picking up speed just making lights or blowing through them. Somewhere in the Palisades he did a few things; lit another cigarette, pulled the cassette out and slammed in another one, looked over at Lise who was in some narcotic bliss he didn't have a code to and again picked up more speed. The rude slide guitar of 'Good Day in Hell' cranked over the engines growl on his Bose system, the whole car filled with it, pushing him in some way he didn't understand to drive harder. Even this far west the hot air and wind was whipping the trees and the cross current in the open car was intense. His foot on the gas, he felt lost inside; someplace he couldn't recognize. He just heard the lyrics as if they were somewhere else, not in the car, and he knew the devil thought he was doing just fine when he sideswiped the first car and started shooting diagonally across the boulevard. In the oncoming lanes instantly he reacted by pulling the emergency brake and turned the wheel to control the skid but the light post was already there and hitting the curb and jumping the side of the car Lise was on took the brunt of it, directly on her and her door. The sheer force of the impact slammed her on the door shredding her above the waist, her torso hitting the pole simultaneously and gruesomely coming down to rest, askew, on her body in the car, her body almost cut in half, the right side of her head already bloody, grey matter visible. Warren, in his lap belt was throttled and snapped his head as it made contact with the corner of the windshield frame, instantly the blood was fanned over his face, and his blonde hair glistening red in the pole's light. Dazed, when he shook the blood out of his eyes he could've sworn when he looked at the grotesque broken doll next to him that had been Lise winked at him. He looked down, seeing her legs open and her panty crotch exposed and thinking he was hungry, he passed out.

  Warren's recovery was not so quick; sutures in his scalp and forehead, neck brace, dislocated shoulder, numerous lacerations and broken fingers on his left hand. His hips, thrashed on impact made walking painful, but he was hopped up on painkillers and sedated to the gills. Headlines were varied. The worst were the tabloids who showed separate pictures of Warren, and Lise posted together insinuating they were lovers with inserts of Loren, the Nazi great-uncle and the Porsche t-boned at the light pole, now called 'the death car' in variations on each cover. One even showed Warren with his great uncle's picture next to him with headline 'Nazi Uncle's Ghost Kills Woman.'

Sympathy fell to Loren.

Warren's only hospital visitors were Big Dutch, Maud, Stanford Morris and his wife Hannah. The hospital threw reporters and paparazzi out, and one almost took a picture of him in his hospital bed before a nurse caught him. He had no friends after killing Lise. He was looking into his father's eyes on the older man's nightly visit and then he saw Lise, her panties…Jesus, Lise, you don't know how lewd that looks!

"Haas-san…wake up! Wake up…it is only a bad dream." Ueda was holding his shoulders. Warren's hair was soaked in sweat; the pillow case damp and the sheets were a second skin. He focused on her face, seeing her age in the cold light by the bed; yet also glad it was there as he came back. He was in the white room where he had awoken earlier in the afternoon feeling so free and at peace. And here he was back at square one, a ghoul to the end.

"Wait here for me…" And she left the room. Momentarily she came back with a bottle. "This is what I could grab on short notice from downstairs," and handed him a small pint bottle of bourbon. He sat up higher and took a long pull off of it.

Ueda watched him, and then took a short drink of it herself before capping it and putting it on the nightstand. "Was she beautiful, sensei?" Ueda asked.

"Who?" Warren asked, surprised by her question and genuinely curious.

"The woman you loved who died in your car. You were screaming her name and saying you were sorry. She is Lise, yes?"

He ran thru his memory making Lise smile, walk, throw her very

Asian hair back and laugh. She looked into his eyes, and thinking of her making love, remembered her lips, her sly kisses.

"Yes. Yes, she was very beautiful. But she was… I don't know what she was." He reached for the bottle again.

Ueda watched him and left again, this time coming back with a towel and started drying his hair and shoulders. Her own robe was loose and pulling off her shoulder as she worked on Warren. She turned to get another dry towel off the edge of the bed where she had laid it, and her robe was off her shoulder, exposing her scapula. He could see plainly the ribbed lines in her skin, the atomic tattoo with three visible keloids, and he knew. She turned back to him, and seeing his eyes, she pulled her robe up farther on her shoulder.

"So sorry, living alone with Megumi I forget sometimes my modesty." And she knew he saw the burns from the lightweight, striped kimono she wore when the initial flash burst had caught them. Warren put his hand on her arm and pulled her to him and she let him pull her body to his and as he laid on his side pulled her back into him, an arm under her and the other holding her hips. She reached up turning off the light, and he was already asleep.

Chapter 35

The snow was falling in light powdery swirls as Yukio saw Tomoko to the *eki* and bid her goodbye, crossing the tracks on the overpass to the other side to await his train. He carried his kendo *shinai* in a sling and his protective sparring gear in a backpack. They met earlier after his lesson for a coffee, as her *juku* was only two stations up the line.

He looked across the tracks to the other platform, thru the white mist of snow, and saw Tomoko waiting for him to see her so she could wave goodnight. They sensed that their eyes finally met as they looked across at each other and lifting his hand first she thrust hers up and waved energetically. Behind her he saw a very dark man who was holding an open suitcase as he came abreast of her. He engaged her in conversation, her wave frozen in the air as he talked and displayed the wares in his case. Yukio recognized him as the African who was outside the station hawking small figurines and feathered jewelry that they had avoided when walking in.

Straining his eyes now he saw the man touching Tomoko's arm. She abruptly pulled it away from him and shook her head no. Yukio could hear nothing as seeing the powdered mist start blowing violently as her train made its approach to the platform; screaming her name to no avail and then she disappeared in the white wind and oncoming train cars, their reflective windows streaming by. Furious, he could only wait. After what felt like days the train started pulling out slowly and after the last car cleared the platform he saw two or three *nihonjin* and the African; Tomoko had gotten on the train.

He saw the man walk to another woman and opening his case for her as he did for Tomoko. The next thing he knew Yukio was already on the stairs to the crossover bridge and once on it racing across as fast as he could run. Coming down the other side he had unsheathed his bamboo *shinai* and looking up saw the woman brush the man off and started to move away from him as he shrugged his one shoulder, the other hand holding the open case. He didn't see Yukio until he heard the words hissing from him.

"Japan for Japanese!" And when the man felt the sting of the bamboo on his free wrist, the shock and the pain of the attack, he dropped his case and the contents spilled out in all directions. He screamed 'Hey!' but the next answer was two quick hits to his face followed by a thrust to his solar plexus. Yukio grunted loudly with each movement and felt elation as never before seeing the wood on the helpless man.

The man, stunned and in pain, turned to run from his attacker and found his effort was now in vain as Yukio had shifted his position to stave off escape and used a flurry of parries to hit the man over and over again, breaking a bone in his forearm as he tried to protect his head. Yukio delighted in his power and backing up, lunged to attack again only to be grabbed from behind by a middle-aged man in a suit who was telling him to stop. Yukio, breaking free, started running and picking up the sheath, looked down track and seeing the headlights of his train estimated he could make it as he bounded up the stairs and streaked across the covered overpass, never looking back. Hitting the platform he bolted in between the sliding doors as they closed.

Out of breath, sweating thru his clothes he started coming down off his high and took stock of his surroundings. The empty car ignored him and he wound his way to a corner seat sliding his hand down the silver stanchion he used to swing into it. His *shinai* was still exposed and shaking, he started sheathing it in the sling bag, excited that he saw blood on it. He smiled. So easy, he thought. He closed his eyes and shaking slightly, still coming back into his body he wondered about the weight of the real *katana* he was going to purchase on the black market. The dealer he contacted did sales under the table without having to register the weapon as per the law, and had promised him a 1944 *Shin-gunto*. He would keep it inside his closet in the recess to the right of the door; inside the space even his mother would not find it cleaning or hanging up his clothes.

He regained his normal breathing and while his clothes were still damp with sweat he just appeared as any young man returning from a hardy workout. Leaving the *eki* he found his bike, unlocked it and pedaled silently in the snow the few blocks to his house. The foyer was quiet. Dropping his gear quietly he slipped his house shoes on and went in search of his parents.

His mother, alone and watching TV looked up at him and smiling asked how his lesson was.

"Very good. I had a prosperous evening, mother. Where is father?"

"In his office upstairs. Go bathe and I shall make a snack for you." And she got up off the small love seat and went into their kitchen. The Moritani's employed a housekeeper but it was her night off.

Yukio bowed his head ever so slightly and slipping upstairs

stripped off and sitting on his stool, held the shower spray of hot water over his head luxuriating in the memory of beating the *gaijin*. Soaking in the tub afterward he thought of Tomoko.

After his bathing he called Tomoko on her new cellular but all he got was her giggling voice message. It was okay; this was to remain his secret. He went downstairs to discover a small cake and a glass of chai laid out for him, and feeling refreshed enjoyed it immensely. Visiting his mother again, kissed her forehead and walking quietly past his father's office went to bed.

Before school the next day, his father came to him as he was dressing, and adjusting Yukio's tie engaged him in conversation, "There's some lunatic who attacked an immigrant with a kendo *shinai* last night at a train station near your dojo. Any of your classmates immigrant haters?"

Yukio laughed, "Father, how many kendo clubs do you think are in Tokyo? And perhaps it wasn't a club participant.... but some someone else?"

His father laughed, "Keep on the lookout for people who say things and do things against foreigners."

"Hai! This was on the morning news?" Yukio was a bit wide-eyed at this report.

"Yes, very big news. You know how these morning reports are very much like they were in America. Lots of excitement and drama."

"Very exciting."

The tone, not so much the words caught Yukio's father off guard as it was said with passion. Looking at his son's face the expression also made him wonder. The old mask, the *Noh* character he used to be for so many years; white and expressionless seemed to melt away. Never before had he seen his son so animated, vibrant.

Chapter 36

Flattery took the intercepted letter home so in no way could he be discovered reading it. When back in his flat and sitting on the floor nursing a beer, all he could do after reading it was lay down on his back and staring at the ceiling smile and picture Ai; on her knees. That he was also in shock was an understatement as he had thought Riordan a hapless wank of the first water and now he needed to reevaluate that estimate.

Ai, pretty little Ai. He thought of how to play this newfound treasure; extract full payment. Riordan losing his job was a given, but what of the collateral dividend of Ai. Could he kill two birds with one stone, as it were? Well, he smiled, *audentes fortuna juvat.* Put that in your fucking pipe and smoke it you American prick.

Ai! Now that was a fine young woman, and while sleeping on this idea he woke up in a sweat twice. 'Seamus,' he told himself when shaving the next morning, 'you owe it to yourself, lad.' He rode his bike, whistling, even in the cold dry air in that week before holiday break. He wondered who they would hire once Riordan was discovered a child molester? Oh, poor Kin Tama, visited by another tragedy, yet *saved* by Mr. Flattery who allowed the school to excise Riordan discreetly, and well done Mr. Flattery! And little Ai will say nothing to save him either or risk exposure

The Deep Slumber of Dogs

to her parents. Sealed with a kiss, he laughed to himself.

He went to the admin support office where the comprehension of English was probably the poorest and making one copy of Ai's letter, he folded the original and placed it in the inner pocket of his jacket. Whistling, he repaired to the NS Dept. and finding Kawakami and Haas the only faculty in attendance, went to the small changing area and shut the door behind him.

Mari looked at Warren, who couldn't resist a schoolboy moment and returning her look put his fingers up and pinched his nose as if something smelled foul. Mari covered her mouth out of habit and stifled a giggle. Mr. Flattery was indeed *akushuu*. Warren had zero trust in Flattery and seeing him arrive and not come straight up the back steps from the bike racks made him curious. I'll have to keep an eye on this prick today, he reminded himself.

Flattery went about his business and waited until the 5th bell when he knew Ai attended a study group of independent seniors who were considered 'AP' in all their classes. There were only six of them, but any teacher from the NS Dept. would not be scrutinized for coming in as they had the preponderance of the classes the students attended, math and science the only exceptions and he knew that Riordan's class was at the opposite end of the building for this bell. All the students looked up as Flattery entered then just as quickly went back to their work, each hoping he was not looking for them. He went directly to Ai and asked her to step outside the class for a quick second. She nodded silently wondering what he wanted and what it was he was holding as she rose from her chair smoothed her skirt and followed him out. Once outside the door Flattery did a cursory look over his shoulder and spoke to her in a very soft English.

"I want you to read this, then I want you to read the instructions at the bottom and if you do, there will be no problems for your friend. Its only a copy, so please understand destroying it is a bit of a futile gesture," he smiled, looking at the front of her crisp blouse, " Now please pay heed to this special lesson plan, lass." And with that he turned and walked back, whistling to the NS Dept.

Ai, staring at the first line of the letter felt the sweat break under her arms and between her breasts; her letter for Philip; her explicit, whimsical caught in the moment letter, staring back at her. Given to her by *Flattery*...how could he...how did it happen? But it did. Her face flushing a deep red, she just walked straight to the girl's room and finding an empty stall, sat and locked the door. She used the toilet paper to dry her eyes and wipe the sweat from her forehead. She used the letter to fan her face and with her other hand pull her blouse away from her body as it was stuck to her like a second skin. She took a deep breath and then finding Flattery's *katakana* at the bottom, read his 'lesson plan.' Once done, she rose off the seat and kneeling vomited into the bowl, her stomach a spontaneous eruption of disgust. Her only saving thought was that once it was done, Philip would keep his job and no one would know of this repulsive interlude.

The night Flattery gave her was a *juku* night and also a planned assignation with Riordan. She could sidestep all of it with a deft fib. She returned to study hall after washing her face and gargling to rid herself of the taste of her vomit. She tried to push Flattery out of her mind, yet every time he appeared or she remembered his nauseating odor she felt she would gag. She avoided Riordan for the rest of the day as well.

Come final bell, and returning to the NS Dept. office, Riordan pulled Marlowe aside and jokingly asked him if Flattery had won the Irish

Sweepstakes, as he was in a jolly mood all day.

"Who in hell knows with that assclown?" Offered Marlowe.

Flattery came in, and slapping Riordan on the back before he left, laughed at him, "*Audentes Fortuna Juvat!*"

"Huh?"

Warren's eyes followed Flattery, "He said 'Fortune Favors the Bold' in latin."

"I hate that prick," Riordan said softly.

"Get in line," Warren reminded him. Flattery's humming in the small changing room caught his attention, and without Felch in the office, he couldn't pump him for info. He got out of his seat and went into the small space, shutting the door behind him.

"What're you so happy about? Kitihara pat you on the head? Find a half filled bottle of Guinness in the men's room at Fussa Station?"

Flattery guffawed, " You're such a fucking tosser, like, Warren, as if I would even entertain discussing my business with a arsehole like yourself." He was pulling on his cold weather leggings for his ride home.

"Don't sell me short, prick. That chip you carry on your shoulder from being on the business end of all those English dicks is no hanging matter to me. Just feeling froggy, all you have to do is jump. But you won't."

"Go the fuck away, Haas-been. Go lay a wreath to your dead nazi uncle or piss up a rope, either or, it's all the same to me, lad." He stood up, "Now get the fuck out of my way."

Warren, smiling, lifted both his hands in mock surrender and turned sideways to allow Flattery to pass him to the stairway. At the door, he turned back to Warren.

"Don't think you're going to like me very much in the near future-

--but then again I could truly give a flying fuck, *yank*!" Smiling, he left.

Warren watched him, every bit of his self control keeping the smile frozen on his face until Flattery was well down the stairs.

"Fuck!" He exhaled, seething. Then he turned and saw it.

In his haste, Flattery left his jacket hanging off the edge of the locker. Warren would've turned and walked out had he not noticed the folded paper in the partially visible inner pocket. Normally, the thought of touching anything of Flattery's disgusted him but he remembered the warning the Irishman shot across his bow on the way out. Warren snatched it out and back inside the office hid it inside his copy of *The Portable Curmudgeon*.

Marlowe, catching his furtive movement raised his eyebrows, "What's up?"

Warren gave him the *nix-nix* movement of his hand at his throat and shoving the book into his briefcase decided he would leave as well. Since the cold snap and poor weather he had taken to riding the train the last two days and grabbing his topcoat from the tree at the office door left.

Riordan looked at Marlowe, "That was a bit abrupt."

"Warren Haas, man of letters and mystery." Marlowe said *sotto voce*.

"Say Marlowe, what do you make of Haas?"

"What do you mean?" Marlowe was sure he would get an installment of Riordan's cluelessness.

"I mean...do you think he's a good guy? On the up and up?"

The older man frowned, "Phil, if you haven't figured out who the good guys are and who're the pricks up here, it's also evident you don't know what Diddy-wah-diddy means either...." He shook his head. Riordan gave him a weak smile.

There was a commotion in the changing room, and the door burst open revealing a red faced and out of breath Flattery, "HEY! Where's that bastard Haas? Right Now!"

Marlowe stood to make sure Riordan knew he would do the talking. "He went to see Kitihara, why? Did you forget to blow him goodbye?"

"Fuck your mother, Marlowe," and he flew out towards the office door, enroute to Kitihara's office.

"He left for the *eki* not to see Kitihara," Riordan said, excited by Flattery's obvious distress.

"Hell, I know that, but whatever Haas did to him, he deserves a head start. He should be on his train by the time Flattery figures it out." He smiled.

Chapter 37

The day after Ai met Flattery, the first Saturday of Winter Break, she decided to drop out of Kin Tama. She cried to her mother that the pressure of college applications combined with *juku* and her studies had oppressed her to the point of losing it. She needed time off. Her mother, incredibly upset met her father in the vestibule upon his arrival home by the car service he took. Ai was so distraught, she told him, that she had called a doctor who sedated her and left a prescription, along with an order to not give her the third degree when she woke up. Her parent's concern for her was paramount, and they made plans for her to relax---they would go down to Osaka and stay at a *ryokan* his corporation used for family and business times. When refreshed, she could reconsider or they could weigh all options. Later, Ai accepted their offer but knew deep inside she would never set foot again in that school.

She could never look Philip Riordan again in the eye.

New Years Eve came and went, and Riordan, heartbroken over the loss of Ai at the chalet due to a sudden illness at least looked forward to her return from school. But she did not return and her cellular was out of service. Finally, he strolled to the admin building and finding the registrar made a professional inquiry as to why this certain student had not returned.

The Deep Slumber of Dogs

The registrar called over one of the younger office girls that spoke better English who explained to Riordan that this student withdrew from classes, signed out by her parents and was no longer in attendance at Kin Tama. In shock, he also knew it was dangerous to pursue the matter, so he walked stiffly away.

For the rest of the afternoon he was in a daze. Did her parents discover the affair? Was there an indiscretion before the Nagano trip? He was in a controlled panic and when he scanned the faces of the of the NS Dept. staff he saw nothing save for some raised eyebrows and a smile Flattery gave him. He was on auto-pilot after work, returning home and pacing, made his dinner and didn't eat it in the quiet of his flat repeatedly hitting the redial and listening to the out of service recording in Japanese. What had happened? Should he seek help from Haas, or Marlowe? Riordan finally settled in a weak sobbing that ultimately accompanied him until sleep took him over.

Warren also noticed Ai's absence as well, and figured she was still on vacation or taken sick over the holidays. Thinking he nipped the scandal in the bud when he removed the purloined letter from Flattery, nothing else entered his mind. That letter was dynamite too, dangerous to both Ai and Riordan. He had burned it at home, but he didn't know Flattery already gave her a copy with marching orders. He never mentioned it to Riordan either because of the obvious freak out that would occur and the other reason being he would have to explain how he came to have it and that might result in violence between Riordan and the Irishman. When Warren had taken the letter from the Irishman's coat it became a silent knowledge between the two men that hung there; another weight and issue that stretched them both like an elastic band to the point of snapping. Flattery conceded to Warren with that 'you got me, pal' look of a conciliatory shrug of the shoulders yet inwardly smiling at the knowledge he was going to cuckold Riordan and savor every second.

When Ai was out several days Warren inquired in the same manner in which Riordan had and taking it farther found out she was enrolled at Chrysanthemum Academy in Shibuya that very same week after holiday, as there already was a records request. He muttered a 'wow' to himself and returned to the department. Something had happened. Ai must've known her letter was compromised, and was protecting Riordan.

When the two were alone, Warren found himself staring at Flattery until the man looked up and engaged him with his eyes. "All misty are we Warren, feeling the surge of love course thru your veins when you see me?"

"You know why I'm looking at you."

"You wish you did, laddy-buck, you wish you knew. But alas, I am but a dim bulb in the marquee of life," and he smiled brilliantly.

Warren just had that feeling that there was something else there between them, almost tangible but slipping in and out of his vision; his ken. He always felt a weakness when confronting Flattery at times in that the energy he expended in controlling his anger and from jabbing a pencil into his neck left him exhausted!

"Mr. Haas, "Felch intervened on his thoughts, as usual. Warren just turned his head, not speaking, "Mr. Haas, I see that look you have. Can we label it the 'pensive writer' look?" Smiling, he turned to Flattery.

"Let's call it the 'washed up shirt-lifter' affect. Remember, he's a sensei now not a writer. In the shitpile with the rest of us he is."

When sandwiched by the Double-F's as he termed them he became a clam and turned inward search the bin of snappy comebacks to discover, again, the bin had been emptied! Looking at Flattery, Ai's letter came to mind and so indeed the word *blackmail,* but it froze on his tongue seeing the ramifications of that accusation playing itself out; nothing positive to come from it.

"Too proud are we Warren? Cannot speak to the unwashed *illiterati?*" Flattery laughed hard, took one of his translation books and walked to the door where at the threshold, stopped and pointing at Warren with his finger let go a loud fart. Laughing, he disappeared out of the doorway. Warren turned to Felch.

"Your son just said goodbye to you." And he got up and went to the coffee mess. Pouring his cup he wondered about the real reason Ai transferred.

Chapter 38

Riordan was about to explode out of his skin. He had finally asked after two weeks and nightly calls to the non-service cellular recordings. He knew Ai was friends with Tomoko and Keiko as they bonded as returnees in their classes. In a conversational, neutral tone that he practiced after walking up to them when he saw them together in the canteen before Haas' lit class.

"Hello ladies," He said matter of factly.

They both laughed self-consciously, and slightly bowing, "Good afternoon, Riordan-sensei."

Tomoko alone asked, " Can we help you?"

"Uh, yes, please…I have, well she left a book, and I wish to return it."

They both looked at each other. Then Hana turned to him, "Do you mean Ai when you say 'She'? Flustered, Riordan cleared his throat.

"Yes, indeed, Ai. She just seems to have vanished," he smiled but couldn't help feeling that his lips were trembling.

"She transferred to Chrysanthemum Academy in Shibuya. That's all I know. You could probably just mail it."

"Thank you," and turning abruptly as if were on a drill field,

The Deep Slumber of Dogs

Riordan walked away.

There was silence between the girls. Keiko looked at her watch. "He was always a bit high strung, don't you think?"

Tomoko giggled, "Like tight strings on a *shamisa*!" They laughed together.

Riordan was already digging thru the English phone directory and thinking of excuses to leave early. Then voices told him don't.

Chapter 39

Close to his birthday in February Warren returned to the Mifuku Surf Bar in his neighborhood. Aiko had stopped falling by when Warren's visits to the bar diminished. He was spending time with Ueda and took to frequenting Marlowe's jazz bar opting out of the Beach Blanket Frenzy of Karoake.

That night after returning from the jazz club he passed the small, hidden doorway of the bar and decided to go in. It was somewhat subdued and quiet, Steve-erino standing behind the bar drying glasses. He recognized the prerecorded tape they used that featured old surf tracks of Dick Dale and other instrumental notables, as no one was slinging it to the karaoke machine. Seated were two couples and a table of three black men. From their style of dress he could see they weren't American Military. His 'suffah' girl wasn't there but her 'sister' was and, seeing Warren, threw him a shaka. He returned the gesture and sat down tiredly to order a nightcap.

"Konbanwa, Stever-ino. Genki deska?" Warren greeted him.

"Hai genki des, konbanwa, Wallen." He looked over his huge black glasses and was markedly depressed. "You bin bizzy?"

"Hai, busy. Work and things. Why so sad in here?" Warren felt like an idiot after he made a downturned smile face, as if he needed to illustrate depression. He wondered if he would ever grow up.

Stever-ino looked around Warren and then pulled his head back, as if indicating the area behind Warren. He did a slow turn and found himself seeing the three black men huddled at their table.

"They scared. There was kendo attack near this *eki.*" Even Warren who never paid attention to the news heard of the 'Kendo Ninja' as they called him in the NS Dept. office. The story made *The Japan Times* with every attack and there were many different theories as to who it was. One had him as a member of an anti-foreigner hit squad or *bosozoku*, nationalistic biker gangs, as they believed there was more than one. Another stated that it was a crazed *gaijin* attempting to hurl shame on the Japanese. Marlowe surmised it was one guy, probably late teens, early twenties. The victims had been primarily African street vendors but there were a few non-African tourists and one airman from Yokota Base out with his Japanese girlfriend.

"I see. Well, are they at least buying drinks?" Warren looked back over his shoulder and the men who just sat gloomily staring at their empty glasses. Stever-ino shook his head in the negative. He looked at Warren.

"Aiko not here tonight. She has a man she see now, salary man working at Casio."

"Good for her!" Warren smiled, thanking the love gods for a respite.

The other barmaid came up, putting her drink tray on the bar top and turned to him, "Hey sensei, suff's up! Where you been?"

He smiled at her, "Busy." He wanted to drain his beer and go home, the entire atmosphere in the bar oppressive. Then a small group of young men came in, obviously on a pub-crawl as they were loud and happy.

"Konbanwa!" They yelled.

Stever-ino and the barmaid yelled back in greeting, "*Hajimimaste!*" To which the barmaid added, "Suff's up!"

One of the young guys went straight towards the men's room and taking in the Africans pointed at them, turned to his buddies and then affecting a kendo stance yelled for his friends' benefit, 'Japan for Japanese!' all laughed loudly as the youth continued onto the bathroom.

The three men at the table looked at each other in shock, and all stood as if on cue. They pulled their coats off the chair backs and speaking in their own tongue cursed the group. On the way out of the lounge, one pulled a glass off the top of the bar onto the floor, the glass shattering. One of the Japanese youths stood and screamed at them.

"*Fuzaken, ja ne-ee-zo!!*" That Warren knew was a facsimile of 'fuck you.' The youth then turned and seeing Warren he took up the kendo pose, screaming at him, "*Chuui!*"

Warren looked at him blankly, tired, drained his beer and slowly placing it on the bar top he then made a finger pistol and pointing it at the younger man told him not to bring a sword to a gunfight.

"Ka-pow." He blew the imaginary smoke from his fingertip and walked out of the bar.

The mad kendo ninja had certainly caused a ruckus he thought as he hit the cold air in the street. His flat was off the main road, across from the bar and so made his way home. He almost half expected the mad ninja to propel out of the shadows and engage him in some weird, Japanese feudal stand and deliver scene.

He was drunk. And decided if so, he would just take the beating.

The Deep Slumber of Dogs

HARU/NATSU

(Spring/Summer)

Chapter 40

He was drinking a coffee and sitting on a bench outside Condom-Mania. He had bought Marlowe a wind-up hopping penis as a joke gift. He almost bought the hopping vagina but it was actually a bit scary looking. He wondered what his sister Maud would say, opening a box and finding this penis with feet.

It was a day off and he just felt a bit mindless and wished to be lost in a crowd. There were always tourists around here, *gaijin* like him, so he didn't feel as if he were alone in that sense, but just wanted to be in a 'message in a bottle' moment. Ueda told him to fall by her studio for another sitting but he just wished to be off leash, as it were, and out of hack. Sweet Ueda, who brought him back from the dead. Maybe she would enjoy a hopping penis as well but he had no means to contact her, still refusing to own even a small basic phone while others sported new flip-tops that covered the assortment of keys. He just didn't want something vibrating or ringing in his pocket. She thought him atavistic for not giving in. She called him *Showa Man* named for the last period to reflect the tenure and reign of Hirohito.

He tried to picture Condom-Mania in the U.S., maybe on Sunset Blvd. at Fairfax near Goldblatt's. Or down closer to the rotating Rocky and

Bullwinkle. Then again, some religious society or a church group would be protesting it. Quite different from how things were run over here where nobody was jumping up into the face of a young man who had on long sleeve jersey with FUCK emblazoned on the front because no one cared. Only we of the English-speaking world saw the blasphemy, he kidded to himself. He actually didn't give a fuck either. He'd enjoy even at his age to walk down a street in downtown L.A. wearing a 'fuck' tee shirt. Wear it in honor of Charles Bukowski Day. Sell hopping windup genitalia for a living.

But, it was spring already.

He started really noticing the difference in Yukio since before the winter break. He knew he'd stopped playing soccer to focus on his kendo, but his grades also seemed to be slipping and at times his work habits erratic. He put it down to 'senior-itis' at first but now wondered if there were other things at work. He never felt he was absolutely a stable unit when they had their first interview, yet he seemed to enjoy the Lit class from fall to winter. Now he was in senior English class with Felch; American Lit, which was a joke with Felch behind the wheel. It meant watching movies based on books. Most of the kids slept in his classes when he showed them. He recalled a few of their conversations discussing Mishima and the subtle beauty of his writing. Warren also explained how a good translator could help a book as well. Yukio was enamored of Mishima, and had branched out, finding his literature on his own.

He liked these interludes when he could train down into Tokyo and just do some foot dangling. Earlier he walked down near some antique stores just to browse and enjoy some of the art pieces when he saw two pretty good sized stone temple dogs; guardians of the entrance to the shrine. But the dogs were at the foot of a steep staircase, and curious,

Warren started climbing the almost sheer attitude they were built. Looking up he asked himself why he undertook this, as he felt winded by the midway point. Once at the top, he was glad he had investigated. It was a spectacular view just from the small area the old shrine took up. There was a meager *torii* gate and a place to make out a prayer and leave it for all or nobody. He never filled anything out, never rang the gongs, feeling that as he wasn't a Buddhist he should just let certain things alone. The shrine itself was a small, and humble abode, and there was nothing of significance inside, yet there it was; Spartan and clean atop this hill inside the city having been a witness to how many prayers, seasons and catastrophes. The spare grounds were tree lined from the top of the stairs and surrounding the shrine. Ivy also grew wild up the trunks of the trees, giving them the appearance of wearing sweaters against the cold and wind. He felt something was wrong for a second, and listening to his own breathing realized he couldn't hear traffic from the street below. He felt good, and again, like at Kamakura, felt at peace. There was a small bench of stone and he sat down. He *felt* like thinking of Lise, and he did. It wasn't some frosty apparition or nightmarish image of her after the accident, nor was she baiting him or calling him 'Dutch boy.' It was just she and was smiling that crazy tilted down smile of hers.

"Hello Lise." He said softly. And she smiled back.

Chapter 41

Riordan's spring was just another dead zone as far as he was concerned. There was nothing to look forward to, nothing to live forward to. His class changes meant nothing. Ai was scheduled to be in his English Comp class until graduation and the empty chair that looked at him daily only made his pain deeper, his affect duller. Warren told him to snap out of it and address his current classes with the diligence that they expected. Riordan had shot back to mind his own fucking business, but was rebuked by no less than Serazowa that Haas-sensei was correct in his assessment. Sulking, Riordan apologized, readjusted and brought himself back to a higher level of teaching.

Chrysanthemum Academy was more prestigious than Kin Tama and while not as popular in their Native Speakers program for returnees they employed *only* English Majors with a minimum of a BA. This alone put it a leg up on Kin Tama, so Ai's parents were happy with her choice as they supported her transfer. She dropped her desire to attend an American University and was looking forward to staying in Japan. Her father felt very prideful when she explained that after living abroad and now back 'home' she preferred to stay here. She also apologized for losing her cell phone and explained that in turning over a new leaf at Chrysanthemum she wished to have a new phone number as well, severing all ties to Kin Tama.

Riordan took a mental hygiene day off and trained down to Shibuya early to get a glimpse of Ai, and perhaps speak to her but became totally lost after exiting the *eki* on the wrong side and by the time he finally located the school classes were already convened and he found himself outside alone save for one tall boy in a black and white check hound's tooth blazer smoking a cigarette. Riordan asked him if he attended the Academy and was met by suspicious eyes. The boy threw down his cigarette, picked up a backpack and throwing his head back to readjust his hair, sauntered to the front door and disappeared.

Depressed, he left to return to the trains. He had no clue what he would do for the rest of the day, feeling guilty that he asked Marlowe and Mrs. Bloom to cover his classes for the day and almost felt obligated to return to Kin Tama. He basically played hooky, and after his scolding from Warren and Serazowa he felt a bit paranoid. Haas had made him feel like a kid.

Maybe he was.

Chapter 42

After the initial attack it started to feel more important than just instilling fear into foreigners. He started remembering instances in the United States he felt belittled and made to feel as if he were the 'other.' It disturbed him yet he had gone inside himself and using his mask face, would steel those feelings behind it. He lived as a shadow for a long time, the only instances where he was exposed was when he dominated his position on the pitch and played against other boys; nationalities of all stripes as an individual with ferocity. He eschewed the locker room and its antics just stripping, showering and disappearing back into his parent's car to return home. He was shocked at the Norris boy's intervention in regards to the religious incident. He attended no parties, mixers, team events outside a mandatory team dinner in which all the boys wore the school blazer to begin the season and an awards banquet post season.

Yukio was a virgin and never kissed a girl until Tomoko entered his life. Just the impact of her first kiss, given him spontaneously when out at the KFC near Kin Tama altered him, knocked his world slightly off kilter. The emotions he felt afterward, he knew, changed him and he could not return to that boy behind that mask again. But at the same time, it unveiled that side of him kept rigidly under a taught rein of sentimental austerity. That kiss severed all control over that. What had been his jealousy and immature reaction to the man trying to sell his wares at the station now became the fabric of his emotions; an extension of his sexuality in striking them down.

Yet inside him he wished Tomoko to remain as chaste as he, to wait until perhaps they could marry at some time, when together they could remain in a state of purity and be as one; untouched by any others. These feelings increased the ferocity of his blows and broadening his victims from the Africans to Europeans and military members who were alone or with women.

The night before he rode the Chuo Line to Kokobunji and getting off strolled around the station and its surrounding areas. There was a kendo academy close by and if stopped would say he was just wishing to check it out. He saw a thin white man staggering up a side street after quitting a bar. Slipping into the shadows he allowed the man to walk by him as he made his way to what was probably the *eki* as he staggered in the direction Yukio had just come. He let the man get 30 meters ahead and then fell in behind him. Then the man stopped.

At the entry of a club he was chatting to a woman, and his demeanor spoke to a familiarity with her that Yukio could see. They spoke softly and he ran his fingers thru her hair and held her shoulder as well. They moved a few doors down from the club and came closer to Yukio, stopping under the *noren* of a bakery that was closed and darkened. The doorway allowed for privacy and in that space they continued their conversation in hushed tones. Then he realized the woman had taken the man's penis out and his hand were on her breasts. Sliding down, he placed his hands on her head and she started fellating him. Yukio was transfixed as her head went forward and back and the man moaned softly, now pulling at her shoulders. He started shaking violently and gasped, the woman reaching up and putting her fingers at his lips to silence him. Pulling her fingers back down seemed to be using her hands to finish whatever they were doing and buttoned his trousers. The man, wobbly on his feet now, attempted to hug her but she laughed and pushed him aside, and standing, straightened her dress and talking in furtive tones to the man, patted his cheek and walked back to the club entrance leaving him as he weaved his way back to the trains. Once back, she reached into her bag and pulled a small bottle out and drinking, gargled quickly and spat on the walk. Yukio hadn't moved a muscle throughout the entire scene in front of him, and realized he was aroused. His confusion at feeling anger at the man and his excitement from the act he witnessed riveted him to the place of hiding. When the man was out of sight, he emerged slowly and made his way from his side of the street to be opposite from the club entrance and saw the woman, half in shadows smoking a cigarette. He slowly walked across to her.

The voice in the dark seemed deeper than he expected, "You were watching. I could see you once I crouched down. Like it?" And then she laughed.

Indignant and also nervous, Yukio blurted, "I did not watch. I happened to just look up and there you were…with this *gaijin*. Excuse me, I must go…" And he turned to leave. Reaching out, she grabbed his sleeve. "Do you want what he got? I can see you're young. I won't charge you." She realized her cigarette had gone out, and lifted her lighter to start it again.

Yukio, immobilized by her offer just watched as the lighter illuminated her face for a second as she dragged on her cheap cigarette. The heavy made up face and wig could not hide, in the light, that she was a middle-aged man. He was shocked and simultaneously enraged, knowing he had been aroused seeing the sex act between the two. Had the *gaijin* known he was with a man? He started unslinging his kendo sword as if an automaton, free of any orders from his heart or his mind; he was pure action now. The man in the dress realized what was happening, and attempting to run in heels was his undoing. One snapped sharply as he turned to run and stumbling cried out as Yukio overcame him and unleashed a blistering array of blows. The wig, black and splayed out as it flew off his head was a large silent spider seeking escape as it crashed to the ground, the man's scalp bleeding from the blow. The man's dress rose on his hips and Yukio showed no mercy on his buttocks and wrapped testicles inside his pantyhose.

    And then it was over and Yukio was walking briskly up the street towards the *eki* as he sheathed his sword and restrung it behind his back. Behind him he could just hear the man whimpering and throwing weak curses at his back. He did not turn around, and then once abreast of the station he decided not to use it and started to walk parallel to it and kept walking, to cover the distance between it and the next station at Nishikokobunji, not wishing to be standing at the station and have the police look for him near the site of his assault as they were suspicious of anyone now with a sling or pack that could hide a kendo sword. He would arrive home very late, but he would escape scrutiny at the next station. He found his decision liberating and in so doing, started to do a hop, skip and jump for a couple of blocks in his march to Nishikokobunji.

    It was a *man*, was all he could think of every time the image of *her* on her knees in front of the *gaijin* returned to him.

Chapter 43

He again took the day off and rode the train and subway to the district Ai's school was in. There had been no communication at all, and a letter sent to her under the guise of the Kin Tama letterhead was never answered. It was as if he never knew her and was all a fever dream. All he remembered with her was behind him and so he stood again, outside her academy clueless and nervous.

Riordan was raised in Tarzana, north of Ventura Blvd., not out in the west valley 'flats' and things in his life had always been smooth, almost effortless until he took the position at Kin Tama. His whole perception of life, at one time sitting so easily, was kicked off its chair and he felt pole-axed in the bargain after leaving home and traveling to Japan. He was three years removed from his fraternity and meeting people like Felch and Flattery vexed him; how did you deal with such ingrained assholes? It was a chore enough in teaching at Kin Tama what with the apathy from some of the kids and Serazowa prowling silently around the edges of the department like a shark. And the weather! He had only encountered small bursts of humidity on family vacations to Miami or Maui, but the Kanto Plain was different. He felt there was a dirtiness to it, an industrial grime that seemed to get into his skin unlike the hot and dry streets of the West Valley that meant nothing once he was immersed in the pool at his parent's house. This was a lifestyle he had trouble dealing with, until that day Ai came into the department. It all became acceptable because she was there, and that was all right. Since December he walked around between a somnambulist and the proverbial ouch cube of paranoiac nerves. He was just perplexed at what went wrong. Now, again in front of her school, he had no plan, no idea if she even walked out or was in attendance to the door he staked out that the smoking boy disappeared into that other day.

As the classes were dismissed, he stood in the middle of a huge wave of emerging students. To make it even more visually chaotic the school blazers of black and white checked hounds tooth with a red crest over the right breast pocket created a sea of blurs. Riordan stood in utter confusion and growing sadness from the incoming waves of loud material.

"Why are you here, Mr. Riordan?"

Her voice startled him, totally unaware she had walked up on him.

"Ai! God, Ai…what happened? Why didn't you talk to me, tell me anything?" He grimaced and cursed himself for whining, his voice shrill and anxious.

Looking past him, "There was nothing to discuss. I switched schools and I didn't need to tell you." Her tone was businesslike, bordering on dull.

He was at a complete loss as her voice; demeanor pushed him off as if she was a stranger.

"You should not have come. I do not wish to see you. I am here now and I have to go. My parents send a car service for me." Her voice metallic and seemingly coming from some place he just didn't know.

"What…what did I do wrong?" She quickly looked around the two of them as his voice cracked and a large tear rolled down his cheek, to see if anyone had noticed his emotions. Unknown to him, it was killing her to see him.

"Nothing. It is as they say, all about me, ok? Now I must go. Please do not come back or contact me," and hiding her own eyes from him she walked briskly away.

Mr. Riordan. Not Philip. Jesus.

That night he went madly drunk into Shin-juku and attempted to get a massage. He started crying in the middle of it and didn't stop until he fell asleep at home.

Chapter 44

"Are you going away for Golden Week?" Warren asked Riordan.

Riordan felt on the spot when addressed by Haas, and also suspicious of why he would ask. "No. I have no plans and am staying put. I have *no one* to go anywhere with."

The younger man's tone told Warren not to pursue it. Their relationship wilted resoundingly since Warren's discovery of the relationship between student and teacher and Ai's subsequent transfer. Warren always had a question mark surrounding the letter he took from Flattery and the man's refusal to pushback afterwards; as if all were resolved. Now he wasn't sure. Things in retrospect went far too smoothly and the small deprecating smiles and raised eyebrows Flattery affected only lent themselves to an unspoken deed. Whatever invisible currents ran between the two men, Warren could not navigate any of them.

The warming days earlier in the month at Easter gave way to the links at Tama Hills, and the NS Dept. staff, as Christians, were given an extra day off over the weekend. After the Friday of golf, Marlowe greenlighted Warren at home, had him throw together a quick ditty bag of clothes and a douche kit and bringing him downstairs and throwing him into a small van with Ueda and three other people, they drove off to a rented chalet near Fuji-yama. Ueda, after hugging Warren sat back and reaching into her oversized bag, pulled a bottle of sake out and taking the temporary cap off it, toasted her companions and drank.

The evening was much a repeat of the first night at the jazz club, sans freak snowstorm, with people arguing the merits of this book or that, or this sax player and the other. The hosts were very gracious and English was spoken most of the night. The chalet was well appointed with a huge private bathhouse that had *sento* etiquette in Japanese and English, as it was a popular rental. Regardless of the rules, no one bothered with the one aimed at gender separation. Warren found himself with a large plastic cup filled with Johnny Walker Black Label soaking next to Marlowe and another man discussing American and Japanese baseball. Thankfully, Marlowe and he staked out a room in a small loft area as overnight guests and Warren, just wasted, bid adieu and with a towel on, found his bed and passed out fast.

There was a push in the morning for the overnight guests to climb Fuji as this Easter Sunday morning looked clear and fine, yet nobody had actually planned for it and the women wore heels, loafers or espadrilles, the men in leather loafers. Ueda, sipping Bailey's Irish Cream at 10 a.m. held up a small foot encased in a ped and declared herself ineligible. The two teachers inspected their footwear and decided Warren's chukka boots and Marlowe's low cut Chuck Taylor's satisfactory. Walking down late, the host got very excited when he heard the two *gaijin* wished to climb Fuji-san. He barked out a few words at the rest of the company, who were either hiding their faces or trying not to laugh. The host then tightening his robe stormed off back to his room, and in Japanese Warren understood the word 'Children' as he spat it out.

"What's the deal?" He asked Marlowe.

"No climbing today. Too many people have died from freakish cold winter; we should wait until summer. He called them naughty children for pushing us."

Ueda, smiling mischievously, said she would accompany them on a small walk in the Aokigahara Forest and protect them from goblins and *kami*. Marlowe gave her a sour look and said no way in hell would he go there. Turning to Warren, who was already on the verge of asking, he explained the suicides that take place quite commonly there, and the belief its haunted.

Warren nixed that idea as well. So they drank, ate dishes the cook threw together effortlessly and listened to jazz and again discussed literature and Ueda outed Warren as an author so he was forced to go down that rabbit hole as well. Later everyone descended on the bathhouse and after washing on their respective sides, all congregated to sit and hang out on the men's side soaking and gossiping. Ueda, who had been busy haggling on the phone with a gallery in Hong Kong came in, and decided to just do her washing on the men's side as well. Slipping out of her robe, nude she started to use her washcloth and apply soap. One of the other women jumped out to assist her in her toilet and like a disciple, helped her to scrub off and rinse, taking care when she washed Ueda's scarred back.

Warren and Marlowe were drinking scotch again and Ueda, done with her scrub down slipped in next to them. The Japanese, used to soaking and socializing this way stayed well into the evening, while Warren had to beg off, and assisted by Ueda, tried to argue he could put himself to bed alone, gave up and like a five year old allowed her to tuck him in.

"I have come to like you very much, Haas-san. There is something inside you fighting back and I like that." She said softly as she left the loft.

Chapter 45

There were no plans at all for Yukio during Golden Week. The seven days holiday would see most of the Kin Tama student body either out of town or country and a third of the senior class were enroute to Okinawa, Thailand or Hawaii. Tomoko asked him about his plans as she and her parents were off to Maui. Scoffing, he told her he was done with anything that was part of America and he refused to go abroad as well. Unknown to Tomoko, Yukio's parents had contemplated perhaps visiting Hong Kong before the treaty ran out but Yukio refused to go. It were as if now that he returned to Japan, he was permanently moored or under a house arrest. His parents were worried about his behaviors, but also felt it necessary to also be discreet and in contacting Mr. Kitihara with some concerns, the headmaster was most happy to tell them their son was among the best of the best, his stock line for every parent.

His father had discovered a small notebook with the folded clippings about the 'kendo ninja' and asked his son why he kept them. Yukio nonchalantly answered that he felt the person attacking foreigners was just a good citizen with a nationalistic pride who wished to keep Japan for Japanese, and he didn't feel anything in regards to it as a crime. His father was mildly shocked by this answer, and wondered if exposure to western TV had given his son this mindset. Yukio already planned to visit Yasukuni Shrine and to pay his respects to the war dead and among them, those *murdered* by the Occupation Forces who put them on trial. The only crime in Yukio's thinking now was to not be the victor.

There were no reports of an assault on the man dressed as a woman and he could only surmise that this person did not report the crime for reasons of discretion. Yukio wondered if he were a well-known business executive, or perhaps a large family man; nevertheless he felt he deserved the beating; on his knees to a foreign white man! His disgust rose quickly inside and then the memory of his arousal would cause him to burn white. His only trigger to returning from this dangerous place was to think of Tomoko, her image soothing and melting the high heat from this candle of hate and wishes to inflict pain on someone.

In his dreams, he idealized Tomoko; always in a brilliantly white kimono, her hair lacquered. She never interacted with him; he viewed her. She was never eroticized or undressed in his thoughts. It had a calming influence and yet with even this analgesic to diffuse his anger he started to pull away from her in school. He left Haas' class after the holidays in winter and now was suffering thru Felch's boring and plodding movie-thons, and overheard him disparage students. Yukio felt he was sleep walking at school and was barely turning in the mandatory work for math, science and his *kanji* writing elective class. There was an idea germinating inside him and he had started moving towards it, slowly at first and then picking up his stride. In the idea he wouldn't need to improve his stroke of the brush in his writing and would himself become the beautifully appointed scripture of his native country.

Chapter 46

After the Easter at Fuji, they settled into the last days before Golden Week. The last Friday, Marlowe scraped up his books and turned to Warren, "Golf next week. Probably Tuesday. Have your shit together and I'll pick you up at like 8 a.m.?"

Warren nodded and sat reading the internet to see how the Dodgers were doing now the season was underway. Mari had come into the office to drop off her books.

"Off to somewhere special?" He asked her.

"Yes, Haas-san. I am taking the *Shinkasen* to Kyoto and staying at a *ryokan* that has an attached *onsen*. I depart from Shinegawa station" She smiled, and then quickly covered her teeth. Warren had come to like her teeth and wished she wouldn't do that.

"Warren," Flattery said, "whyn't you go to Miyajima and take the tram to see the monkeys. Might find a few you know," laughing, he left the office.

There was a pregnant silence; Mari always nervous when any of the men exchanged rude conversation. Warren just kept cleaning his area and desk, stacking books that were strewn about. He looked at Mari and spontaneously he stuck his tongue out at her; she burst out laughing.

Chapter 47

Yukio barricaded the Natives Speaker Department doors to the main hallway it issued out into but he had not locked the door to the small changing room accessible from the back stairs in the garden; hidden in the bushes and used by Warren and Flattery when they rode their bikes. Yukio was unaware of the passage. Felch, secured with line and duct tape to his chair and sweating thru his clothes kept his small blue eyes to that door in hopes the cavalry would crash in at any second, his eyes bugging out for rescue.

He left the *katana,* his Pacific War sword on the desk in front of Felch, as if he desired him to study the object of his impending demise. He sat quietly smoking as he attempted to write out his death poem, his *jisei.* He pondered this task and had yet to find a proper metaphor. He loathed mentioning the seasons, as that was such a cliché. He felt his stance warranted a statement of war per se, and his nationalistic voice need be heard. The word *decay* kept surfacing in his mind and every time his eyes fell on the sweating and corpulent Felch he felt disgust and disturbance. This man, Yukio thought, would be a proper mess when he finally dealt with him. The image of this old fat sensei that way gave him a warm feeling.

"Hello, Zipperhead-sensei." He smiled at him. His eyes met

Felch's. The small blue pebbles were bulging in their fear. Yukio, having returned to his passive mask that betrayed nothing as he took a measured drag on his cigarette. He was still wondering in which style he would write his poem; the longer *kanshi* or *haiku*? He had trouble finding anything to use and so decided he would just write it and let flow to its own borders, the terminus of his feelings. Haas-sensei told him, '…don't feel bound by fences as there are classic and honored boundaries for all poetry, but sometimes we need to roam farther and find another means of egress for our souls…' But Yukio was not a strong writer and the thought of an epic poem started to recede.

This memory of Hass-sensei made him smile and he wondered if he were outside now. His American sensei who helped reintroduce Nippon to him; find the voice for his anger and emptiness. Now these thoughts were punctuated by Felch's moaning thru his gag and extremely loud flatulence; his stomach on fire losing control of his bowels. They had cut the AC off to the NS's wing and along with being stifling hot, it smelled putrid. Yukio smelled Felch; his body as if a rotting, rancid pile of old dairy products. The room temperature made it almost swamp-like in its own repulsive humidity.

Yukio turned on Flattery's desk fan that ran on batteries to cool down, while turning Riordan's on Felch, to hopefully keep his stench in check. They did not cut all the electricity off yet, as the phones that obviously ran on another circuit and they already called once before he slammed the receiver back. He would not go near a window for fear they may have a sniper watching. American TV had some merits.

Unable to start his poem, and cursing himself in not writing it prior to occupying the room he turned his attention to Flattery's desk drawers. His dislike for Flattery ran almost as deep as Warren's. He was put off by the Irishman's constant smile and deprecating way he treated the students being able to understand their whispers in class and using it against them. He had also heard his shared bigoted remarks concerning students with Felch. He felt certain he would find something to disgust him in Flattery's desk as well. The first two drawers on the right were full of paperwork reflecting Flattery's pursuit of his Class 1 translator certificate. The third drawer down held treasure.

There was a small metal lockbox under a stack of football magazines from the UK and a hardbound copy of *The Viz*. It was a common metal box with a small key lock and handle. Yukio searched the top drawer, in the center of the desk for a key, hidden maybe under pens and paper clips and the pile of discount tickets for a local sushi-ya. He found nothing. In Marlowe's desk he found a Swiss army knife and used it to jimmy the lock, cracking open the top of the box and found its contents. His rage erupted.

Flattery had, over the years, collected a trove of 'upskirt' photos of Japanese girls and women. Some were on the train, standing no doubt and not able to see what a seated Flattery was doing and some were obviously taken at Kin Tama as the skirts only looked too familiar. Yukio was sickened at seeing the white cotton panties of who knew which schoolmate or who's sister they were. The older women wore a variety of lingerie, and one was nude save for her hose, clipped to a garter belt; her vagina a forest of dark hair. Then he saw one that was too familiar. Her face was slightly visible, as it seemed it was taken from somewhere below the level of an instructor's podium. Her legs were carelessly open, panties exposed and Tomoko's face was turned as if in conversation with her seatmates. His anger was at boiling point and he wished that Seamus Flattery were trussed up in the chair instead of this fat, stinking pig.

Felch was watching Yukio as he went thru Flattery's desk and how his countenance changed once he opened up the small metal style cashbox. He saw the ferocity appear in Yukio's eyes and his skin flush strongly, bright red as he looked at what appeared to be photos. His fear mounted as he watched the student start to raise up in his chair, hissing and speaking in a deep guttural voice, Felch not comprehending the words. He strode forcefully towards Felch and when before him, he picked up the *katana* and backing up assumed a fighting stance. Felch's screams behind the duct tape went nowhere.

Chapter 48

The police were having a discussion with Kitihara in regards to blueprints of the building and air ducts. They were also concerned that Yukio may have been telling the truth when in his letter he said he had explosive devices as well as firearms. After the serin gas attacks they could not afford to discount anything. Kitihara, as per his character, was nervously at a loss to formulate any answers or plans of action. Serazowa stood by stoically, his face impassive, in no hurry to assist Kitihara. He listened to the police and as he was not asked to offer his advice, he remained silent. The other department members stood off to the side talking amongst each other furtively. The students had been all taken off to the athletic field, and awaited pick up by parents, escorted off thru a back lane that ran next to the facility and was nowhere near the NS Dept.

Riordan lit a cigarette hurriedly, "Why in hell take Felch hostage? Why him?" he fanned the smoke away erratically after taking a drag.

Mrs. Bloom also waved his smoke away, "He was alone in the department when Yukio took the office, that's why."

Warren looked up to the glass windows that reflected large serene clouds punctuated by blue patches. He knew the blinds were all lowered and wondered what Yukio was doing. Marlowe shrugged and looked with flat eyes at Flattery.

"I can think of others he may have wanted besides Felch."

Flattery understood the point, avoiding Marlowe's eyes. He turned to Warren,

" Ya think he forgot the back way we use from the bike stands in the bushes, like?" His eyes nervously moving to the blank, cloud painted windows of the 3rd story department.

Warren thought about it. " I think he'd lock it from the inside as the door is down by Kawakami's desk? I wonder what in hell poor Felch is doing? Christ, he must be shitting himself."

"Better him than us, boyo!"

Marlowe said with utter contempt, "Yea…buddy is only half a word for you."

Flattery smiled wolfishly, "Sincerely Marlowe, if it were you or Haas I wouldn't mind at all." His voice started getting louder, "Yea I wouldn't mind it at all if it were you Haas, but as Yukio was *your* pet Jap I suppose you would've been freed by now, eh?"

"The fuck does that mean?" Warren edged closer to Flattery.

"You know exactly what it is I'm saying. He's *your* boy. *You're* his sensei. You're the one who shoveled this entire Mishima-nationalistic kill the foreign devils shyte into his head. Now poor Felch is up there paying for it!" He jabbed Warren in the chest when the first punch took him on the jaw. His head rocked to the side when Warren upper cutted with his left throwing Flattery backwards and he fell on his ass; his face a flurry of twitches. Marlowe watched it unfold and let it play out. He stepped away from Riordan and Mrs. Bloom, both with their mouths open, and took Warren by the shoulders.

"Done Warren. Over." He said in a low soothing voice. Looking at

Marlowe, Warren cleared his throat all of a sudden feeling very dry.

"He shouldn't have touched me. He's human shit." Warren stepped towards the prone figure of Flattery; Marlowe put a hand on him and pulled him back.

"I know, Warren…just leave it." He turned to Flattery, now up on one elbow rubbing his jaw with his other hand, "Get off your ass, Seamus, start thinking of Felch."

Flattery got up slowly, keeping his eyes on Warren. "Fuck the both of you, fucking yank cunts."

Serazowa had watched the developments as well, as he continued to listen to the police plan of perhaps offering food and a phone call to the boy's family as they waited for a hostage negotiator to arrive from Tokyo and while he enjoyed seeing Haas-sensei punish the Irishman his face still showed no emotion. He was surprised at the quick and violent exchange and how long it was in coming between those two. He was also most interested in Flattery's accusations of Haas that in some way thru his teaching, he was responsible for the Moritani boy's commandeering of the NS Dept. and taking Felch hostage. He walked now very briskly following Flattery until the latter was out of earshot and view of the other Native Speakers.

"Flattery-sensei, I wish to speak to you." Their conversation was in Japanese and in very low tones.

Chapter 49

"So…there is another way up, Haas-sensei?" Kitihara was in disbelief.

"Hai. A small stairway we use from the bike stands behind the hibiscus that was a service entry for laborers or janitors when it was first built post-war. It terminates in a small changing room and that contains a door that opens to the NS Department."

"This is unacceptable!" Kitihara squealed. "Why is there no such entrance in the blue print diagrams?"

Warren, standing next to Marlowe shrugged his shoulders, "Maybe the originals were lost and during the 1960's renovation new ones were produced that missed the stairs."

Kitihara smashed a fist into his open palm, "Hai! Hai!" And turning went to the head police detective who was speaking into a small cellular phone. Warren watched as Kitihara puffed himself up, a common procedure before talking to anyone, and animatedly informed the detective of Haas' revelation.

The cop spoke to Warren with no accent, "Show me, please."

They walked over to the towering hibiscus at the end of the building and Warren led him to the door. "Thank you, that will be all sensei." The lead detective again took out his cellular and speaking quickly turned to Kitihara. "Please go back and take care of your teachers...or make sure the children are being picked up, yes?" He said in a dismissive tone.

Marlowe raised his chin to Warren as he walked back to the NS group. "What's up? Any change?" He looked up at the windows, and then back at Warren. "I don't think this will end well, dude. I'm getting that 'spider walking over my balls' feeling and that ain't good!" Coming from Marlowe, that wasn't a good omen. "How is your hand? Flattery's jaw like glass?"

Warren had already dismissed Flattery from his memory, "It's fine, little stiff from not having punched anyone since I was 12. Jesus...this whole thing is going to end bad isn't it? Maybe I should ask to talk to Yukio?"

"I'm surprised you didn't unload on that prick long ago. Maybe you shouldn't, I saw Serazowa walk thataway to Seamus after he accused you of Yukio being your fault. I smell trouble there too. Watch your back."

"I will as soon as we get old Felch outta there. He must be having a heart attack."

Marlowe smiled grimly, "Or he bored Yukio to death and is just sitting there fucking with us!"

They both laughed, working out the nervousness they felt when the glass of an upstairs window blew out; a crystal explosion raining down like frozen ice. At that moment the faculty outside froze as they saw the police rush to the area where the glass showered near the small stand of Japanese maples. Serazowa came rushing around the building where he had been interviewing Flattery and Warren freeze-framed him in that moment; his suit fitting like a glove and his hair smooth and glossy stirred ever so slightly, as if in slow motion. Where everyone else showed fear and stress, his demeanor was one of controlled calm, a Buddha in the midst of calamity, the police active around him like startled ants after a child has stomped on the hill while he stood there now a sturdy tree in the face of a gale, Serazowa, unbending and always secure.

Then all at once it got crazier. Yukio's sword tip emerged from the hole left by the shattered glass and the object that created it. The sun catching the long blade but only reflecting a part of it, and his screaming deep guttural bark, the words unintelligible to Warren. Then one of the policemen screamed from the maple grove. Looking away from Serazowa and up at the brandished sword, Warren wondered what it was that was occluding the sheen of the sun's reflection on the blade. Marlowe grabbed his shoulder and also Mrs. Bloom's, his head bent towards the maples and the fierce voices issuing from there. It was a simple reason the blade wasn't shining. It was mottled in blood, and the police had discovered Felch's head after its explosive ride thru the window accompanied by the glass, laying sideways peacefully in the small grove where it came to rest, the duct tape over his mouth half intact.

Chapter 50

The detective with no accent called out to Kitihara. He wanted to know for sure if the *gaijin* sensei had been the only known hostage. He needed this old fool who kept on about Kin Tama's unblemished reputation to ID this most ugly head. He also listened to the young man's screams from upstairs calling for the Irish sensei to 'bring his *skebbe* self to the NS office if he were a *man*.' The detective, while listening, was giving hand signals to his men to encircle him. Kitihara was waved away violently; ashamed, the older man moved, his head bobbing wildly as if he were an invertebrate. The detective asked one of his men if he recorded the rant against Flattery and was given an affirmative nod.

"Kitihara-san, I have a most distasteful chore that only you can perform. You, as headmaster, need a spine of steel now."

Kitihara pulled his shoulders back and then resembling a puffer fish expanded before the detective's eyes, "Hai! Whatever it is you ask of me."

The detective took his arm gently and moving into the maples gestured another police officer to unveil the object on the ground. "Who is this, Kitihara-san?"

Kitihara dropped his gaze when the small towel was removed. He looked into the faded blue eyes, one of which was fixed in an upward attitude as if cynically eyeing his old headmaster. Kitihara felt the nausea and convulsing, vomited hitting near Felch's head and the policeman guarding it. He shook violently.

"Felch-sensei." He said as if he were being strangled.

The detective was thinking how unfortunate that an American had been killed and the consulate must be informed and more red tape for an awful situation, getting worse.

Yukio was still calling for Flattery's head and seeing that the situation changed from hostage to no hostage, it merited another course of action. The detective quickly informed his men they would attempt to capture Yukio now using tear gas, and a flash bang grenade. He picked four men who were starting to strap on protective clothing, making a quick call to Tokyo, informed his boss of where it all stood now and was given a reluctant go ahead. The negotiator was still inbound.

Outside of Kin Tama, on the perimeter of the school grounds, news stations had deployed cameras and crews for the intense standoff. Another officer told the detective that Yukio's mother was downtown, and due to the train and traffic congestion situation that already held up the negotiator, she was unable to get onsite, and they were attempting to have her call him now, but it was a poor connection. His father was in Kobe on business.

Marlowe had been consoling Riordan and Mrs. Bloom who were still shocked at Yukio's taking of Felch and the department. He then pulled Warren aside and behind the anxious group of mixed faculty and staff. No one knew yet what the object was they saw Kitihara vomit over. Serazowa also listened with interest to Yukio's repeated calls for Flattery and his branding him a *skebbe owaji*, or 'filthy old man' and an 'imperialistic leech of Great Britain.' Perhaps he need not talk to Haas-sensei at all.

Chapter 51

Yukio felt immersed in white heat, a blinding flash of light branding him when he threw down the pictures from Flattery's cache. In that moment, he melted into pure fluid, pure action. Cowering, Felch could feel this moment intensify. He knew he was dead. He watched Yukio approach him, a blur in his blue *yukata,* school uniform in a disheveled pile on the floor after he took the sensei hostage. Felch's last conscious thought centered on the soft rushing sound Yukio's clothes and the whisper of the blade cutting the air towards him; a nanosecond of clarity.

Yukio marveled at the destruction his katana achieved. Felch's head just flew backwards and the arterial spray was caught by the small fan and rained over parts of the desk and floor. His disgust for that head coupled with his adrenalized state, enabled him to pick it up and with one savage throw over his head as if he were on a soccer pitch hurled the staring head thru the window.

When he had cooled down, lit a cigarette and after screaming out of the window, demanding Flattery return he then nonchalantly wiped the blade on a sweater Mrs. Bloom left draped on the back of her chair He noticed a book of poetry on Haas-sensei's desk, decided his poem would be somewhere inside that.

Chapter 52

After the positive identification of Felch, the lead detective was informed that the stoppage on the highway and trains were due to a suicide of a female student and a simultaneous multiple vehicle accident he was on his own as there would be no negotiator at all. Had all the students gone mad at once? There were reports from one of his men that out on the athletic field students were fighting, smoking and attempting to leave and take trains downtown as if it were a holiday!

Yukio went to his backpack and taking out a folded pennant, thought about how he would deploy it from the department windows without being shot. The flag was a World War II sunray battle flag and it was imperative that it be unfurled and visible to all. The line he brought would enable this and he set about rigging it, all the meantime screaming for Flattery's head. As he worked he was unaware of the small group of men assembled and dressed in riot gear. They were almost at the door to the small vestibule the sensei's changed in.

Chapter 53

Warren and Riordan were chain-smoking; Marlowe comforting a distraught and shcoked Mrs. Bloom who repeated a quiet mantra almost no one could hear of 'poor Mr. Felch.' The horrible revelations of the last few minutes made all the NS Department and their counterparts shudder.

"Would he have killed me had I been there?" She asked Marlowe.

Marlowe felt she would not have been killed but kept his opinion to himself. He acquired a feeling that Felch, while not targeted, become a victim of opportunity or design during the hostage period. She was processing it, he thought. His own inner voice asked the same thing, and in that icy cold zen moment when the voice answered back, it said yes, he would've killed you Marlowe, but not her.

Warren tried to accompany the police, explaining he could attempt to persuade Yukio to give up and was told no, so sorry. They had slipped quietly into the staircase and darkened hall behind the doors he and Flattery used. Watching them, Warren knew they would kill Yukio now. He would not surrender and the police would have to kill him. He wondered what things flew thru Felch's mind before his death and was hit by a violent shiver; an affirmation *he* was alive.

Kitihara slipped up behind Warren without him knowing. When he turned to ask Marlowe a question he was face to face with the headmaster. He could vaguely smell the vomit on his breath as he spoke.

"Haas-sensei…this is a most unfortunate day. I am embarrassed our faculty must be witness to this." He said meekly.

Warren for an incredulous second, remembering Felch's head flying out the window and associating 'embarrassment' to it said "Huh!?" Then hearing a noise from upstairs looked up to the window of the NS Dept. in time to see the flag unfurling. The red sun and spokes of sunrays on the white background was in stark relief to the faded sandstone brick of the building. Then at once the windows blew out and rained crystal shards as a flash bang grenade exploded.

Chapter 54

The night before, Yukio and Tomoko had shared a bento outside a 7-11 in Tachikawa. He felt bad that he could not afford two but he was on the scrounge since his parents cut off his ATM account after they discovered he was the 'ninja' attacking foreigners, and had been sleeping on the lanai at the house.

Of this he told no one, least of all Tomoko. They sat on a stone bench that was in front of a handbag store. As Yukio talked, she stared attentively at the shoulder bags hanging from the two mannequins in the window. She had taken to start tuning him out when he went on his speeches concerning Mishima, and most especially *Sea and Sunset*. She envisioned herself as the deaf and dumb protégé of Anri, the old *gaijin* who settled in Japan, and as he told his tale, he knew it was falling on deaf ears and so too Yukio knew in a sense, that she was too. Yet as he talked he could start to feel the reality of who he was, and why Haas-sensei and he were bound together. They were foreigners, the two of them who through a vision restarted their lives; wishing to bring others with them to a place of enlightenment. Tomoko wondered how that shoulder bag would look with her school uniform. Looking at him, she finally really noticed how disheveled he looked. He also smelled. Was he not showering? Was it his endless kendo lessons? She started to worry about his plummet in the academic standings as they were only a week from graduation and he had not applied to any schools, and stopped most of his associations and talked only of Japan returning to pre-war glory. The old *gaijin* at Kamakura...again! They had read the story in Haas-sensei's class months ago, and she was so tired of it. She felt sleepy with all of it. Where was the old Yukio?

"Tomo-chan...did you like the story of the young army officer and his wife, the story *Patriotism*?' He looked at her. Could she, Tomoko, honor her vows as a wife and follow her husband into the void, honoring *bushido?*

She looked at him a minute wondering if it were a trick question, a test. She didn't know what to expect from him anymore. The question, she felt, for whatever motive on his part was unanswerable. They were in high school, not in pre war 1931 during the *Showa* era. This was not her reality. She looked into his eyes, he anxious for an answer and decided to take a subtle, easier avenue to meet his nervous look. She took his hand and laughing softly, turned to again look at the shoulder bag.

"But Kio-chan, how can I give you a good answer, when I am not *samurai?*"

Chapter 55

The blast from the grenade startled everyone below. The rain of glass again scattered people much the same as cats and dogs in a sudden and violent thunderstorm. Warren was reminded of the noise he heard when the Porsche finally made contact with and wrapped around the pole and felt a moment of nausea. Kitihara made a small shriek and fell to the ground. Marlowe had instinctively covered Mrs. Bloom by wrapping himself around her and spiriting her away. Warren then heard mixed voices screaming and small popping noises. Then silence. He found Riordan staring at him; blank and empty as he cried. Warren let his eyes drift back to the window frames and saw smoke seeping out, and out the window came a policeman's arm, shoulder and then his face. He waved down to the others and then went back inside. He looked to the ground where Kitihara fell and saw he was gone.

They all just stood there, Mrs. Bloom crying into Marlowe's shirt, Riordan standing alone like a windless pennant, and Warren watching the police move about and send men with small crime scene suitcases up into the building. Flattery left to who knew where and Kitihara was speaking to Serazowa and another detective.

The police were now moving slower, more methodical. It was as if the clock had slowed and everyone seemed to be walking on a plush carpet, slowly and easily. Looking over to the remaining NS faculty, Serazowa walked slowly up to Warren.

"Sensei...we are going to adjourn to the conference room adjoining Mr. Kitihara's office. We are arranging a small debrief in there with the police. There are things to discuss." He spoke, as he always did, no difference in his voice as if it was just another day at Kin Tama and things needed to be worked out concerning some mundane issue. "Can you ask the others to please go there now?"

Warren nodded and turning to the other three explained what they wanted.

"Want to keep us away from the press, no doubt." Marlowe spoke over Mrs. Bloom's head, looking at the throng of news vans and boom mics hanging over the Kin Tama fence line. His arm was still around her.

Kitihara and Serazowa then went to the athletic field to see how the evacuation was going. The coaches were in charge of the field, the administration people allowing them their domain.

After a bit the four of them made their way to the admin building and Kitihara's office. A policeman had accompanied them 'for their safety' and once inside the beautifully wooded room with its plush carpet and dark padded leather furniture they all found a chair and pulling them out, respectively sat down in each.

"Nice leather." Riordan said to nobody. They all nodded their heads in agreement without speaking. There was a noise at the door and Kitihara's major-domo, Mr. Kimura entered followed by the office girls that had been procuring refreshments from the school canteen for the faculty. There was green tea, coffee and small tasteless cakes. It was a solemn gaggle that brought the goods in and staged them ever so neatly on the large oval shaped conference desk. One of the admin girls came in with a tray of small sandwich wedges that went uneaten in the canteen.

Warren spoke out, "Jesus, I just realized how parched I am, all that time in that crazy heat. Is that water in that one carafe?"

"Think so." Riordan said grabbing it and peeking into the top. He stood up and leaning over the table handed it to Warren. Mrs. Bloom sat next to Marlowe, her head on his shoulder, saying and looking at nothing. The doors then opened and two policemen in their riot gear sans helmets entered, and Warren recognized them as two of the small force that went upstairs. The lead detective entered and after him as if in tow, the silent Serazowa and Kitihara who was rubbing his hands and went directly to the table to ensure the girls laid everything out as he had instructed. Serazowa then sat to the side, away from the table on a chair next to the wall. The lead detective then turned and motioned to a person outside the room. A woman came in, was identified as a stenographer and behind her a man in a well-cut suit who was not introduced yet exuded lawyer.

Mrs. Bloom, moving away from Marlowe coughed, ran a hand thru her hair and asked of no one in particular, " Do we need a representative from the airbase, or the embassy present?" Under the table, Marlowe pressed a reassuring foot against hers.

The lead detective, in his unaccented English replied softly, " Mrs. Bloom, isn't it? You do not need any representative or advocate as this is merely my request and none of you are at any risk of legal jeopardy. Serazowa-san was so kind to organize, to get some background on today's unfortunate events. The people from your Embassy are enroute to be with the late Mr. Felch's wife, who is being consoled by the commanding officer at the base. Mr. Flattery is enroute and due any minute as he had retired to his flat." He allowed them all to focus on his words and to gain their attention. His voice was soft yet held a noticeable intensity.

"I realize this is a traumatizing day for all, and my questions will be brisk and to the point. Please allow me to begin by saying, that along with the sad fate of Mr. Felch, Moritani Yukio is also dead. He refused to surrender his *katana* and in that act of refusal also committed to an attack on my men and I, and he was mortally wounded." At this Mrs. Bloom started tearing up, and lowered her head. Riordan looked at the ceiling and his eyes filled as well. Warren just felt numb.

The detective started again, and his eyes met Warren's. "Those who had Yukio as a student, could you see any noticeable changes, hear any espousing of anti-foreigner language? Did he ever show any obvious contempt for Mr. Felch, his teacher of record, and Mr. Flattery beforehand?"

Warren had Yukio in his lit and humanities classes last fall and answered most of the questions asked, studied intently by Serazowa. He started to feel as if he were being centered, cut away from the group and only surrounded by them to feel a sense of security. Then the detective asked him what he and Flattery argued about prior to Warren hitting him. Warren felt Marlowe's spider crawling across his balls now…so this was what it was about.

He cleared his throat, and looking into the man's eyes told him, "In my early discussions with Yukio he was depressed at leaving the West and returning with his family to Japan. He barely knew it from when he was a baby, even though they kept their house Japanese style and visited their homeland throughout the years. When we talked he started rediscovering his home here, *his* country, and I recommended some literature…Mishima, this new author Murakami, and Abe. I used a Japanese author in lieu of western Caucasian authors and specifically Mishima."

"Hmm, the Mishima Incident of 1970," the detective said aloud.

"Yes, but I didn't teach about that. I used a short story and one novel. The rest, Mishima's history, his other works, *The Sea of Fertility* books and the failure at the JDF facility were never introduced. These were more than likely researched on his own, his own discoveries. These prejudices you ask of, perhaps he felt they affected Japan, were his thoughts concerning foreigners. I don't know." He ended weakly, he knew, but didn't know what to say.

"Do you know of a reason why he killed Mr. Felch? Or ranted about Mr. Flattery being a sex criminal?"

The words 'sex criminal' took Warren and the others by surprise. "No idea." Then he remembered Ai's letter. Had this to do with it?

Marlowe asked if he could make a query. "Wasn't Felch just in the wrong place at the wrong time? This wasn't anything personally about him, was it?"

Here Serazowa cleared his throat and spoke for the first time, but very softly. "We believe Mr. Felch was as you say, a target of opportunity...wrong place, but there seems to have been a lot of anger directed at Felch-sensei as a representative of certain things this young man detested."

Here, the detective took over, " From interviews with some staff and students, by my men when they were on the athletic field, it was said Mr. Felch also disparaged students. He was overheard to use the term 'zipperhead' in regards to Japanese and that it was brought to Kitihara-san's attention, related to us by a staff member"

Kitihara seemed to have awakened from a deep slumber, and his eyes opened wide, reptilian in their wariness.

"Yes, Kitihara-san?" Serazowa asked, his eyebrows rose ever so slightly.

"Well, yes, indeed, I gave him a stern lecture and threatened to dismiss him as a teacher." Kitihara raised his brows dramatically after he spoke.

Marlowe laughed loudly, "Sorry, but when Felch returned to the NS offices he laughed and said he threatened to cut off your golf privileges at Tama Hills, and you *believed* him! Then, sorry Ktithara-san, he called *you* a zipperhead." Marlowe smiled ruefully while Kitihara pulled his collar and smoothed the sides of his scalp.

"Not true!"

"Enough," the detective said. "There seems to be grounds here for perhaps a grudge felt by this boy. Haas-sensei, did he ever argue with you about western values in regards to things in Japan?"

Warren kicked around the definition of argue in his head. "If you meant a rant, it never happened, but we did discuss Mishima's nationalism *after* Yukio learned of it on the Internet. But no sir, he did not. Nor did he ever mention any disrespect for Mr. Felch or Flattery."

As if on cue, Flattery entered the conference room, a policeman behind him.

"What the hell is all this here? Why're we being questioned without advocates or consular people?" Flattery spat out sharply, his lilting brogue gone.

"Thank you for returning," The detective said. Serazowa looked at Flattery passively.

"As if I had a bloody choice…and then they told me Poor old Felch had been killed, fucking beheaded! He was my friend," turning on Warren, "And you sent that bloody fucking tosser Yukio out there, Haas, with his big hard on for us. That little wanker didn't have a clue in him until you be filling his fucking zip...his head with this samurai and bushido rubbish." He turned to the detective, "if you want who incited this bastard to kill poor fucking Felch, its this arse-hole," And he hooked a thumb at Warren.

"Yes, it may well be as you say, but why would this unfortunate boy rail at you, Mr. Flattery? Why would he scream out the windows that you were a dirty sexual old man, a sexual deviant? This occurred as you left the school and after the death of Mr. Felch, and the subsequent throwing of his head out of the window."

Flattery was horrified. Again he turned and hissed at Warren, "You stupid bastard...his head out of the fucking window? You used that kid to even scores, and the like." Then he turned to the detective. "I'm sorry, I have no idea why he would say those things in reference to me."

Looking in Flattery's eyes, the detective took from a chair seat, not visible to those seated a small lockbox, a piece of paper taped to it, and written in flourishing and beautiful *kanji*, "Please investigate, thank you."

Flattery fainted.

Chapter 56

The flash bang grenade stunned Yukio and staggered him yet he did not relinquish his grip on the sword. Then a canister rolled across the floor, emitting smoke. He could make out three to four dark figures issue from the locker room dressed in heavy gear, the lead man with a gun who was screaming at him to drop the sword and surrender, but his ears were still wringing and he didn't quite catch it all. He shouted to them once, 'Never!' and then satisfied he had copied at least a good poem, arranged the lockbox to be discovered easily, screamed, "Long Live the Emperor!" and charged the group.

The lead man shot him three times, dead before crashing backwards into Warren's desk, an exit hole tracking stream of blood peppering the desktop. The note he left for Warren was inside his copy of *The Temple of the Golden Pavilion*, now adorned with small flecks of Yukio's blood.

In the aftermath, as the detectives visually took in the NS office; the headless duct-taped corpse of Felch like an ugly, obese stump in a field, the start-stop pieces of paper from Yukio's attempts at poetry all seemed so surreal. The fresh bowel movement on the one desk with the box and note asking for an investigation was another strange item on a terribly strange day.

The detective studied the face of the boy leaning on Warren's desk, sitting on the floor. His headband was askew from the violent fall the bullets had given him yet he was taken by the serenity of his countenance, even in death, as if this were the best proposition he could hope for. The detective, unseen by the others, bowed towards Yukio ever so slightly at the waist.

Chapter 57

The next two days were a blur to Warren. He was told to report to work but the NS Dept. was still being processed by the police, so all business would be run out of the conference room; a temporary staging area. All senior classes were terminated and they were readied for graduation to help with the bottleneck of students. There was also the problem of cancelled classes and those doubled up when possible due to the loss of Felch and pending deportation of Flattery, who dodged all criminal charges due to intervention by the consular people in the Irish Embassy, that while he owned those pictures and they were in his possession, they could not prove he had taken them. He was, though, still in jail and police had 'cleared' his flat of any and all photos they deemed contraband and pornographic.

Felch's family were arranging for his body to be flown back to his native Iowa for burial so he, Warren, Mrs. Bloom, Marlowe and Riordan taught classes and filled in when they could. They discovered Felch's stash of lesson plans that were all simplistic bunk that relied heavily on watching movies. Those compared to Flattery's massive worksheets to be done in some *rote hell* while he worked quietly on his own translator side business. Discovered also was the camera inside the book he used to take his pictures, too late as he was already back in Dublin. Marlowe coined him *the panty spy.*

In a quick move by the board Serazowa was now Headmaster, Kitihara being sacked after the secretaries at the impromptu conference room meeting leaked the 'zipperhead' story, after the incident. Kitihara, his nerves shredded from the ordeal, decided he would enjoy retirement as he was given a generous pension when fired.

After a week, the detective who was on the scene and who shot Yukio to death in the office met Warren at the bike rack early in the morning. Warren had been arriving earlier due to the extra workload and graduation planning.

"Haas-sensei," he called out.

Warren really took the man in this time in eye so very different from *that* day. He noted the man's quiet strength and absolute control, and wondered if he were related to Serazowa. Warren asked what he could do for him.

"I want to do something for you, sensei," he handed Warren an envelope. On it Warren noted faded red flecks. "This is for you. It was left inside your copy of *The Temple of the Golden Pavilion.* I would normally never do such a thing but in this case I felt it necessary."

Surprised, he guessed it was a communiqué from Yukio. Unknown to him the detective also paid a visit to Yukio's guilt and grief filled parents. They filled in parts of the story of his growing nationalism and isolation, his visit to Yasukuni Shrine and Kamakura, and ultimately their locking him out after discovering he was the kendo assailant and harassing *gaijin.* He also attempted to fly his battle flag from their house. The detective, in the hopes of giving solace, said any and all investigations and publicity in regards to the attacks would be dropped and not spoken of. For their sake the assailant would remain a mystery.

Warren weighed the letter in his hand and recalled the last time they talked. Yukio asked Warren why he read Mishima. He thought about it, and instead of giving the stock teacher-student answer of hoping to expand his world knowledge thought of meaning of the tetralogy and said in one word, *samsara*.

"Was he a good student, Haas-sensei?"

He smiled, "He was like a sponge. He sucked up literature and information. It were as if he were sterile his whole life and then exploded onto this fertile field where anything and everything could grow. I'm sorry for the direction he took." He caught himself then, in what he was saying. He had planted a seed inside Yukio, and what it grew wasn't what he expected. The detective caught his pause.

"Please, I do not view it that you corrupted this boy. Teachers are but alarm clocks. You can wake a student but what they do for the rest of their hours is *their* lives, yes?"

He reached a hand out, to Warren's surprise. It was the first time he had ever shaken the hand of a *nihonjin*. "It was necessary I read the letter, you understand, as it was evidence, but I was the only one."

Warren thanked him. Then shaking his head, "Your English is flawless. Where?"

The detective smiled, but not happily. "Like the boy, I shared his experience living abroad and found many times divested of myself, my harmony, my core." He bowed ever so slightly at the waist, Warren returning the gesture. As he walked away, over his shoulder Warren heard ever so faintly:

"Virginia Tech, y'all."

It was Serazowa who broke the silence.

"Was that Detective Kimoto, Haas-sensei?"

"It was. We had a brief word" Warren was placing the envelope inside his unslung backpack as he spoke knowing full well that Serazowa probably spied on the whole exchange. "So, how is your new job title working out, Serazowa-san?" He started moving towards the building, to keep Serazowa on his turf, in his rhythm.

"Decision making causes stress we perhaps haven't encountered in other positions." He asked Warren to stop. " I have a proposition for you. And I wished to make it to you privately before work. Perhaps you would consider running the NS Department? Substantial raise and living allowance as well, think about it." Then he walked away.

After a bit, Warren said very softly, "Fuck you."

Chapter 58

"Haas-sensei---

You will not agree with the path I have taken, but I am speeding down it, like the Runaway Horses in Book Two. I cannot stop my headlong sprint to where I see that sun, in its glory, reigning over my Japan.

I wished to thank you for stepping outside yourself and allowing me an avenue to open up inside myself, to make discoveries and to apply them to the world as I see fit. Again, you may disagree with how I succeed at this, but it is <u>my</u> choice.

When I was at Kamakura, humbled in front of the Daibutsu...for the first time in my life I felt pure peace within. I know by nature I could never hope to have the patience of meditation---so I was taken by that feeling in the simple act of lighting a joss stick and sitting beneath Him. Your lectures in the lit/humanities class instilled that desire and in my short life, I am grateful. And I am Japanese! Please do not judge me harshly; it is my karma, and mine alone. Be easy on Tomoko in preparation for her graduation speech as she is nervous.

This is my poem. Again I have you to thank, as I am incapable of writing my own!

"Looking back at the beach
Even my footprints are gone"

(Ozaki Hosai)
Yukio

Chapter 59

In the NS Dept. he was dressed and at his desk when Mari approached him.

"Ohayo, Haas-sensei."

"Ohayo gozaimus, Mari-san."

She looked at him, her usual closed smile, and teeth hidden behind the curtain of lips like a bashful chorus line. She recalled the touch of their hands that day and how aroused she felt; the stark relief his erection displayed in his trousers for *her*, and the embarrassment for him, so obvious in public. She felt nothing now in the wake of the incident. She felt a void between him and her as a barrier that allowed no affection or ardor to breach. She dipped her head slightly in a silent acknowledgment of a scheduled departure that was missed; a decision averted, ardor restrained. She wondered why she felt distracted by these thoughts. She looked back at Warren and he was writing something in his journal book as though he were dismissing those very thoughts. She looked at the two clear desks of the departed and wondered if there would be new hires soon, and if once again they would mine the local airbase or place an ad in *The Japan Times* and try and obtain some *gaijin* who was living and teaching here for a bit and had experience. With the loss of the two teachers, she felt it would only get better. Giving herself an inventory after the fact now, she found that while she felt bad about Mr. Felch's death and the continued sadness for his family that his absence did not bother her at all, nor did Mr. Flattery's. She heard him speak one day to another Japanese teacher, recognizing his baritone voice, even speaking in her language, and they were joking about women. Her countryman asked Flattery what he thought of Mari, working with her in the department, and that he felt she cut a very nice figure. To this Flattery had answered that he couldn't remember whether she was 35 or what, and that he likes them with bigger arses. Then he reminded the other man that you know, Mari is 'Christmas Cake'…no one wants day old cake, past the 25th, and Mari was a decade past her 25th. Angered, she returned to the NS Dept., and then leaving that to attend the lady's room, found she started crying.

    No, she did not miss either of them.

Chapter 60

That afternoon the letter arrived from his father in a large manila envelope. The handwritten name and address in the familiar old school cursive with the flair of the W and H. Taking it back to the NS Dept., he was greeted along the way by some faculty with a slight bow of the head that he returned; as well as small polite verbal exchanges with some students in the NS program. Climbing the stairs from the faculty offices and mailroom he looked out into the gray, clouding sky that was threatening to rain. These almost summer days held more volatility that the sturdy spring of May which had been almost an endless stream of high pressure sunlit warmth that caressed one.

The classes were still combined but Serazowa scheduled interviews for this week and there were at least ten resumes to read thru to make a final cut. One traveled all the way from an English teaching position in Holland. Warren wondered if they too had Nazis hiding in the family closet. There was no talk lately of the tragedy. The school called it the 'June 7 Incident' and not relegating names felt it was safely sanitized. Serazowa was firmly in place and his will was being enforced in slow, subtle ways and Warren knew the next hires would reflect more of his character, his ideas for an institution than all who came before. The mistakes of hiring indiscriminately as Kitihara did were at an end. Warren gave him another two months and shirts would be forever tucked, jackets buttoned, hair above collars, no dye, and skirts another six inches longer.

Riordan, who had started making plans to find a job for fall in California, gave his notice. He could barely meet Warren's eyes when he came to work and repositioned his desk so he did not face any of the other *gaijin* in the NS offices. He felt deep down inside that Warren, in some way, damaged his relationship with Ai, being the only person to his knowledge who knew. Mrs. Bloom also broke the news that she would be returning to the US mainland as something happened, no explanation and no goodbyes. It was as if the death of Felch and Yukio splintered the whole department. Marlowe and he were the only teachers who did not discuss leaving; and Serazowa's offer was still on the table. He talked about it with Marlowe, feeling the other man was more senior to him, and Marlowe good naturedly told him to take it yet also warned him about getting in bed with Serazowa, whom he felt could not be trusted. He made short work of Kitihara, and where he was a weak yet pleasant moron, Serazowa was Godzilla in a Brooks Brothers.

The letter from Big Dutch sat on the desk in front of him. It had been forever since they talked and while there was a few e-mail exchanges with his sister post the 'incident' as she was concerned with his mental outlook, Big Dutch was never part of that conversation. His lookout was if he could live thru dismembered limbs and charred torsos, burning oil and seeing your friends eaten by sharks, Warren should be able to handle what transpired at Kin Tama without his assistance. Warren could respect his position on it, whether he liked it or not.

"Fan mail from a flounder?" Marlowe asked smiling.

Warren had to laugh, "Yes, Bullwinkle." He picked up the

The Deep Slumber of Dogs

envelope as if weighing it. "No guilders in here. Hmmm...probably some bills and a notice to appear forwarded here. I'm probably being sued again."

"Maybe its good news. Maybe its some old residual check from your days as a hotshot so we can go to the jazz club and you can spring for a round, you cheap Dutch bastard."

"Alright already. I'll open it." He took the letter opener and slicing open an end reached inside to find a small piece of stationery and another envelope. Ignoring the envelope he read the letter:

> *It looks important, thought you should see it.*
> *Dad*

Knowing his father and the economy by which he lived, Warren wasn't upset by lack of any content. He turned his attention to the envelope and saw it was from the Doyle Agency, one of the most prestigious agencies on either coast. Lise did some work for them when very young and freshly married. He couldn't remember what or why. His old agents had no connection with Doyle so now he was curious.

Marlowe spoke up, " By the look on your face, I'd say curiosity is about to claim another cat."

"You're right." Warren split the envelope open and after extracting the letter read:

> *Dear Mr. Haas,*
>
> *An esteemed client of ours, Loren Oppenheimer, has submitted to us a collection of short stories you wrote some years ago that was in possession of his late wife, Lise Dreyfus*

Oppenheimer. As it was a gift, so noted by you, it became his possession upon her passing.

Mr. Oppenheimer has asked us to represent you in the matter of the publication of these stories in the hope you may see your way to becoming part of our 'family' at Doyle. Any and all business arrangements can be conducted either in person, telephone, fax, e-mail by yourself or a designated advocate of your choice.

Presently, this is the only known address we have for you and it was obtained from court documents. Please contact us at the address and numbers provided at your earliest convenience, as we are anxious to get this project off the ground.

A stipulation made by Mr. Oppenheimer is that you do not contact him without agency knowledge and you dedicate the book to the late Mrs. Oppenheimer. Between you and I, when Mrs. Oppenheimer passed her memory was shall we say, somewhat in distress? In publishing this, her husband also wishes to write a preface concerning her talent. Other than that, the content stays intact. Looking forward to hearing from you.

Cordially,

Skip Doyle

Warren had to reread the letter twice. When writing his 'Turner' stories he wondered what Lise did with those stories he gave her and figuring they went into the black hole of her life she often joked about. And Loren? What happened? He couldn't even begin to wonder. Had Loren read the stories just recently, or sat on them for years? The best story he felt was the one he wrote from Loren's perspective. In Doyle's words he saw Loren resurrecting Lise in a way. Breathing a second wind into her legacy. He had no objections. Even the dead deserved a second act these days.

He looked at the date and saw two weeks had passed. He would call Mr. Skip Doyle and fill him in on where he was hanging his hat and how they could proceed. Why not? Ueda told him his art, his true self, needed to wake up. Ueda, with her tireless soul creating something daily, always moving like a shark, her back forever branded in 1945 yet always on the move forward. He would be a coward to turn this down, and ashamed to stand next to her.

Next day the two men went outside to stretch their legs on the break time.

"So?" Marlowe's eyebrows were raised.

"It appears I'm a writer again." He said simply.

"Really? So it was truly some fan mail. You're definitely buying at the club."

Warren leaned back, stretching his out and clasped his hands behind his head, "Just very unexpected news. Like the last thing you would ever expect."

"I could offer a veritable cornucopia of questions, yet I will resist with exception of did you submit something recently on the sly?"

"No. Try like almost 8-9 years ago. It was something I wrote for my editor and I believed it long gone."

"And it just turned up?"

"Don't know when it surfaced but it's out there now. I do have a set of stories in the same vein I can submit now...but I want to see where this is going."

"So what'll you do in the long run here...tender your resignation? I know you don't wish to be Serazowa's lap dog." Marlowe asked. He had always admired Warren's fluid ability, and then at the same time he wondered how close to reality his perception was to what Warren really felt; how he operated inside. Still, that perception was grounded in what he saw the other man doing and how he conducted his business. He watched him thru the crisis with Yukio, and how he started to, without provocation, reshape the department to run in the midst of a calamity and knew it wasn't the Haas of celebrity lore; this was a new and different man. He thought at one time very early on to recruit him but realized it was a whim, a *beau geste* out of friendship and not hard facts. His *colleagues* that met Warren at golf had also nixed any ideas that way. Warren was an asset at Kin Tama, but not in the way he needed him. If only his Company friends could meet *this* Warren. Oh well…

"Its weird, I didn't know what I would do. I have Serazowa on the one hand giving me reign over the NS Dept., and I can make it a real educational department and now this offer from the Doyle Agency and actually reentering a literary orbit." He paused looking out over the koi pond in between the building where the NS Dept. was housed and the large, old admin building with the façade like a huge shrine entrance. Warren was watching one rather large orange koi with dappled white splashes on it swimming languidly. "Then, last night after I talked to this agent guy I played *Highway 61 Revisited.* Listened to the entire CD and I started to miss America. I was actually remembering the words to *From A Buick 6* and I sang along to it; it hit me. I wanted to go back to California. I'm just not this expat stuff, never was. I was practically an expat in Honolulu---fish out of water. Even my patented Manhattan Beach boy look didn't fly there. I was broken." He wasn't allowed to smoke on school grounds but he pulled a cigarette out of his top pocket and lighting it, inhaled deeply.

Marlowe laughed, "That's so juvenile its funny. You are a fucking caution, Warren."

"Marlowe, you saved me. Seriously, you were, are, my friend. The only one here that kept me safe, involved, and you also gave me Ueda who pulled me back into a reality I had forgotten. It's like you arranged all that. I turned a corner in life. I walked for so long as if in a dream, half asleep hitting things and stumbling into them never making headway. And here I am. I'm 41. I saw Felch's head fly thru that window and I thought that was it. Like everything was over. It was all finished really…is that weird?"

Marlowe scratched his chin, "That deal with Felch and Yukio, and then Flattery. Jesus, it was a trifecta of sheer intense insanity. That hot, hot day and Yukio just planning that, losing it. I never asked you then, was he losing it?"

Warren stared at the koi, wondering if Yukio had been reborn yet. "I knew he changed, but to what extent, no idea. We had a lot of discussion, appropriate discussion about Mishima's work and view of Japan." He took a drag on his cigarette. "It affected him after being away his entire life, as if he were a new person here, found a new body and mind. I didn't know about the assaults on the foreigners." Marlowe jerked his head back; "they just made him for that, you know. The detective, the lead guy during the assault let me know about it, and gave me a letter Yukio left for me. That guy attended Virginia Tech of all places."

"Wild how Flattery became collateral damage---his whole fetish just laid out for the cops. And Yukio shitting on his desk…how classic is that? Do you think he took the office to kill Flattery instead of Felch?"

"Not sure. He didn't say anything about it in his goodbye letter to me. I had to laugh though…ironic sense of humor…'Be easy on Tomoko, she's shy,'" Warren laughed stubbing out his cigarette.

"So, are you going to blow this popstand soon?"

"Dunno, there's so many things to do. I just kept listening to *Highway 61* and it was like this huge mainland magnet. Mainland. I picked that up in Hawaii. We pick up a lot of things, don't we?"

"Those guys talk money with you?"

Warren shook his head as if such a question were below him, and sniffed, "I shall be among the gentrified once again, old sport." Laughing, Marlowe got up and stretched.

"Have you talked to Ueda?"

"I did. I used the phone upstairs. I could feel that Ueda smile over the line too, as if she knew everything was going to happen this way."

"Did you and she...?"

Warren remembered the night she came to him when he had his very last dream of Lise, "No, but we have slept together, sleeping slept. I'm attracted to her in so many ways, and yea, physically too, but its just not going to happen. And I think without that pressure, it makes it easier. Make sense?"

Marlowe smiled, remembering his night with Ueda years before. "I totally get it, chum." He sat back down. "You know she was fifteen when Hiroshima was bombed. She had her back to a window, as she and her mother were prepping what little food they had for breakfast. Her father was some sort of civilian quartermaster who managed to ferret away a bit of grub here and there. You know how badly Japan was on the ropes by then. Anyway, so she has her back to the flash and heat wave, then the whole house pretty much disintegrates. They lived like a mile from ground zero, which is why she is around today. Seriously, you've never been intimate?"

"I saw her back that first night, like in those pictures of the wounded in books and museums, the pattern burned into her skin like a negative of a photograph. No…once we made out after drinking a lot, then laughed at how lame it was to do that."

"Her family was wiped out, and subsequently she took up with relatives who lived in Kanagawa. She's pretty amazing. Making out?"

"She's used me as a model a couple of times. That's sort of embarrassing to say, now that I hear it."

"I'd take it as a compliment. She was definitely impressed by your balls when you were passed out. So when are you coming into all this filthy lucre?"

"Don't worry, for fucks sake, I'll buy you a drink!"

"You had better, you cheap Dutch prick."

Warren thought for a moment. "Any clue as to what happened with Mrs. Bloom? I mean like wham, all of a sudden she's packing up and flying home. Off, like shorts in the night."

Marlowe was quiet for a moment, looking up at the windows of the surrounding buildings. "Her husband was in trouble. You know he was part of the communications command. He was busted for communicating with the wrong people, and let's leave it at that."

Warren whistled. "Wow…like right out of a movie!" He looked at the other man, "Marlowe?"

"What?"

"Thanks."

"*The Long Goodbye.* The quote you had that first night we went to the jazz club, it's from that book. I read it. Sad ending. Poor Marlowe."

"Yes, sad ending." Warren looked at his friend, smiling, "What is it you really do, man?"

Chapter 61

It was a month since the June 7 Incident and the NS Dept. seemed to be functioning well. The graduation had been a hard day to get thru, and there were many people, faculty, staff and students who were in tears. Tomoko was excused from her speech, as she did not feel she could complete it without feeling emotional. Warren advocated for her, as Serazowa was at first adamant she deliver the speech, then backed down and allowed her to withdraw. They finally had their talk, he and Serazowa, and there was no questioning as to Warren's decision. Serazowa asked if he stay on after the new hire and help brief whoever it was that filled his position, while still being salaried. Marlowe was asked to take the helm and after a bit of hemming and hawing he conceded and accepted.

Warren told him it was the worst performance he ever saw, when sitting over a martini at the jazz club.

Even on break, the teachers were still within the offices cleaning up, getting rosters ready for the next term in August, and readying for their vacations. There was not a whole lot of conversation in the Department, as if one thought that the two spirits of Felch and Yukio still stalked the spaces, not wishing disturbance. Warren took to just filling out lesson plans and curriculum for the new teachers. He would give them to

The Deep Slumber of Dogs

Marlowe and show him how to make a general file for the respective grades to follow.

Mrs. Fukuda, who missed the entire Incident and the repercussions of Flattery's arrest, confided in Mari that she was glad they were rid of the two.

"It's a divine wind that swept those two out of here, and Kitihara as well. Such a useless invertebrate"

Mari hated to admit it, but when she even tried to feel anything, she could not. She had never liked Felch and Flattery, and felt bad for Riordan and Warren, who took the brunt of their poisonous tongues and silly antics. Mrs. Fukuda cursed the two out.

"I know I should have respect for the fat, dead one, but I am more saddened by the boy and what a waste his life was. His poor parents!"

Mari agreed. In the office, she found herself again staring at Warren. She knew he had tendered his resignation and would soon start his return to America. He looked up and she quickly averted her eyes and picked up a pen, just to have something to do. His memory of the daytrip to Meiji Shrine and her wet shirt returned. Closing his eyes he could see the image of them parting at the *eki,* yet knowing he should leave it alone, whatever the spark of the moment. Mari, having looked away thought of the many times she had spied on him in the changing room; once not being enough. She cleared her throat and found herself speaking.

"Haas-sensei?"

Warren stopped his writing and looked up, "Hai?"

"I was wondering...how you have been? I feel I have not responded in the manner of a friend, since the death of Yukio, and Mr. Felch." She then averted her eyes and looked back down at her desk. "I apologize."

Warren hoped the surprise he felt didn't register on his face. It was the last thing he expected. Serazowa, in a moment of reflection, when alone with Warren had also given voice to the Incident but with a different outcome.

"You detested Mr. Felch, and he was an embarrassment that Kitihara tolerated for his personal gain. Fate is a strange bedmate is it not, Haas-sensei? It would appear things have been realigned in an extraordinary way, yes?"

And that was all she said. Looking at Mari, Warren almost felt like walking over and giving her a hug. "Thank you, Mari. That's very thoughtful."

He watched her pick at a pink eraser, and smiling, nod her head in gratitude. She looked up at him again.

"Will you join me for a drink, this night, the 7th?"

Warren said, "Of course," remembering her story in the *izikaya* on that rain swept day, of Tanabata. The stars had come back into realignment and there stood Mari in the path of his orbit.

Chapter 62

"What did he write you Haas-san?" Noriko Ueda sat under the fan on her outdoor deck, burning punks to ward off mosquitos had also been placed along the perimeter of the covered lanai.

"The police found a lot of starts and stops balled up and thrown into the waste basket. His attempts at poetry were pretty awful, but I guess he was also under strain." He leaned forward and flicked an ash into the crystal bowl in front of him.

Ueda laughed, "Everyone else uses the floor up here except you. You're so funny, Haas-san. And did your parents do the same?"

"Actually, they would just flick the butts into the yard, near the empty bottles they threw. I just like your deck out here. It makes me feel good, so I enjoy treating it with respect." Warren smiled, then looking off into the lights of Roppongi, he continued about Yukio. "He found a two line poem by Ozaki Hosai in a book I had. It goes:

Looking back at the beach,
Even my footprints are gone

There was a silence, as his words just seemed to stay there, like the smoke of his cigarette in the windless air. Ueda looked out over her deck to the lights Warren seemed to be fixed on.

"It can be anyone's poem. It's very beautiful. How sad he was so young. Again, such a waste." She looked now at Warren as he sat quietly in the dark across from her.

"You miss him, yes?"

"I do. I miss the rest of his life that he and no one will ever know."

"Did he believe in Shinto faith or had he been Christianized in America?"

"Shinto."

"Then he will be back again, many times. Perhaps next time he shall find a longer peace. And what of you now? Are you the same Christian *gaijin* you were when you first arrived in Japan?"

Frowning at the word 'Christian' Warren thought about it for a minute. " I wasn't really a Christian per se, in the true sense, ever. We didn't take that route in life but no, I am not the same man anymore; the man who bottomed out in Hawaii, scraping by philosophically and morally, good salary but owed too many legal fees and debts and vices. *That* guy. That man is gone. Somewhere in Japan he just unraveled and I was underneath. Now I'm what you see, what you hear in this instant; this moment. I feel as if I have never been so much in the *now* as in my whole life. And you're right, anybody can use that poem, as it fits me perfectly now. If I walk out that door, there's no trace of me...I just keep moving forward. I feel as if that finally happened to me in Los Angeles; my high water mark didn't mark how good I had been, it just erased all that came before that...does that make sense? But I also never felt so grounded. Contradictory isn't it? But it's real for me." He looked at her and she smiled with her eyes.

The Deep Slumber of Dogs

"In your rather strange and roundabout way, yes, Haas-san, it makes sense." She reached for a cigarette on the table between them. "I feel about my art in much the same way. I feel it, paint it, and then I am over it and again in the *now* of the next moment, the next inspiration. I am happy for you, sensei." She smiled sweetly.

He recalled the evening of the Incident where he brushed off entreaties from Marlowe to stay at his flat, or call Ueda and put on a good drunk at her place. He just wished to be alone and be away from Kin Tama and at his own speed. He went back under the police tape to the edge of the building where the bikes were in their racks in the bushes; his parked alone and how peaceful it looked in the early evening. It was twilight and he could just make out the landscape as it slowly blurred in the dwindling light. He looked up and saw that the windows with blown out glass were now covered in a plastic wrap that billowed in some sections from the AC within the office. The police had placed it to protect the crime scene and in the early evening the lights from the office were evident behind the plastic, the police still busy at work.

Yukio, he asked himself, what visions did you have? He looked away from the windows and wondered, was it my fault? Have you met Lise yet and did she make you enjoy a good laugh? She'll make you laugh. He walked on to the trains and when riding home did not get off at his station. He had fallen asleep; his head bowed slightly, his arms resting on his thighs, the overhead lights of the car creating the halo of light on the top of his yellow hair. His was the deep slumber of dogs.

The End

About the Author

Doc Krinberg is a California native who while living in Southern Cal, Northern Cal and the San Joaquin Valley had various jobs to include taxi driver, truck driver for a scrap metal company, strip club barker, sailor, hard hat diver and finally when desperate took a doctoral degree in education. He has lived and taught overseas, on the US Mainland and currently resides in Virginia, awaiting the return to glory of the Oakland Raiders.

Other works include a novel 'Polonio Pass' (Aignos Publishing), Poetry anthologies to include '58 Stones', 'Bellwether Messages' and 'Running From the Pack' (Savant Publishing), 'The Black Rose of Winter" and 'Temptation' (Lost Tower, UK)

Made in the USA
Charleston, SC
31 May 2016